Kry
gather above the fallen g...

She couldn't say where it came from. But it seemed almost as if it were being drawn out of Mariah. Like all the blackness in her tortured young soul.

Krysty wondered if her adrenaline-pumped mind was playing tricks on her, but the orange-haired coldheart standing nearby was clearly seeing it, too. She gave a strangled cry of fear, stumbling back a step. She raised her longblaster as if to ward it off.

The blackness was unquestionably spinning, though Krysty would be hard-pressed to say how she knew that. It began to drift away from Mariah toward the woman who had clubbed her down.

"Get away!" the coldheart yelled. "Back off."

The cloud seemed to whirl faster. The woman jabbed at it with her rifle butt.

The stock sank into the cloud. And was suddenly yanked into it. The butt shattered, pieces whirling briefly in the cloud before seeming to dissolve.

The coldheart let go of the weapon. But not before her right hand was drawn into the whirlwind of shadow. She screamed.

Krysty saw blood spray, caught in the cloud like water swirling down a drain, and pink shreds of skin. The blackness sucked the coldheart woman in, tore her to pieces and consumed the fragments.

Other titles in the Deathlands saga:

Rat King
Zero City
Savage Armada
Judas Strike
Shadow Fortress
Sunchild
Breakthrough
Salvation Road
Amazon Gate
Destiny's Truth
Skydark Spawn
Damnation Road Show
Devil Riders
Bloodfire
Hellbenders
Separation
Death Hunt
Shaking Earth
Black Harvest
Vengeance Trail
Ritual Chill
Atlantis Reprise
Labyrinth
Strontium Swamp
Shatter Zone
Perdition Valley
Cannibal Moon
Sky Raider
Remember Tomorrow
Sunspot
Desert Kings
Apocalypse Unborn
Thunder Road
Plague Lords
(Empire of Xibalba Book I)
Dark Resurrection
(Empire of Xibalba Book II)
Eden's Twilight
Desolation Crossing
Alpha Wave
Time Castaways
Prophecy
Blood Harvest
Arcadian's Asylum
Baptism of Rage
Doom Helix
Moonfeast
Downrigger Drift
Playfair's Axiom
Tainted Cascade
Perception Fault
Prodigal's Return
Lost Gates
Haven's Blight
Hell Road Warriors
Palaces of Light
Wretched Earth
Crimson Waters
No Man's Land
Nemesis
Chrono Spasm
Sins of Honor
Storm Breakers
Dark Fathoms
Siren Song
End Program
Desolation Angels
Blood Red Tide
Polestar Omega
Hive Invasion
End Day
Forbidden Trespass
Iron Rage
Child of Slaughter

JAMES AXLER

DEATHLANDS®

DEVIL'S VORTEX

A GOLD EAGLE BOOK FROM
WORLDWIDE®

TORONTO • NEW YORK • LONDON
AMSTERDAM • PARIS • SYDNEY • HAMBURG
STOCKHOLM • ATHENS • TOKYO • MILAN
MADRID • WARSAW • BUDAPEST • AUCKLAND

First edition November 2015

ISBN-13: 978-0-373-62635-9

Special thanks and acknowledgment to
Victor Milan for his contribution to this work.

Devil's Vortex

Printed in U.S.A.

It is not light that is needed, but fire; it is not the gentle shower, but thunder. We need the storm, the whirlwind, and the earthquake.

—Frederick Douglass,
1818–1895

THE DEATHLANDS SAGA

This world is their legacy, a world born in the violent nuclear spasm of 2001 that was the bitter outcome of a struggle for global dominance.

There is no real escape from this shockscape where life always hangs in the balance, vulnerable to newly demonic nature, barbarism, lawlessness.

But they are the warrior survivalists, and they endure—in the way of the lion, the hawk and the tiger, true to nature's heart despite its ruination.

Ryan Cawdor: The privileged son of an East Coast baron. Acquainted with betrayal from a tender age, he is a master of the hard realities.

Krysty Wroth: Harmony ville's own Titian-haired beauty, a woman with the strength of tempered steel. Her premonitions and Gaia powers have been fostered by her Mother Sonja.

J. B. Dix, the Armorer: Weapons master and Ryan's close ally, he, too, honed his skills traversing the Deathlands with the legendary Trader.

Doctor Theophilus Tanner: Torn from his family and a gentler life in 1896, Doc has been thrown into a future he couldn't have imagined.

Dr. Mildred Wyeth: Her father was killed by the Ku Klux Klan, but her fate is not much lighter. Restored from predark cryogenic suspension, she brings twentieth-century healing skills to a nightmare.

Jak Lauren: A true child of the wastelands, reared on adversity, loss and danger, the albino teenager is a fierce fighter and loyal friend.

Dean Cawdor: Ryan's young son by Sharona accepts the only world he knows, and yet he is the seedling bearing the promise of tomorrow.

In a world where all was lost, they are humanity's last hope…

Chapter One

"Wait—there has been a slaughter here!"

A scarf muffled Doc Tanner's words. Each of his companions had one wrapped around his or her face to give what protection the garment could from the powder snow and dust whipped at them by the unforgiving North Plains late-winter wind.

The seven friends staggered across a bright desert of white. Ryan Cawdor had to lean hard into the bone-cutting wind to keep it from pushing him upright. The snow wasn't falling, so far as he could tell. The mat-trans jump had delivered them to the rolling prairie of the eastern Badlands of what had been South Dakota, near the border with the former Nebraska, as near as they had been able to tell from J. B. Dix's minisextant and Doc's calculations.

Ryan drew his SIG Sauer P226. Doc's warning cry had indicated no present danger. Had the old man detected an immediate threat, he would have called it out. Doc had been trawled from his time in the 1880s to the 1990s by the whitecoats of Operation Chronos. Doc had proved to be an uncooperative test subject, so he had been thrust one hundred years into the future to what was now known as the Deathlands. The multiple time jumps had addled his brain, and sometimes he wandered in a fog that filled his brain.

But when it came to danger to himself and his friends, he snapped back to the here and now. He had spoken very clearly in the past tense—but Ryan was not put at ease.

If people had been slaughtered, that meant coldhearts, and they might still be in the area.

"Weapons out, people," the one-eyed man called. He knew that his companions would most likely have their blasters in hand, but he had to be sure. They were all seasoned Deathlands travelers and fighters, but everybody made mistakes. And they were all worn down by hunger, fatigue and the biting cold.

He had his six companions winged out in a vee formation: his lover, Krysty Wroth, to his right; then Ricky Morales; then J. B. Dix, the Armorer. To the left walked Doc, Mildred Wyeth and Jak Lauren. They were spread out far enough they could just keep each other in sight in the storm.

Jak, a slight, skinny albino youth, normally walked, not point, but ranging in advance of the others to scout out danger. Not today. In this nasty storm, which was worse than a thick fog because the wind-blown dust and ice particles stung the eyes and constantly threatened to clog them, Ryan wanted J.B.'s judgment and skill with a blaster, and Jak's hunting-tiger senses guarding the rear.

That accounted for why the least likely of them all, Dr. Theophilus Algernon Tanner, had spotted something first. Although Doc looked to be pushing seventy hard—if not powering right by—in fact he was roughly the same age as Ryan in terms of years actually lived. It was his time jumps and the abuse he had suffered at the hands of twentieth-century whitecoats that had prematurely aged him and addled his mind.

"Swing left, everybody," Ryan called. "We need to see what we might be up against—"

A man suddenly appeared, stumbling toward them blindly in the hard driving snow.

"Black cloud," Ryan heard him mumbling. "The black cloud!"

The one-eyed man raised his handblaster. The man showed no sign of even seeing the companions, even though he was about to blunder right between him and Doc. Ryan had not kept himself alive—to say nothing of his companions—across the length and breadth of the Deathlands by taking anything for granted.

And then the shambling man clearly did see them. Ryan could actually make out his eyes going wide in the gore and filthy mask of his face.

"You mutie bastards!" he screamed. Suddenly he was raising an ax above his head with both hands. "You won't take me alive!"

He charged.

THE GOGGLE-LIKE SHADES, with slits of polarized glass, protected Hammerhand's eyes from the wind-lashed snow, dust and grit as he scaled the peak the Plains folk called Gray Top.

Nothing protected the rest of his massive frame. His muscle-packed six-foot-six-inch body was nude from the black topknot surmounting his side-shaved head to the soles of his feet. Susan Crain, the Crow Nation healer and medicine woman he had sought for counsel, had told him that he had to be naked to complete the vision quest.

The rugged granite rock cut into his palms and feet, but he ignored the discomfort. He was inured to hardship, from the abuse and poverty his tribe and own family had inflicted on him, growing up among the Káína people of the great Blackfoot Confederacy of the short grass plains to the north.

Of course, the nuking mushrooms I ate might be helping with that, he thought. The magic mushrooms made him hyperaware, his senses unnaturally keen. Yet they made him somehow less vulnerable to those sensations.

They also deadened fear. But he was used to fighting down the terrors that beset him. He'd done that all his life, as well.

The mountain, which took its name from the gray granite cap rock that rose above its pine-clad slopes and the surrounding Black Hills, stood near the Dead White Man Faces Mountain. It was the tallest in the Hills. It was held to possess great power.

It seemed as good a place as any to find the key to his destiny.

Hammerhand wasn't sure he believed in all this mystic shit. Then again, he wasn't sure he didn't. For nuking sure he'd had to put up with the taunts and barbs of those smug bastard Absarokas in order to consult their well-known shaman.

After a generation or two of peace, the two nations, his Blackfoot Confederacy and the Crow, were back to an on-again, off-again war of mutual raiding and occasional battles. The only reason they hadn't shot him on sight was that he was a known exile from his native Blood band, a wild child whose wickedness and ambition alike were too great to be constrained by tradition and stick-up-their-butts elders. But his judgment wasn't trusted widely enough, even by other adolescent warriors, for him to raise his own war band and probe his inner self in any kind of way anyone on the Plains would pay attention to.

Painfully and painstakingly he made his way to the top. That had always been his strength, he reckoned: that he could act with precision or passion, as the need of the moment required. Mebbe both.

It was why he knew himself fit to rule.

The question was how.

And mebbe *who*. Those questions were what had brought him here: blasted out of his mind, freezing to his marrow and a hundred feet in the air up a cliff of granite made slick by blowing snow, cold enough to dangerously numb the fingers and toes that scrabbled and fought for holds every inch of the tortuous way up.

But Hammerhand persevered. He was good at that, too. That was another way he reckoned he was superior to the people who'd given him life: although they could endure almost anything, and had wizard survival skills, they had a tendency to fly off the handle at random moments. Not at something that required persistence in a physical craft—like skinning a chilled elk or even curing its hide for use in making clothing and lodges—but at anything abstract.

They didn't have what it took to envision Empire and make it happen. They didn't have the *horizon*.

Hammerhand did. That part of the vision he had. But he knew he was missing key pieces.

He could see barely past his fingertips when his arms were fully stretched out. For a moment, when through the whirling whiteness he glimpsed rugged gray with only more white beyond—just above his reach—his brain, altered as it was, couldn't process what its eyes were showing it.

His body came to the rescue. Locked in "climb" mode, it commenced to haul his mass up the cliff again, fingers and toes seeking cracks and jutting icy gray stone. The image of the lip of the cliff resolved itself into his brain: the top!

Seeing a bright line of red and yellow halation following the outline of the rock-sky interface, Hammerhand let his mind ride shotgun as his body pulled itself onto the angled and uneven upper surface. Exercising the power of suggestion as much as his powerful will, he stood upright, bracing slightly against a wind, fierce now that it was unrestrained, that sought to bash him right back over the cliff to oblivion.

"I'm here," he called into the storm. It seemed he could hear the individual impact of each tiny particle of snow, ice and grit as it banged against the lenses of his glasses.

He looked around and could scarcely see more than ten feet from the tip of his nose. The hilly, wooded country surrounding the peak was invisible.

And then, suddenly, it was before him: a masculine figure, as nude as he was and at least twice as tall, floating six feet above the wind-swept granite. Its every muscle was seemingly molded with great precision out of white light. The brightness of the faceless figure didn't hurt his eyes. But the golden radiance that surrounded it dazzled him through his shades, making him blink and try to turn away.

He found that he could not.

"Hammerhand," a voice said like thunder. *"Kneel before me."*

"Who are you?" he demanded. He was determined not to let the...thing...see his fear. Even though he had the drug to deaden it, his knees were so loose he was only keeping himself upright by the force of his will.

"I am your destiny. Kneel before me."

"I'd rather die standing!"

"It is not permitted," the voice boomed. *"Nor is disobedience. I am Fate."*

The willpower that held his knees locked shattered like glass struck with a hammer. His legs folded abruptly beneath him. It was all he could do to keep from going over backward on his buttocks.

Then, irresistibly, he felt his torso being winched upward, until he sat up straight. He could feel his muscles doing it, but not by his will, nor under his control.

"You see that resistance is futile, Hammerhand."

"What do you want from me?"

"Only to give you that which you most desire, what you have come here to obtain, naked, freezing and electric.

"Now, hear me..."

Chapter Two

The boom of the stubby shotgun barrel beneath the longer main barrel of Doc's gigantic LeMat revolver beat the blast of Ryan's SIG Sauer P226 by half a heartbeat. The man was already staggered by the charge of buckshot when Ryan double-tapped him at the center of mass, which was still more shadow than apparent substance.

The .44-caliber upper barrel of Doc's revolver spit yellow flame and crashing noise. The man's head snapped back and he crumpled into the snow.

"Offer accepted," Ryan said, lowering his weapon.

"Maybe we should've tried to keep him alive," Mildred said as Ryan cautiously approached the fallen man. She wasn't doing it just to be contrary—although she was perfectly capable of that. She, like Doc, had been taken out of her own time in the distant past by science. But in her case the motivation was the opposite of Doc's: doctors had put Mildred into cryosleep when a routine abdominal operation had gone terribly wrong, hoping that she could be cured sometime in the future.

"It might have been helpful if he could've told us what happened here," she continued. "And who did it."

Ryan began to see signs of what had inspired Doc's original call-out: ruined buildings and scattered trash on the ground beyond the man they'd chilled. Some of that trash, he saw, was bodies. Much of it appeared to be body parts.

Ryan grunted. "Abstract knowledge doesn't load many magazines," he said.

"I'm a big fan of not getting my skull split by an ax," J.B. commented.

Then he frowned and stepped up to kneel by the chill, pointing the muzzle of his M-4000 shotgun skyward.

"Look at this," he said, while Jak, who had appeared at the fringes of visibility when the blasterfire erupted, vanished back into the blowing snow. Ryan thought about warning him not to get too far from the group lest he lose sight of the rest. But then he knew how ridiculous that was. The albino would find a way to track them through a sealed-up cavern at midnight. As long as Jak lived, his companions would never have to worry about finding him. He'd find *them*.

Also, Ryan knew the danger in giving orders he knew might not be obeyed. The albino accepted Ryan's leadership. But he had his own notions of how to do his job as scout. And since he was the best there was, Ryan had learned to give him his head in such matters.

Instead he allowed himself to take his eye off the surroundings, where he saw little but still-vague shapes in the blown snow anyway, to look at the man. As expected, he was dead. His remaining eye, bright blue, glared at the keening white void above.

His other, his right, was a bloody socket rimmed with semiliquid aqueous humor. He'd suffered its loss recently, along with the other wounds visible on his face and chest through his ripped-open plaid flannel shirt.

The Armorer pointed to, without touching, red-rimmed rings on his cheek and jaw. Sucker marks.

"Stickie," Ryan muttered. "Ace on the line."

He looked up and around. What little he could make out through the wind-blown snow and grit suggested structures that had never been much to start with but were probably worse now.

"Eyes skinned," he commanded, straightening. "We don't know if the muties are still around."

"Some are," Mildred observed, sounding grim. "The bodies I can see from here are stickies. Or stickie parts, mostly. They're everywhere."

"It looks as if a bomb went off in a stickie colony," Krysty stated.

Ryan moved on from the chill. Almost at once he came close to stumbling over a lump that he quickly realized was a green stickie torso—headless, limbless, about the size of a ten-year-old norm's body. It was partly covered with drifted powdery snow.

"Could they have been fighting?" Ricky asked warily. He'd had to make some adjustments to his outlook on muties when joining up with Ryan and his group. His homeland, Puerto Rico, was called Monster Island, not just because it was overrun with savage monsters—it was—but also because large colonies of humanoid muties, including stickies, lived side by side with the human majority in perfect amity. Whereas on the mainland mutation was considered a taint—such that even the gorgeous Krysty Wroth faced discrimination or even violence whenever it was found out that she was, though nearly perfect in face and form, a mutie.

Of course, on the mainland, stickies had *earned* their reputation as monsters a thousand times over.

"Mebbe," Ryan said.

He was starting to wonder himself. *Abstract* knowledge might not load many blasters, it was true. Which was why he'd long since learned—the hard way—to suppress his own lively natural lust for knowledge for its own sake. *Staying alive* took all the brain power even a man the likes of Ryan Cawdor could bring to bear.

But this was shaping up into a mystery whose answer might well affect their survival.

"Or maybe that dude we chilled killed them all with his ax?" Mildred suggested.

Ryan grunted. "Mebbe," he said.

"That'd be an irony," Mildred stated pointedly. "If that guy's reward for heroically taking out a whole colony full of stickies was for us to blast him out of his socks."

"Spilled blood won't go back in the body, Mildred," Ryan said. "You of all people should know that. Anyway, you might remember he thought we were stickies and was fixing to proceed accordingly."

"True," she said.

As Ryan cautiously advanced among the scattered stickie bits with his blaster ready, details of the handful of buildings became apparent. Clearly this had been a farm. Like so many others, buildings seemed to have been thrown together and rudely nailed in place from whatever could be scavvied, traded for or stolen. Planks. Timber scraps. Flattened tin cans. Cracked and sun-discolored plastic sheeting. A few rare chunks of corrugated metal. Sad and sagging but no more than most to be encountered in the Deathlands. And the farm had to have been relatively prosperous, judging by the number of structures.

Ironically, their number and size suggested that this had been a prosperous location. Relatively. A marginally better style of hardscrabble life.

"Looks like a sizable group lived here," Mildred said. "Normal people, that is." Stickie colonies could take numerous forms—like the rubbery-skinned little humanoids themselves—from massive piles of rubbish to what looked like outsized wasps' nests. But never as orderly as this place was.

Even now.

"Might've been an extended clan," Krysty said.

Ryan had seen no sign of norms other than the man he'd helped chill. But as Krysty spoke he saw a little girl lying facedown on the ground. Snow had already half drifted over her. She was clearly dead.

Neither Ryan nor any of the others made a move to examine her more closely. Her rough smock was torn and bloodied on the back. That she'd died by violence told them what they needed to know. And despite all being hardened survivors of years in the Deathlands, none of them wanted to see more horror than they had to. Not even Ryan, and he was reckoned a hard man.

They came across other chills, adults, both men and women. All bore the telltale sign of stickie violence: the red sucker imprints on their flesh left by mutie fingertips that could peel skin from muscle and muscle from bone with their terrible adhesive power. Some bore bite wounds, as well, divots scooped from sides or limbs, throats torn out. Some varieties of stickies lacked external mouths. Others had mouths filled with needle fangs.

These were that second kind. Or had been. Ryan saw a couple more or less intact stickie chills, one with a lower face and throat obliterated by what had to have been a point-blank shotgun blast, another with an ax still embedded in its round head.

"Blasters up, and stay ready, people," Ryan called softly to his comrades.

A beat later Jak called out from somewhere, lost in the snow-swirl, "Hear something."

Ryan crouched, handblaster at the ready. Beside him he saw Krysty and Ricky do likewise—the redhead with her full-auto capable 9 mm Glock 18C, the youth with his old Webley revolver, rechambered for .45 ACP.

Then Jak said, "Girl crying."

Krysty's pale and beautiful face, which had been an ice sculpture a moment before, softened. She straightened, lowering the boxy muzzle of her blaster.

"Don't let your guard down, lover," Ryan growled. "We don't know it's not a trap."

She cocked an incredulous brow at him. "What? A stickie crying out in a little girl's voice to lure us in?"

"Other muties have been known to do that trick," J.B. reminded her. "Who knows what stickies might come up with. Some of them are bastard smart."

Krysty's other eyebrow arched up to match the first. She nodded. "Good point. But we still need to check. Just *carefully*."

"It's not our problem anyway," Ryan said. He was talking to the woman's back as she moved purposefully ahead among the eerie cluster of farm buildings. She had a mind of her own—it was one reason he loved her. And she had as keen a survival sense as he did. After all, she'd met the same brutal and deadly challenges he had across their years together on the Deathlands. Some he even hadn't, when they were split by circumstance or necessity. She knew what she was doing.

But he also felt concern that her big, soft heart might dull the edge of her wits.

At this point the only thing to do was follow. He heard a rustle and glanced over his shoulder to see J.B. slide in behind him, his M-4000 riot scattergun held slantwise before his hips in patrol position. The little man flashed him a quick grin.

Getting my back, Ryan thought. Automatically. As usual. They were all sharp-eyed and sure shots, and none of them compared to Jak Lauren in the sensory-keenness department. But Ryan just felt better when it was his best friend and right-hand man in particular who was watching their asses. Especially going into an unknown situation.

He grinned to himself. Every situation in this life is unknown, he thought. And forgetting that little fact is one of the best and quickest ways to end up with dirt hitting you in the eyes.

The main structure was one story, big—half a dozen rooms or more. It had a peaked roof to shed snow as it fell. Now the wind was spooling the powdery stuff off its battered galvanized and corrugated metal in swirls and skeins, flinging it at their eyes. A screen door, hanging open and sagging, banged against the frame periodically as it got kicked by vagaries of that killing wind.

But the sobbing was coming from a much smaller side building. *Sounds like a kid,* Mildred mouthed to Ryan. He nodded.

Jak crouched outside, covering the door with his Colt Python revolver. The albino loved knives and preferred them over blasters. But given what had happened to the farm folk here, if there was a nasty surprise waiting for him in that shed, he wanted to be able to answer it straightaway with a bigger, louder surprise of his own.

And shed it was, Ryan judged. His first glance suggested it might be an outhouse—the cold sucked his sense of smell away, and if the farmers had had sense to lime it, it probably didn't give off an eye-watering, knee-buckling stink except on the hottest days of a Black Hills summer. But it was too big for a one-holer and not proportioned right for two or three. The structure had to be used for storage, he thought. Mebbe tools.

The door opened outward. It hung invitingly, just a hand span ajar. As he approached, J.B. slid past him, as smooth as an eel.

"Let me," he said with an upward tip of his shotgun's barrel.

"Go right ahead," Ryan said. The 12-gauge was an even bigger surprise than Jak's .357 Magnum blaster for lurking bad things. Lots of strange predators or scavengers could follow behind a marauding stickie clan. Some of them not even muties.

Standing well clear of the doorway proper, the Armorer reached forward, gingerly grabbed hold of the door, then whipped it open. Neither a lunging feral form nor a blast of blasterfire greeted the sudden movement. Holding the M-4000 leveled from his hip, he sidestepped quickly across the doorway, left to right, staying outside. He wanted to clear the fatal funnel of the door without plunging into a completely unknown environment.

"Easy, little lady," Ryan heard him say. "We're not here to hurt you."

Cautiously Ryan joined his old friend. He saw that J.B. had been right not to do the usual room-clearing drill, stepping quickly inside and then immediately side-stepping left or right out of the doorway, to make a perfect target of himself for as short a time as possible. They were in a toolshed, and the tools were in some disarray, scattered here and there. Had the Armorer driven ahead, he might've tangled up his feet and pitched face-foremost onto the packed-dirt floor. Or worse.

A little girl huddled inside, just visible in the gloom of the far side of the crowded little room.

"HOW'D IT GO, BOSS?" Hammerhand's chief lieutenant asked as he strode into camp. Joe Takes-Blasters's big broad face showed a frown of concern. "Reckoned you'd stay at the Crow camp longer."

"No need," Hammerhand said.

"So, you decided you didn't need to go chasing visions after all, eh?" Mindy Farseer asked with her usual half-mocking tone of voice and one eyebrow arched.

"No. I did. I got what I wanted."

The Blood encampment was a collection of about one hundred "lodges," tepees of hide or canvas, yurts standing up from carts. It was the standard dwellings of Great Plains nomads. The brutal wind had subsided to a breeze that came and went, snapping their flaps occasionally like little whips. A few skinny children chased one another, sending chickens squawking from their path.

A handful of assorted battered trucks, modified to burn alcohol as fuel, were parked in the center of the camp, along with a selection of motorcycles, from dirt bikes to powerful but stripped-down choppers. Most of their transport took the form of a substantial herd of horses.

Hammerhand thought that they looked like a sorry-ass bunch of draggle-tail coldhearts, not the kind of people with whom he could build an empire.

But he meant to do just that. With them. And this morning he had received a clear and compelling vision of *how* to accomplish that.

It was time to kick ass.

And whatever Power it was—he didn't know or care because the fact that it was a big and badass Power was enough—had anointed him as the chosen one to do it.

Now he had concrete goals and the beginning of a plan.

"The Crow elders are still here," Joe said. He sounded uneasy.

He pointed with a jerk of his chin toward the group of four who stood expectantly nearby, at camp's edge. Three men and a woman, with gray in their long braids, were wrapped in colorful blankets against the wind's chilling touch. Their weathered faces showed strong bone structures and jutting noses, with skins the color of old leather. No doubt as a reproach to the mixed-breed Hammerhand, the Council had sent four elders to speak to him and urge his return to the fold.

As if.

After the Big Nuke, most bands of the Blackfoot Confederacy had taken in numerous refugees from fried-out cities, as had many of the First Nations groups that survived the war and skydark. And as most continued to do. The Blackfoot had thrived in doing so and now were preeminent north of what had once been the US-Canada border.

But while they had accepted their share of refugees, and continued to adopt new members regardless of heritage, the stiff-necked Blood people had chosen to maintain an unusual form of discrimination within the tribe—not against mutants, but ceding social standing on the basis of supposed purity of breeding. It was a policy they termed Traditionalism. And one that younger fire-bloods, many but not all mixed race like Hammerhand, disdained as "Trad."

He looked at them now, standing there all mock humble but really demanding his submission—whether in renaming his band, or better, disbanding it and crawling back on his belly to beg the Council for forgiveness. Arrogant pricks.

He knew in his heart what the dazzling figure from the top of Harney Peak would tell him to do. And although obedience was not in his nature, no more to glowing, floating sky people than the grubbier terrestrial kind, he would follow its words. Because that was the vision he had sought and had gained. And because he knew in its heart it was righteous.

Black Bear, the shortest and stockiest but most senior member of the group, extended the ceremonial coup stick, hooked and feathered, toward Hammerhand.

"Return with us, and become once more one with our land and blood, young man," he said.

"It's not too late for you, boy," said John Tall Person, who as might be expected, was the tallest of the group. Had his back still been straight he'd have been only an inch or three shorter than Hammerhand, which made him a tall man indeed.

Hammerhand's anger at their arrogant imperiousness was beginning to smoke. "And if I don't?"

Deer Woman scowled. "Then we shall make you! It will be war."

"Your answer?" demanded Crow Legs, the final member of the group. His gray hair had been braided into a sort of unicorn horn jutting from the front of his head. Hammerhand thought it made him look comical.

"My answer?" Hammerhand gave them a long, hard look.

Then he turned to his lieutenant, Joe Takes-Blasters.

"For my answer, send their hides back to the Council," he said. "Without them inside."

Chapter Three

Krysty's heart melted as a whimper escaped the form lying on its side in the fetal position on the dirt floor. She felt an overpowering impulse to run to the girl and hug her.

But she fought it down. She was a seasoned campaigner, almost as much as J.B. or Ryan. She knew the girl could be bait in a trap. Or even, unlikely as it seemed, a danger in herself.

She scanned the corners of the cluttered toolshed. There was little to see but shadows. The structure seemed sturdily made, with no cracks to let even the feeble light from outside leak in.

"No danger," Jak said, then vanished from Krysty's side into the blowing white clouds of snow. He knew his companions could handle whatever menace a sobbing, freaked-out girl with black pigtails might pose.

"Right," Ryan said. "Let's move on."

"And just leave her?" Krysty demanded.

Ryan looked at her and shrugged. He was a hard man, because he usually needed to be.

Krysty usually did not try to temper that hardness, but when the time came, she reckoned it was part of her job.

But it was J.B. who spoke up first. "I'd like an account of what happened here," he said. "Best way I know to have a shot at keeping it from happening to us."

Ryan bared strong white teeth, but he nodded. The little man in the scuffed leather bomber jacket, fedora and round wire-rimmed specs was the ultimate technician of survival. He was even more purely practical than Ryan himself, and when he spoke, he spoke to the point.

Taking that as all the assent she needed, Krysty holstered her Glock 18C and picked her way quickly but carefully through the disarrayed tools. She hunkered down by the girl, who wore a simple black shift with long sleeves.

"What's your name?" she asked gently. She mostly wanted to try to pierce the other's veil of uncontrolled emotion before doing anything like touching her. Gentle tones and innocuous words seemed the quickest way.

The girl didn't look at her. Her eyes were screwed so tightly shut in her snow-pale face that it almost seemed as if she was resisting attempts to pry them open. But her shivering began to slow. The rhythm of her heartbroken sobbing began to break up, like the steps of a runner slowing down.

"It's all right," Krysty said. "My name is Krysty and I want to help you."

"Here, now," Ryan protested from behind her. "Let's not go overboard with this."

"Out of the way, Captain Sensitivity," Mildred said brusquely. "A healer needed here."

"But—"

"Healer *working* here."

Although Jak had butted heads with Ryan a few months back, that was all in the past now. The two had discovered the hard way how much they needed each other. Same as everybody in their little crew needed everybody else. Before, during and since that time, the other member of the group to challenge Ryan's authority was Mildred. Krysty reckoned he endured it as much to help keep himself from getting too full of himself and thinking he was infallible—which was a sure recipe to end up with dirt hitting you in the eyes, triple quick. But like every one of the companions, she had a specialty. And when she or anyone of them was engaged in his or her work, Ryan knew to back off.

The way, of course, they did with him. Mostly. Krysty had to grin to herself.

"My friend Mildred is coming to help you, too," Krysty said—fortuitously a moment before she heard the clatter of a tool inadvertently kicked by one of Mildred's combat boot, and a suppressed curse. "You're safe now. Why don't you talk to me? Tell me your name."

An eye opened. It was brown. It looked startlingly dark in that bloodless face. Krysty had to hope that trauma and terror had drained color from her skin. Otherwise she could hardly be healthy.

The eye rolled, then fixed on Krysty. The sobbing dwindled to a sniffling.

"I—I'm Mariah," she said.

"Are you hurt, Mariah?" Mildred asked briskly, kneeling next to Krysty. She subtly shouldered the redhead a bit to the side to make room. The two were best friends. As such, Krysty knew that when she was in full-on healer mode, Mildred was as bullheaded businesslike as her man, J. B. Dix, tinkering up a busted blaster—or using one to chill a room full of stonehearts.

"Any blood? Any broken bones? Any bad pains?"

"No," Mariah said. She moistened her lips with a pale pink tongue. "Can I have some water?"

Mildred promptly pulled a canteen from her belt. With plenty of snow on the ground here near the Black Hills, fresh water wasn't hard to come by. Fresh chow was another thing entirely.

"Come on," she said. "Sit up to drink it."

She let Krysty urge the girl to uncurl her arms from their death grip on her shins. Then Mildred firmly grasped her shoulders and pulled her up to a seated position. Krysty suspected that her friend's bedside manner, as they would have called it in predark times, would have raised some eyebrows, but no matter how abrupt the dark, stocky woman with the beaded hair plaits might be, she treated her patients far more gently than a girl like this was likely used to. It was how the world was.

Mariah took the canteen and drank thirstily, her eyes squeezed shut. Krysty noticed that she didn't spill a drop.

After a moment Mildred eased the canteen back from the girl's lips. "Not too much at a time, or you'll just throw it back up again. Breathe."

For a moment Mariah clutched at the bottle like a nursing baby at the breast. Then she dropped her hand to her lap. Her eyes focused, first on Mildred, then Krysty again. Then they swept over Ryan, J.B., Ricky and Doc, looking in from the doorway.

Jak's friends had put themselves in position to counter whatever threats may have lurked in the toolshed. He, of course, had moved on. His business now was to secure the rest of the small farm settlement and report back to the rest.

Mariah appeared to become more in control of herself. Some color was coming back to her cheeks. Krysty still reckoned she likely was as naturally pale as the redhead was herself.

"I'm Mariah," she said again. "What do you want from me?"

"That's a good question," J.B. said, scratching his neck. Evidently deciding the scared child—she looked now to Krysty to be in her early teens—offered little immediate threat, he had tipped the barrel of his combat shotgun toward the slanted roof. "I can't really think of a thing."

"Information," Ryan rasped. "What happened here? And who did it to whom?"

"What do you mean?" the girl asked.

"That's Ryan," Krysty said. "He's the leader of this crew. Tact isn't his strong suit." She and Mildred hastily introduced the others. Mariah seemed to listen attentively, nodding shyly at each in turn.

"What our fearless leader was asking was two questions at once," Mildred explained.

Krysty saw Ryan frown a bit at that, and she flashed him a grin.

"Why don't you tell us what happened first?" Mildred asked.

Mariah moistened her lips, then she looked down at her hands, lying in her lap like crippled white birds.

"Stickies attacked us before dawn," she said. "The, uh, Baylah family lived here. Actually, a few families did. They were all related to one another somehow, I reckon. I never did get it straight, and no one bothered explaining it to me. Paw and Maw Baylah owned the 'stead, though, and ran the show.

"Just all at once I woke up and there was screaming everywhere. Screams of people and animals in pain. And that awful screeching the muties make."

"Ones with mouths anyway," J.B. said, nodding.

"You were sleeping in your dress?" Mildred asked.

"I do a lot," the girl explained. "In case somebody decides to rouse me out in the middle of the night to do chores."

Krysty watched her closely. If those chores included the sort of sexual favors that were sometimes demanded as the price of boarding—even of children—she wasn't giving the fact away in her face and manner any more than in her words.

If that sort of abuse had happened, the guilty had more than likely paid by now. For what that might be worth.

"You got away?" Ryan asked.

"I was sleeping in the pantry," she said. "They didn't find me. At first. But when I looked out the door to see what was happening, they spotted me. They were... feasting already and across the kitchen. I ran out the door and hid in the first place I hit."

"This shed," Krysty said.

She nodded. "I shut the door. They started hammering on it. Dust flew all off it—I could just see by dawn light seeping in through the little window. I hoped they would get tired and go away. But they knew I was there and didn't give up. Then the door sprang open, and I curled up in a ball like the way that you found me, closed my eyes tight and started to scream."

From the doorway, Ricky made a strangled sound.

"Relax, kid," Mildred told him without looking around. "We know the stickies didn't eat her."

"Why not?" Ryan asked.

"Ryan," Krysty said.

He raised his eyebrows at her. "What? It's a fair question."

Mariah just shook her head. She still didn't look up.

"What happened to the stickies?" Ryan asked carefully, his lone blue eye on Krysty.

Mariah shook his head.

"I don't know. The door burst open. The wind was howling. A big bunch of snow and dust blew in. And the stink—the stickie stink, and fresh blood. And worse—"

Worse likely meaning the reek of torn-open guts, Krysty knew. She was double glad the cold wind tended to carry off the charnel smell and deadened such scent as remained.

"But the stickies didn't come in. I waited and waited to feel their…those awful sucker fingers on me. And those teeth. But it never happened. I still didn't open my eyes because I didn't want to see the world anymore."

"Hard to blame you there," Mildred said.

"Any idea what happened to the muties?" J.B. asked.

"Why?" Mariah sounded confused. "What did? I wondered if something scared them off."

"Something chilled them," Ryan said. "More than that—it was like they all got blown up or chopped to pieces."

"Never seen anything like it," J.B. added.

"And from this outlandish collection of humankind," Doc remarked, "that is a remarkable statement indeed."

Mariah continued to shake her head in what Krysty took for incomprehension.

"We found a man with an ax outside," Mildred said. "We, uh, chilled him. We had to. He thought we were stickies and came rushing at us. We found stickie blood on his ax and stickie wounds on his body after we took him down."

"That'd be Elias," Mariah said. "He always did have a temper on him."

"Enough to chill an entire pack of stickies?" Mildred asked. "Enough to wipe out the whole rest of the farm?"

Mariah just shook her head. "He was big and strong. And you know how men can get when the anger comes upon them."

"Yeah," Ryan said.

Jak called softly from the doorway, "All chills inside. Wind dying." No one had heard him approach. His friend Ricky started at his sudden speech, banging his head on the top of the door frame.

Ryan had been hunkered down beside Mariah, his weapons sheathed or slung, hands on the thighs of his sun-faded jeans. Now he nodded decisively and stood.

"Right," he said. "Well, thank you kindly. That's all we needed to know. We'll be leaving you to it, now."

"Ryan, we can't just leave her," Krysty protested.

He looked at Krysty in what seemed genuine consternation.

"It's time to go," he aid. "Shake the dust of this place off our boot heels."

"But what'll happen to her?"

"She'll find her way. Or she won't. She made it this far, anyhow, and that's a thing. It's not our problem what happens to her now, though. One way or another."

As Krysty scowled at him, the girl abruptly launched herself at her. Blasters whipped up, but instead of attacking her, Mariah was suddenly clinging to her and sobbing. Krysty judged herself lucky she'd been on her knees; otherwise the girl, slight as she was, might've bowled her over backward.

"Krysty's right," Mildred announced as the redhead began to stroke Mariah's head and murmur soothingly to her. "We can't just leave her out in the middle of this god-awful wasteland."

"But she's been living here just fine all along," J.B. said.

"When she had a family and a working farm around her," Mildred shot back. "What is wrong with you, John? Where's your compassion?"

He blinked at her through the round lenses of his specs. "Compassion?" He sounded as if the word was unfamiliar to him.

"There's food," the girl said, still sobbing and her face pressed sideways to Krysty's neck. "Supplies. Powder and shot."

"Jak," Ryan called out. "You still out there?"

"Yeah?"

"How trashed is the place?"

"Chills everywhere," the albino said in his customary clipped and often cryptic speech. "Chill parts, too."

"They get around to pissing down the well?" J.B. asked. "Or tossing any chills down it for poison?"

"No," Jak said.

"So the mutant blackguards got no chance to indulge in an orgy of wanton stickies vandalism," Doc said.

"Before Elias put the chop on 'em," J.B. added.

"Sounds like," Ryan said. "Thanks. We'll make sure to leave plenty for you. And now—"

Krysty put her arms around the girl's thin, shaking shoulders. She was actively shivering now, not just to the timing of her sobs.

"Ryan, no," she said.

"You know as well as I do we can't go picking up every stray we stumble across," Ryan said. "We've got to look out for ourselves."

With a final sniffle, Mariah stopped weeping, or at least stopped weeping as vigorously. The trembling subsided, too, but did not stop.

"What are you doing here?" she asked.

Ryan looked blank. "You mean stumbling around in the storm?" Mildred supplied helpfully.

Mariah nodded.

"Let's say we're new in the district," Mildred said.

"Yeah," Ryan said—grudgingly, because information was a trade good itself. But clearly he saw nothing to be lost by imparting a few morsels to the foundling.

"You looking for work?" Mariah asked.

"Well, yeah. Now that you mention it. We could use a gig."

Their supplies had gotten low. The stocks of food and such the girl had mentioned—and fresh water from the well—would tide them over for a spell. But they were always looking for ways to sustain themselves, and mebbe get ahead, even, for the lean times that inevitably followed.

"I know a place," Mariah said. "A ville nearby. The baron's always looking for help, and he ain't triple bad, as barons go."

"We don't hire on as mercies," Ryan said.

"No. Not that." Mariah paused. "I—I can take you there."

Ryan sighed. "We're outvoted, J.B.," he said. "Even if it's just Mildred and Krysty against the rest of us."

"I don't mind her coming along," Ricky said.

"Put a sock in it," Ryan replied without heat.

"I have no objection to it," Doc put in. "Perhaps performing the occasional humane gesture might remind us of our own humanity."

"I don't see how that loads any blasters for us," Ryan said. "But you can come with us as far as this ville."

Mariah let go of Krysty to spring for Ryan. She caught him around the waist in a powerful hug and pressed her cheek against his breastbone.

"Fireblast!" he exclaimed. "You can come as long as you don't hug me anymore, understand?"

Chapter Four

"Please," the painfully gaunt blonde woman said, falling to her knees on the short, winter-scorched Badlands grass before two glowing avatars. "I did what you told me. Now let me have my daughter back. I beg you!"

"What wretches these people are," Dr. Oates said to Dr. Sandler over the suppressed channel. *"Hardly worth the trouble to rule."*

He might have reminded his colleague that they could just as well speak aloud in this vile, cowering being's presence for all the difference it would make. But he did not. Habit was key to discipline, in communications as in every area of life. Discipline was a goal in itself.

Especially when one's collective goal was full-spectrum dominance over this entire timeline.

By the same mode he told her, *"They can be shaped into useful vessels, into which to pour our leadership and enlightened thinking."*

"Of course, Doctor."

Aloud he said to his supplicant, "What have you done? Report, that we may judge your performance."

"I told him to go up Harney Peak to seek a vision. I told him to eat the magic mushrooms to put himself in the proper receptive state. I betrayed my people, because you told me that's what I needed to do. Isn't that enough for you?" the blonde woman asked.

"How did you betray your people?" Dr. Oates asked. "Inasmuch as your people are Absaroka, and Hammerhand a Blackfoot—and a coldheart outcast at that?"

The woman wrung her hands. "Because their trust in me encompasses the sanctity of my visions! If it were known I gave…false advice to Hammerhand, we would suffer disgrace, loss of standing in councils and even mebbe war!"

"The advice we told you to give was not false," Dr. Sandler said. "The subject climbed the peak as you instructed him to. And there he received the vision he desired. What falsehood was there?"

"But the vision wasn't real. It was an illusion you created. Wasn't it?"

"What a pathetic beast," Dr. Oates said inaudibly to the wretch. *"To imagine there can be any such thing as a 'real' vision."*

"The credulity of our two-legged cattle has long been a mainstay of our power, Dr. Oates. Do not forget the fact."

"I apologize, Doctor."

"Who are you to say our powers are not those of the gods or spirits?" Dr. Sandler asked the woman. "Have we not amply displayed them to you? Did not Hammerhand experience them, for that matter?"

"If I may ask, why do you bother justifying yourself to this belly crawler, Dr. Sandler?"

He deigned to answer. *"Because I cannot abide this creature not understanding her inferior status, however transient that misapprehension proves."*

And if Dr. Oates takes such sentiment as evidence of weakness on my part, he thought, that error will prove her own unfitness to serve Overproject Whisper. And be a self-correcting problem.

His colleague, wisely, chose to say no more.

Meanwhile, the woman had gone back to groveling and whining. "Please. You *promised*."

"We did," Dr. Sandler declared. "You have done as we instructed. And as we promised, we release your daughter to you now."

On cue the silent white-coated lab techs removed the duct tape from the child's mouth and pushed her through the portal into her cold and desolate space-time.

Dr. Sandler's viscera twisted in disgust at the sight of the girl, with her mud-colored hair and dust-colored skin. The feeling did not come from any superstition as vulgar and ignorant as racial prejudice, but from the clear evidence it gave of the unrestricted breeding, without regard for genetics, that prevailed in the Deathlands.

The groveling woman reared back on her knees. Her green eyes went wide, then she spread her arms wide.

"Mommy!" the girl cried. She ran to her mother and threw her arms around her.

"Thank you," Susan Crain sobbed into the juncture of her daughter's neck and shoulder. "Thank you, thank you."

"Go now," he said.

"We are finished with you," Dr. Oates added.

"I'm free?"

"Yes," Dr. Sandler said.

Hastily the woman detached herself from her offspring enough to stand. Taking the child by the hand, she hurried down the slope of the mesa on which she had met the doctors.

Waiting until she was thoroughly out of sight, and

thus splatter range, Dr. Sandler made a certain gesture. Thus activated, the bomb that had been implanted in the child's stomach while she was under sedation went off with sufficient force to blow her mother, as well as her to bits.

"Was that truly necessary, Dr. Sandler?"

"Sentiment, Dr. Oates?"

"Not at all. Rather, practicality. Might the shaman have been of further use to us?"

"No such prospect presented itself, Doctor. Her people belong to the past now. They are retrogressive. They will join the new order our subject will establish, under our guidance and control. Or it shall exterminate them."

"I see."

"And now we have further duties to attend to," Dr. Sandler said and closed the portal that opened between worlds.

"I DON'T KNOW where I was born," Mariah said as they trudged along what looked like some kind of game path trodden by the hooves of deer and elk. The sun had come out that day long enough to melt off much of the snow on the ground. "I don't know who my mother and father were. I don't remember anything but a life of wandering."

Krysty walked beside the girl. Mildred trudged behind the pair. Flat prairie stretched to her left. About half a mile to the right the land rose into badlands, rocky heights, wind-carved and striated in shades of brown and yellow. Ahead of them the Black Hills were visible as dark serrations on the horizon.

"What did you do for the Baylahs?" Mildred asked.

The girl shrugged. "Chores around the 'stead. Chopping wood, cleaning, cooking. The same as I've done my whole life."

"How did they treat you?" Krysty asked.

Another shrug. "Like I was disposable, mostly. Not bad. But mostly like they couldn't be bothered to be mean to me. Also the same as my whole life, mostly."

She seemed to think about it a moment. She was a mighty serious-seeming little girl, Mildred thought. Even though "little" mostly meant "skinny." Mariah seemed maybe thirteen or fourteen and wasn't more than an inch or two shorter than Mildred, who, granted, wasn't a tall woman.

"Not that the Baylahs were mean," Mariah said. "Not like some. I mean, they fed me all right and didn't hit me too much. Didn't...try other stuff."

Mildred grunted, softly enough that the girl couldn't hear. She hoped. Sexual abuse of minors wasn't all that unusual in the here and now.

Not that the life Mariah described, of being a poorly regarded and poorly compensated servant, sounded a whole lot better. Then again, it beat being an outright slave. On the other hand, keeping an extra mouth to feed could only be justified if it freed up enough time and energy among the other members of the group to generate the wherewithal to keep feeding the extra person while feeding themselves just a little bit better.

They didn't call the country *Deathlands* for nothing, Mildred thought.

The girl had made herself useful in camp the previous night, gathering relatively dry brush and even making a fire without being asked. She had taken over cooking the brace of rabbits Jak had hunted and chilled with his special leaf-shaped throwing knives. She'd done a pretty good job, too.

Enough that Ryan stopped grumbling about letting her tag along.

"So you don't know how old you are?" Ricky asked from behind Mildred.

"Not really," Mariah said. "Like I said, I don't remember much. Wandering. Working."

"Don't you get lonely?" Krysty asked.

"Compared to what?"

Mildred laughed, but then she realized the girl had spoken in her usual flat-serious tone. Maybe she hadn't intended a joke. Maybe she was asking seriously.

Mildred felt guilty.

"Know where those stickies came from?" J.B. called to her from the tail end of their procession.

"No. I heard rumors about them around the farm. Stories about people disappearing—travelers, folks out working alone late at night or hunting. Even once or twice about them attacking a few isolated places north of there. Everybody's scared of them—"

"Highly sensible," Doc said from his own position behind Ricky and Ryan in front of the girl. As usual Jak was scouting the terrain ahead.

"But nobody took them none too serious as a threat to them, you know?"

"I wonder why they chose to attack when they did," Doc asked, "and in such force?"

"Who knows why stickies do what they do?" Mildred queried.

"Nevertheless," he said, unfazed, "it might benefit the chances of our own survival if we could obtain some insight into the workings of their minds. Dark and twisted though they are."

"I agree with you, Doc," Ryan said. He was carrying his Steyr Scout cradled in arms crossed across his chest. "Knowing how your enemy thinks can be half the battle or more."

"I wish I could help you." Mariah almost mumbled the words. She seemed to be, on the one hand, desperate to justify her accompanying the others in any way she could and, on the other, terrified by Ryan.

"Don't mind our esteemed leader, Mr. Gruff," Mildred told the girl. "He's always that way before he gets his morning coffee."

That got Mildred a glance and a perplexed look over Mariah's shoulder, which turned to a look of near panic when the others burst out laughing. Even Ryan mustered a brief chuckle.

"When's the last time we had real coffee, do you reckon, Ryan?" J.B. asked.

Ryan rubbed his chin.

"A few weeks for sure, the time we traded a homie blaster for a dozen old MRE packs."

"She did report stickie attacks coming out of somewhere north of where we found her," J.B. said. "Reckon that's a good clue."

"Of somewhere to stay away from," Mildred said.

"That's the truth," Krysty stated.

"So you're sure you got no idea why they attacked the Baylah farm?" Ryan asked. "Or why they wound up leaving you alone?"

"No, sir," Mariah said.

He sighed, looking skeptical.

"If that man we shot went berserk with his ax and

chilled all the stickies," Krysty said, "that would explain why Mariah was left unharmed."

Ryan frowned but said nothing. He grunted and turned away.

For her part, Mildred was far from sure that one man with an ax, no matter how strong and crazy he might be, could do the kind of damage and sheer amount of it they'd seen.

But she was in no mood to gratify Ryan by feeding his paranoia just now. She focused on putting one boot in front of the other.

Chapter Five

Hamarsville was a curious sight: a log palisade made out of straight, peeled tree trunks, sticking up out of a meadow nestled among pine-wooded heights on the northeast fringes of the Black Hills. The most prominent features inside the expansive wall, visible to Ryan from the brush on a ridgetop to the south and east from which the companions were scoping the ville, included a watchtower, a lot of bark-shingled roofs and prominent clouds of white steam and darker smoke arising from various chimneys.

What they were making in that stockade was apparent by a light westerly undulating breeze over the low mountain range.

"Turpentiners," Mildred said from Ryan's side, sniffing at the air.

"That's right," Mariah stated. She sounded almost eager, which even Ryan acknowledged was more emotion than she'd showed over the three days since they'd picked her up at the massacre site. "Mostly distill pine oil. Old Paw Baylah said they been at it a couple generations."

"It is a sizable settlement," Doc observed. "And just from what these old eyes can observe at this remove, a relatively prosperous one."

"Yeah," J.B. said, pushing his fedora back on his head.

He was hunkered down to Ryan's right. "Looks like it must run two hundred people. Mebbe more."

Ryan raised his recently acquired World War II–era field glasses to his eye. It was something of an affectation for him to carry them, big and rather bulky as they were, and built specifically for the one thing he didn't have—binocular vision—but they had triple-good optics. Besides, using the low-powered Leopold sight on his Scout longblaster to scope a place out was considered a mighty unfriendly act.

Although they were well concealed up here in the scrub—and Ryan had known better than to let sunlight reflect off the object lens of a scope to heliograph his position to potential enemies since he was a sprat—he avoided doing it on principle when there was reason to suspect the people under observation weren't hostile.

Ryan heard a rustling sound from his left as he focused the binocs. It was Jak. The fact Ryan or any of them had heard the albino meant he had deliberately made the noise so as not to startle his friends when they were already on yellow alert, which they customarily were this close to a settlement.

"Wag coming," the scout announced softly. "Ox-drawn. Driver and lever-gun guard."

It was a long speech for the slight young man and one that came perilously close to delivering a second full sentence on top of his opening statement. But it was all potentially important information.

"Ace," Ryan said. "Thanks."

He didn't need to be told that Jak assessed the approaching wag as posing little threat any more than he had to be told that Jak, having delivered his information, had faded instantly back into the wilds around them. Had he detected even a whiff of danger he would have said that straight off. Ryan had spent years in the employ of the enigmatic man known as the Trader, in whose company he had met J.B. He knew full well that the last thing a pair of wag drivers would be doing would be looking to start trouble. Their livelihoods—and lives—depended on avoiding as much of that commodity as they could.

The road ran to their right, along the stream that passed directly through the ville and out under the log-fort walls. The wag in question not being visible yet, Ryan went ahead and took a leisurely look over the ville.

It confirmed Doc's and J.B.'s assessments, as well as his own: a big place, with sturdy defenses and well-built structures. It was the kind of place to attract plenty of unfriendly attention. And because it had clearly been there a spell, just the way Mariah had said, the inhabitants knew how to repel unwanted attention. When he raised his glasses to the watchtower, he saw a sentry, clearly female despite the shade the roof gave from the afternoon sun, leveling a scoped longblaster and pointing it at the approaching wag. The wagoneers likely recognized that having a bead drawn on them was just a necessary precaution.

The vehicle appeared, rolling in ruts worn in the hard earth by years of previous traffic. With less interest in commerce than he had in the back side of the moon, Jak had neglected to mention whether it was laden or not. But in fact it carried a load of crates and bags woven of some rough fabric, likely hemp, the sorts of things traders might be expected to carry.

The gate, which was also constructed of peeled logs like the surrounding walls, was drawn to the right to open the way for the wag. It rolled inside the stockade without apparent challenge or formality.

"How do they take to strangers showing up on their doorstep?" Ryan asked Mariah as he handed the binocs to J.B.

"It happens all the time," the girl said. "Don't cause them any fuss at all. They take in a lot of jack through their gaudy, which Baron Hamar owns, and the boarding house, which is run by his sister, Agnes."

"What happens if their visitors misbehave?" Ryan asked.

"They usually leave their chills strung up outside the walls," Mariah said without inflection. "As a warning to others. Till they start to smell bad anyway. Leastways, that's what Chad Baylah said. He was the youngest, a few years older than me, and not much given to fibbing, for fear of his maw."

J.B. halted in the act of raising the binocs to his face. He looked at Ryan, who shrugged.

"Fair enough," he said. "Let's go see a man about a job."

"YOU GOT PLENTY of blasters," Baron Hamar said, running his pale blue eyes up and down the newcomers in the dusty street in front of his establishment. "Do you know how to use them?"

Though J.B. was a man not much given to trying to puzzle out another person's feelings, he had learned across the span of his long and eventful life to pay attention to certain basics. It was hard to make it out of boyhood still breathing, especially when you were as skinny a little runt as J.B. had been, without noticing whether a person was obviously hostile.

This stocky baron did not sound overtly angry or suspicious. As for the niceties, such as how likely he was to be dissembling, J.B. left that to the others—to Ryan, who did pay more attention to that sort of thing, because he paid attention to anything that might affect their chances of survival, and to Krysty. The redhead disavowed any suggestion that her mutie powers gave her any sort of psychic insight as to what other people were thinking and feeling, but she was good at sniffing out their emotions.

"We had occasion to put them to use a few times," Ryan said. J.B. had done his time with Trader, too, longer than Ryan had, in fact. He knew from observation that what his friend was engaging in was not self-deprecation. Rather, in the Deathlands, where swaggering braggarts were plentiful, that kind of understatement was just a good sales pitch.

Baron Hamar clearly took it as such. "Good," he said, emphatically nodding his square head. He had close-cropped bronze hair and a well-tended beard, both liberally streaked with white. He wore a soiled apron over a simple flannel shirt and denim pants, with a blaster belt strapped over it and a Model 1911 handblaster riding in the holster, hammer back and held in by a thumb strap.

"Got use for men and women who know how to handle themselves in a fight," he said, "you betcha."

"We don't do mercie work, Baron," Ryan said. "Got to make that clear up front."

"Oh, no, no. I've got a sec team, and my people can fight, too, if anyone makes trouble for us. We do business. We do not look for trouble."

"Ace on the line," Ryan said. "What do you need, then?"

"Come, my friends," Hamar said. "Walk with me."

He turned and nodded pointedly to what J.B. took to be a handful of his staff and a couple of young, gaudy sluts standing on the elevated plank walkway in front of the gaudy house. It was called Sailor's Rest, according to a weathered board sign, obviously hand painted with some care and skill. What a sailor might find to be doing here in this thoroughly landlocked part of the world, J.B. had not a clue. He suspected resting was a good bet, though, since according to Doc they weren't far from the spot farthest from any coast in all of North America.

The employees took their boss's hint and vanished back inside. Hamar guided the companions west at a brisk walk along the main street toward what was clearly the turpentine distillery, from its size and appearance. Not to mention its ever-increasing smell.

"Hard times have come to this part of the Plains," Hamar said.

"That's not exactly breaking news," Mildred muttered.

Ryan turned his head back toward her, ever so slightly. "Shutting up now," Mildred said.

J.B. loved the woman, but she did have a tendency to run her mouth. It was a good thing Baron Hamar had a solid rep for being as easygoing as his manner suggested, or almost. Mariah told them that the patriarch of the Baylah clan considered it a scandal just how liberal he was. But the calluses on Baron Hamar's strong square hands made it clear that, baron or not, he was no stranger to doing hard work.

And the condition of his knuckles told J.B. loud and clear that Hamar was also no stranger to bouncing them off the odd skull, which might have just been how he delivered gentle warnings to gaudy patrons as the step before hanging their hides out on his stockade wall to dry. Whatever the case was, even the most scandalously liberal-minded baron was still a baron and unlikely to be well disposed to getting back talk.

"We've got coldhearts," Hamar said. "Of course we do. Every five, ten years, they've got to make a run at us. Just to learn."

J.B. saw Ryan nod appreciatively. They had to teach some pretty tough lessons in that subject hereabouts, if the learning lasted that long among the Plains bandit bands.

The Armorer kept his eyes roving from side to side, taking in the surroundings—and the onlookers. Jak, as always when he found himself surrounded by anything that might even attract the accusation of being civilization, walked as warily as an old trading-post tomcat who stumbled into a coyote conclave.

"But we've got a new bunch moving in," the baron said. "Muscling in on the other gangs. Getting bigger, stronger. Even enough to start worrying the Plains nations."

That got J.B.'s attention. From what he knew of the area, the Native Americans could be spiky to deal with on their own. Though they generally gave grief to each other more than to any outlanders, depending on who was allied with whom and who was currently blood-feuding, none of them were the sort of people a man would care to rub the wrong way.

"Heard they roughed up Red Knife's Arapaho crew pretty good on the Mussleshell two or three weeks ago. No pushovers, that bunch."

They reached the end of the street. J.B. would not have minded an invitation to inspect the turpentine-distilling equipment, fragrant as it was. It looked mostly like a random collection of pipes and boilers. But it was still something that had been built and fixed with a person's hands. As such, it caught J.B.'s interest.

But apparently Baron Hamar had just felt like stretching his legs. He stopped in front of the operation, far enough away not to interfere with workers wheeling barrows of wood chips from the water-wheel-powered grinder and such to the hoppers.

"Not just bold for coldhearts, but genuinely badass, then," Ryan said. "Have they got a name?"

"Bloods, they call themselves."

"Fireblast! You mean, the Blackfeet are doing this?"

That signaled that it would be an ace time for them all to turn right around and shake the dust of the whole district from their heels triple-fast. The Confederation was one of the biggest and strongest tribes. If they were making a hard move south, it meant that this whole part of the Plains was on the verge of bursting into a wildfire that could easily consume Ryan and his companions. The companions knew the area. The bands that already roved here, such as the Absaroka and the Lakota, would be looking to teach the invaders some hard lessons.

"Not the Confederacy, no," Hamar said. "Nor the actual Blood band. Freelancers who are using the name."

"Black dust!" J.B. was moved to say. "Real Bloods aren't likely to cotton to that."

"Mebbe that's the point," Hamar said. "Rumor says these new Bloods' boss man is a Blood renegade, a young firebrand who calls himself Hammerhand."

"You can just tell *he's* a people person," Mildred said

under her breath. J.B. started to frown at that, but then Krysty gave a half-stifled snicker.

Ryan showed no sign he'd even heard her, although J.B. didn't doubt he had.

"They give you any trouble yet?"

"No. It is just a matter of time, I'm sure. But we weathered such storms before. No, they haven't even been reported within three days' ride of here. But they're starting to hit trade harder and harder."

"So where do we come in?" Ryan asked.

"Do you want us to help guard your caravans as part of your sec force?" Krysty asked.

"Oh, no," the baron said. "It's not goods I want to deliver. It's information!"

Chapter Six

In a single panther-like leap, Hammerhand sprang into the bed of the rebuilt pickup truck. For all his bulk he landed lightly enough that the Buffalo Mob sentry, leaning over the roll bar onto the Tacoma's cab roof to enjoy a smoke under the cold, starry sky, was only alerted to danger when he felt the vehicle rock on its spring beneath his feet.

By then it was too late to dodge. Or even to scream.

Hammerhand felt the man's bearded chin dig into his biceps as he wrapped an arm around the coldheart's throat. He snatched hold of that chin with his free hand and violently torqued the sentry's head to the right.

His thick neck snapped with a sound loud enough to turn even Hammerhand's bowels briefly to ice water. He froze as he felt the dying bandit convulse and his nostrils filled with the rich, wet reek of his sphincter letting go in his camo pants.

Inside the circle formed by the score of power wags parked on the nighttime prairie, the Buffalo Mob's rowdy reverie continued unabated around a dozen or so campfires. The woman playing on a harmonica with surprising skill never missed a beat. Neither did the pair of women dancing drunkenly to the tune.

Hammerhand had spent an hour crouched in the scrub nearby, scoping out his target. So had twenty of his best Bloods, split up into three teams led by himself, Joe Takes-Blasters and Mindy Farseer. It was a risk taking the whole top leadership to a single raid, but this was all a high-risk gamble for high stakes.

That was the point. Not just to score a number of power wags and start a serious upgrade on the mobility of his insurgent Plains nation, but also to do so with sufficient demon style to act as a beacon to the bold and ambitious by its very own self.

That had been part of what the Glowing Man told him. Not giving him the idea. Far from it. Telling him that the idea he had was righteous, as was his dream of establishing a Plains empire in blood and fire, and that he was destined to go for it.

And succeed.

When Hammerhand was certain no one had heard him inside the camp of more than a hundred coldhearts, not even the sentries posted in the other circled wags, he slowly lowered the chill to the pickup's bed. As he did, he eased the slung M16 off the dead man's back. A quick check showed a round in the chamber and a full magazine of 5.56 mm ammo in the well.

After another look toward the campfires, Hammerhand gave the corpse a quick toss, relieving him of a crumpled-up, greasy wad of local jack and a nice Cold Steel lock-back folding knife. Then he stooped, grabbed and, with a muffled grunt of effort, deadlifted the considerable weight high enough to roll over the wag bed's wall on the dark side. Then he hunkered down again.

The Buffalo Mob, as they called themselves, had certainly been exercising diligence in securing their wags and their scarcely more valuable own personal asses. Every other wag had a guard in it, constantly casting watching eyes across the surrounding grassland for just this kind of sneak attack. At least theoretically. The chill's slackness—going so far as to actually smoke on sentry duty, spotlighting him to any sharp-eyed watcher within hundreds of yards and any decent nose downwind—showed how little the Buffalo Mob's sentries regarded the possibility that any prairie pirates would be bold and skillful enough to try creeping on them and seizing the precious vehicles by stealth.

But *bold* and *skillful* were the criteria Hammerhand used to pick his Bloods, even in those rough first days when he, an outcast without a clan and without a reputation, had been struggling to get by with whatever he could scrape together. He had always been picky about who he chose to ride with him—at least as picky as he could afford to be.

Of course, *crazy* was another trait he selected for. But that kind of fell into the general territory of *bold*, to his way of thinking.

And of course, those without the proper mix of boldness and skill tended to get winnowed out of the band fast. With mebbe a bit of a push from Hammerhand's own hands. He hadn't had to chill any of his own for stepping out of line, past the occasional feeb who turned up thinking he might challenge the big man for the role of boss cock. But before he'd got his size and strength in the middle of his teens, he'd had to rely on his wits to get his ass out of the cracks his rough, rebellious nature and smart mouth got it stuck in. Early on he'd figured out how to talk the overly bold into throwing their own stupe lives away and even how to goad the overly cautious into taking fatal risks.

And when it came to fatal risks, apparently the invading coldheart mob never reckoned on a local gang with the patience to spend ten days shadowing them and scoping out their ways and numbers before making a move.

From his left he heard a strange, soft, gobbling cry. He grinned. Joe Takes-Blasters did a piss-poor impression of a prairie grouse. Not that these tenderfeet would know the difference. Or even notice over their own noise.

The Buffalo Mob ran somewhere north of a hundred strong. Well armed, well mounted and surprisingly well fed, they had in recent weeks made a move into the North Plains west of the Misery River, seeking richer pickings than what was offered by the deeper Deathlands to the east and south, where the land was parched and pocked with deposits of still-lethal rad-dust.

But they weren't looking to live by hunting the herds of bison that roved the prairie. Life wasn't easy for those who lived out here—settlers, traders or nomads alike. But by the standards of the day they did pretty well.

Nor did it matter a bent shell casing to Hammerhand what their business was. They were outlanders—interlopers. Meaning they had no family or other allies in the area to concern him. More to the point: they had something he wanted.

Needed.

He slipped over the side of the wag bed, carefully holding the plundered longblaster so that neither it nor the plastic buckles on the sling would clack against the wag. Then, quietly, he opened the cab door and slipped in.

At least the Buffaloes had the sense to park their wags in a counterclockwise nose-to-circle tail, meaning the driver's-side doors faced inward toward their fires.

A quick check by feel revealed the dangling wire bundle of the ignition. Like most wags left over from skydark these hadn't come with keys. So the owners had set them up for quick, efficient hot-wiring.

He rolled down the left-hand window and leaned the M16 against the driver's door with its muzzle brake pointed up. Then he settled in to wait.

He didn't have to wait long. From the far side of the coldheart camp he heard a sudden shout of alarm cut short by a blaster shot. One or more of his raiding party had been detected. Bad luck, sure, but it was nothing that he, and his plan, hadn't counted on. They had hoped to get away with every last wheel of the Buffalo Mob's rolling stock in one stroke. But they were prepared to take what they could.

He quickly fired up the engine, which started right away. At least the Buffalo Mob had competent wrenches and kept their fleet ready to go.

As soon as the engine caught, he picked up the long-blaster by the pistol grip, shoved it out the open window with its nylon forestock resting on the sill and triggered a burst.

He aimed deliberately low, so as not to endanger his own people on the other side of the circle. The point wasn't to hit anybody anyway. It was to panic the cold-hearts, to encourage them to keep their heads down while he and his band made their getaway with what-ever wags they'd managed to snag.

Firing another short burst into the grass, he gave the pickup some gas, or at least the alcohol fuel the vehicle had been modified to run on. The wag's deep-cleated tires dug into the grass and the vehicle started to roll. Muzzle flashes flared orange from the camp itself and points along the perimeter of parked wags. One bullet cracked through the planking fixed crudely over the busted-out rear window on Hammerhand's side, to add a second star to the glass on the passenger side.

"That best not have been one of mine," he said aloud.

He triggered another burst. "Eat that, you mutie fuckers!" he screamed joyously.

Behind him he was pleased to see several other wags pulling out of the circle behind him. Like him, the Blood drivers were leaving their lights off. They knew the surrounding land well enough not to need them. Or he'd know the reason why.

Laughing aloud in sheer exhilaration, he drove toward the rendezvous spot at reckless speed. Mere unseen obstacles meant nothing.

He had Destiny on his side. And more, he had a Vision.

A TERRIBLE, RINGING scream ripped Ryan Cawdor awake.

He snapped at once into full consciousness and was already in the act of rolling from his bedroll and reaching for his longblaster, which lay on a drop cloth beside it. Whatever had made that sound wasn't human.

But it was at least as big. A 9 mm handblaster wasn't going to be enough to deal with it.

It was their last night on the road to Duganville. Baron Hamar was paying a good amount of jack and supplies in exchange for them delivering a wax-sealed pack of documents to the baron. Both J.B. and his hero-worshipping apprentice, Ricky Morales, had begged to be allowed to winkle the papers out, claiming they could do so without breaking the seal or leaving any sign Baron Dugan or his wiliest sec men could detect. Ryan had told them no. It wouldn't load any blasters for them that he could see. Whereas if they screwed up—unlikely as he had to admit that was, as skillful, meticulous and sneaky as the two of them were—they could get stiffed of their pay. Or worse. He had no fear they'd use those traits to try it anyway. When his word was freely given, the Armorer kept it. And the kid was too in awe of his mentor—not to mention stone terrified of Ryan—to try to pull anything on his own.

Aware and alert, Ryan rose to one knee. By habit he wrapped the loop of the sling around his left forearm to give added stability to any shooting stance he may need to assume, however rapid and ad hoc. The night was dark and clear, the sky infested with stars. The low, brushy hills they'd chosen to camp among for security, rather than the mostly flat surrounding lands, brooded dark and silent.

Dead silent. The usual night sounds, of birds and early insects, had been cut off by that scream. Even the breeze seemed to be holding its breath, and his friends, awake, alert and armed around him, made no more noise.

Beside Ryan, Krysty gave him a quick squeeze on the arm with her left hand to reassure him that she was unharmed. Her other hand held her Glock 18. But Ryan heard Mildred mutter softly, "Ricky! The kid's on watch."

He could hear the consternation in her outburst—soft-voiced instead of whispered, since whispers carried as well as conversation at least and attracted double the suspicion when detected. As much as Ricky exasperated her at times, he was part of this group, this family, and she cared for him.

Jak sprang up and went bounding off into the night, clutching his trench knife. He hated leaving his self-appointed duty of watching over the others at night, but Ricky was his close comrade, as the only member of the group younger than Jak.

But here, through the middle of the camp, vaulting the carefully buried remnants of their campfire, came Ricky. He clutched his Webley handblaster in one hand and his dark eyes were wide and wild. He was racing from what Ryan realized was the opposite direction the scream came from.

"Where's Mariah?" Krysty asked softly, despite the boy's noise.

Ryan shrugged. He wasn't sure why the girl was still with them. It had been his full intent to drop her off at Hamarville. But somehow she was still tagging along, keeping the pace, keeping her mouth shut unless spoken to and taking on the bulk of the camp chores.

Plus Krysty seemed to be growing attached to her. Mebbe too attached. Ryan would have to speak to his flame-haired mate, who had already set off in Ricky's noisy wake. The youthful sentry had jumped over a low bush and disappeared. Ryan could only grunt and follow her, aware that J.B. was right behind with his M-4000 ready, and Mildred and Doc were following the Armorer.

Past the bush, as Ryan knew from giving their environs a thorough recce before settling down for the night, the ground sloped quickly to a shallow, sandy-bottomed dry wash, winding down through the hills to the cultivated fields Mariah had told them they'd find near Duganville. The girl herself stood in the gully, arms held rigidly down by her sides, fists clenched.

Jak was crouched on the bank, gazing intently at the sandy bottom. As the others came down the slope, he held up a white palm to them, to stop them from coming any closer.

Krysty ran to Mariah's side. "Are you all right, sweetie?"

Sweetie? Ryan's mind echoed. This has definitely gone too far. Krysty had a huge heart, and he loved her for it.

But if this weird inward kid was starting to make her maternal instincts get the better of her survival ones—that could be a problem for all of them.

"I'm fine," he heard Mariah say as he pulled up alongside her and began to scan the night and darkened landscape beneath with his lone eye.

He could not help but feel a thrill of alarm that with them all gathered there in the arroyo they were making themselves ace targets for anyone or anything ill-intentioned that happened to pop up on top of its banks. Then he spotted J.B. standing guard from atop the slope the rest of them had just rushed down like triple stupes and felt reassured. If not less stupe.

"What was it?" Mildred asked.

"A tiger," Mariah said. She never looked up, nor did she change the near-flat, quiet tone of her voice. She might as well have been remarking that the water for their chicory-and-tree-bark coffee sub was commencing to boil.

"A *tigre*?" Ricky asked. He stood just up the bank from her, where his buddy Jak had stopped his forward progress. "You mean, like a mountain lion?" In American Spanish, *tigre*—tiger—could mean any kind of big cat, including a cougar or a jaguar, although it was way too cold up here this time of year for the latter.

"No," she said. "Tiger tiger. Big, stripes."

"Bengal," Jak said. "Real tiger. See prints?"

At that positive verbal outpouring from the reticent and cryptically spoken young albino, Ryan squinted his eye harder at the sand above which Jak was hunkered. He saw them then, plain enough: tracks as big as hands with fingers splayed.

"Fireblast," he said.

The others muttered surprised concern. He felt the tension rise as they all looked harder at their surroundings, lest the giant bastard come springing down on them. Descendants of zoo beasts released by compassionate, or perhaps foolhardy, humans in the wake of the Big Nuke, some breeding populations of big exotic cats like leopards, lions and tigers, had taken root in various parts of the Deathlands. They were nowhere common, but where they ranged, they were nowhere rare enough—the big cats were not hesitant to snack on human flesh.

"But where did the brute go?" Doc inquired. He had both his swordstick and his outsized LeMat drawn and ready. Ryan reckoned all of the companions might *just* be enough to heat a leaping tiger past nuke red by the time its five hundred pounds landed on one of them.

Mariah shrugged as if the question bored her. "Away."

"'Away'?" Mildred echoed in alarm. "Just 'away'? *Where* 'away'?" She started whipping her head left and right.

The girl just shook her head.

"Nowhere," Jak said.

Everybody looked at him.

"You care to be more specific?" Ryan said.

Jak stared at him if he were a complete feeb, which was how Ryan had commenced to feel the moment the question left his lips. What could be more specific than "nowhere"?

Not that "nowhere" made a lick of sense.

"Mebbe you could explain that a bit more to us mere mortals, Jak," J.B. suggested.

"Tracks come. Don't leave." A white hand waved his Python handblaster in a semicircle. "No tiger."

"By the Three Kennedys, he is right," Doc said. "An impeccable syllogism, as well."

"Congratulations," Mildred murmured. "You win a cookie."

"So where did it go?" Krysty asked Mariah.

"He was just there," the girl said. "Then he wasn't. I don't know where he went. He just did."

Ryan let go of a breath he wasn't even aware he'd been holding in a long, exasperated sigh.

"This would have to make triple more sense than it does," he said, "to make none at all. Jak, don't you have anything?"

"No."

"You don't see any sign of where it disappeared to? Mebbe like it jumped off into the bushes out of sight?"

"Looked."

"Look again." Ryan was on the verge of telling everybody else to keep their eyes skinned and their blasters up. Then he realized that'd be a waste of words.

Frowning resentfully at the imputation he might have missed something—especially something as large as tracks made by a leaping tiger—Jak started to turn away to make another circuit of the area where the prints led and stopped. Then he froze and looked back to the bottom of the bank. His white features were still knotted around the brows and tight round the mouth, but it was no longer a frown of anger.

It was plain puzzlement.

"There," he said, pointing at a small fourwing saltbush sprouting right on the verge of the empty streambed.

Ryan, still unwilling to move forward and risk disturbing tracks that he couldn't see but Jak perhaps could, hunkered down and looked hard at the bush.

"What is it?" he asked.

"Blood," Jak said. "Fresh. Still shiny."

Then Ryan saw it: a few dark patches spattered on the branches and skinny little leaves. He could just make it out by a glint of starlight.

"Some there." Jak pointed to the grass across the bed. "Drops fell there."

He pointed at three randomly spaced depressions in the sand. They were smaller than even baby ant-lion larva traps. The albino's red eyes hadn't missed them—they didn't miss much—but he had dismissed them as insignificant. Before he recognized blood spill.

"Tiger blood?" Mildred asked.

It was her turn to be on the receiving end of Jak's furrowed-brow, tight-lipped glare.

"We don't have any way to know," Krysty said, compassionately throwing herself on that hand grenade of pointing out the obvious for the sake of her best friend. "Seems like the best bet, though, doesn't it?"

"Could it be from a kill?" Ricky asked.

Ryan grunted. "Could be." He tended to take the kid for granted, even though he had proved his value to the group by saving everybody's life several times over.

It occurred to Ryan that he was the *last* stray orphan they'd come across. Before the strange girl.

Doesn't mean I'm not dropping her off at the next ville, he told himself sternly.

"That's a possibility, too," he said. "But we need a clean sweep of the area to make sure the bastard's gone. All together, vee formation. Me on point, Jak scouting up ahead so he won't pout."

"And when we're done, double watches the rest of the night."

Mildred scoffed.

"Ryan," she said, "after something like this, do you honestly expect any of us will sleep?"

Chapter Seven

"Did you see the way I counted coup on that bastard coldheart?" Hammerhand was pumped and strutting back and forth between a pair of pickups parked twenty feet apart with their noses facing each other at the rendezvous spot. "I broke his nuking neck. Bang! Like that."

"Yeah, yeah," Mindy Farseer, leaning against the other truck, said. She had boosted it and driven to this low mesa several miles from the Buffalo Mob's camp. Two other stolen wags were already parked a little farther off. A fifth was just pulling up, a big cargo wag, well loaded from the way it rode low on its suspension. "We saw it, Randy Macho Savage."

"Uh, it was 'Macho Man' Randy Savage," Joe Takes-Blasters said as he got out of the newly arrived wag and started walking over. He was literal minded and had a fondness for predark professional wrestling. He had the tattered remains of several wrestling magazines in his pack.

"I meant what I said. Like I always do."

Hammerhand showed Mindy his teeth. "You could keep in mind the 'Macho' part and do something about the 'Randy.'"

His lieutenant gave him the finger. "In your dreams." She was the only one who could get away with that.

Just as she was the only one who could get away with calling him a "savage." He knew she'd never put out for him, which was a slagging shame because she was a thermonuke fox. But he had to give her shit about it.

That sort of thing could not be permitted to flow only one way.

The other Blood raiders were acting more visibly excited, dancing in circles, whooping and high-fiving. Hammerhand joyously joined them.

"How many more did we get away with?" Mindy asked Joe, louder than necessary and looking at Hammerhand. A couple more wags were just pulling in.

"Not more than half," Joe said. "Somebody blew our shit up."

"Us or them?" Hammerhand asked, suddenly interested in how it had happened.

Joe shook his head.

"I don't know yet. But I hope we get more skinny when the others get here."

"If they get here," Mindy added darkly.

But as she spoke, several more wags arrived.

"We're it," said a woman named Steeltongue, jumping from the bed of a Dodge Ram with several other raiders. It wasn't exactly a traditional First Nation name, but the Bloods were all about the present. Anyway, not even Hammerhand's home tribe, nor the rest of the Blackfoot Confederacy, really stuck to their own ancient traditions, and they hadn't for generations.

"That's, what, ten wags?" Joe said.

"Outstanding," Hammerhand stated.

"Not quite half," Mindy said sourly.

Hammerhand shrugged. "Everybody accounted for?"

"We lost Cody Blackfeather," said Lou Shine, a lanky, dark-skinned man with long, tightly curled hair.

"How did it go down?" Hammerhand asked.

"That's what blew up the surprise," Lou said. "Cody ran smack into pair of coldhearts slipping off to get it on in the bed of a pickup. Dude gave a warning shout before Cody blasted him. Then the woman gave him both barrels of a sawed-off in the gut."

"Ouch," Joe said.

"Where's Cody, then?" Mindy asked.

"He killed himself," Lou told them.

"Ace," Hammerhand said. "He acted right. Like a Blood warrior!"

Mindy wasn't so sure. "If you say so."

Along with the ten wags, it turned out they'd come back with six longblasters, three full-auto—including the M16 Hammerhand had liberated himself—and a Smith & Wesson .357 Magnum revolver, all in good shape. The Buffalo Mob apparently tended to their weapons as scrupulously as they tended to their wags.

That to Hammerhand justified his choice to move by the stealth route on this attack. He had wanted to rack up an easy strike, low casualty, for his own budding tribe, to build morale, esprit de corps, and reputation—though mostly he was concerned about the wags themselves not getting shot up.

Warriors, he could replace. Even good ones. Wags, not so much.

"This is ace on the line," he said, walking back and forth amid his people and rubbing his hands in unaffected glee. "We win. We win!"

"But they've still got eleven power wags," Mindy pointed out. "And a mess of blasters."

"Why, then, we'll just have to get our shit together and go back and grab the rest of the wags, won't we?" he asked with big grin.

"How?"

"Strategy," he said. His grin widened. "You're good at that, right?"

She frowned, then she nodded.

"Reckon so."

"Ace. Then let's saddle up and get back to camp. Reckon the rest of the Buffalo Mob is swarming out looking for us, hot past nuke red, like yellow jackets from a dug-open nest. Plus we got us a lot of celebrating to do. And we have to sing Cody Blackfeather's spirit safely to the Other Side."

He pumped the M16 over his head and shouted at the top of his lungs, *"Bloods ride!"*

"WHY ARE YOU so set against her staying with us, Ryan?" Krysty asked.

"We're not a walking orphanage," Ryan rasped in answer to her question. He'd indulged in a shot of the baron's personal brand of whiskey. It had roughened his voice up some, so Krysty judged it hadn't been exactly smooth. "We've dropped off kids at worse places than this and never looked back."

The bar in the Brews'n'Booze, the Duganville gaudy house owned and operated by Baron Budo Dugan, was hopping that evening. Duganville was a small ville in a low, wide, fertile valley, protected by a fence made mostly of crude planks and topped with coils of razor tape. As Hamarville had, it smelled of the product that brought it its fame, and a comfortable enough measure of prosperity to make it worthwhile guarding with that kind of a barrier, and that kind of a hard-eyed sec force mounted in watchtowers at all four corners.

But in this case it was hard liquor they made in their cookers and pipe contraptions from grain grown in the surrounding fields. As well, beer was brewed by several leading families, including the baron's. Ricky claimed the smell made him nauseated, but even he decided it was better to spend the night beneath a roof than outside the wire with the stars, the wildlife and the ever-present possibility of coldhearts.

An old woman was banging enthusiastically on a dilapidated piano with enough verve and skill to make up for the decades that had passed since it had seen a tuning. Mostly. People were drinking and joking in a mostly good-natured way. A pair of sturdy sec officers, a shaven-headed man and a woman with a black-dyed Mohawk, standing at either end of the saloon with muscle-thick arms crossed over their chests, may have had something to do with that.

The bar was made of long planks laid across the tops of stout barrels. The tables and chairs were made of decommissioned kegs and barrels, as well. Mildred had remarked that the place reminded her of what she called a "fern bar" from her own time, but Krysty thought the reason for the furnishings was simple thrift. The rest of the party sat together at a long table, eating a not-bad meal of buffalo stew and various vegetables, with chunks of coarse bread on the side.

Mariah was sitting at the table with the others, staring into her plate as if it were a working vid screen, and ignoring Ricky's earnest efforts to talk to her.

"Is she slowing us down that much?" Krysty challenged.

"Not a bit," Ryan admitted.

"Is she pulling her weight?"

Ryan squinted his good eye and scratched the back of his neck beneath his shaggy black hair.

"And then some, mebbe."

"You looking for a good time, handsome?" The gaudy slut who appeared out of nowhere to rub her hip all over Ryan's right shoulder wasn't bad looking. Blonde, if not naturally so, faded blue eyes and full breasts only nominally concealed by a low red bodice. She was probably just shy of thirty years but looked as if she was a decently preserved forty.

The slight slurring of her words showed she'd already been dosing herself against the hardships of her nightly shift. Krysty had to give her credit for boldness, no question. Even if her courage was the kind Baron Dugan was famous for distilling and selling.

Ryan shook his head. "I'm pretty well set up in that department," he said. "Thanks anyway."

The blonde made a kissy mouth at Krysty. "I see," she said. "She's a real firecracker, isn't she?"

"You noticed," Ryan said.

"How about it, Red? You good to go?"

"Thank you for the offer," Krysty said sweetly, "but I'm well set up, too." There was nothing insincere in her tone. She felt sympathy for the woman, who was just scrabbling to get by, like anyone in the Deathlands. And she certainly didn't feel threatened by her.

"Both of you at once, mebbe?" the woman asked with desperation just starting to tinge her voice. "You're both good looking. Better than my usual run of customer by a long shot. Give you a two-for-one special?"

"Sorry," Krysty said. "But we've got business to attend to right now. So, if you'll excuse us—"

Still the woman didn't move off. Krysty twitched her red hair, which was hanging unbound to her shoulders. Just a little.

The woman blinked, flashed a nervous smile and quickly left.

Ryan raised an eyebrow. Krysty read his thoughts loud and clear: Aren't you running a risk, flashing your mutie hair like that?

She smiled sadly and shook her head. "She's tipsy enough to doubt her own eyes," she said. "And she knows nobody would believe her anyway."

It was a harsh reality that Krysty was none too enamored of. But she was alive precisely because she always made a point to recognize reality and adjust her wishes and desires accordingly. And this wasn't the first time she'd made use of a tool she'd been born with.

"So what's the problem with letting Mariah come along?" she asked him.

"Why do you care so much about her?"

"Honestly? I don't rightly know. I could say she reminds me of me, somehow. But that'd be double strange, since just to start with, I was never that shy or quiet."

"You can say that again."

She arched a brow at him. "If you want to spend some quality time with that blonde woman, all you have to do is ask."

"Ouch. I deserved that."

"You did. So what's wrong with Mariah accompanying us?"

"It's not safe for her to be with us."

"Where is?"

He sighed. "Come on, Krysty. You're being obtuse. Our lifestyle leads us into more killing scrapes in a month than the average sodbuster out on the Plains sees in a hard lifetime."

"You might underestimate the dangers of farm life."

"Mebbe. Point still stands."

"It does."

She thought about it a moment. She hated being at odds with her life mate. Especially since, in the end, she willingly placed her life and survival in his hands on a daily basis.

But if he'd wanted a meek and mild little helpmate, their track was littered with potential applicants for the job. He'd picked her, which meant he wanted what she had to give. Her fire and her honesty were two of those things.

"As I say, I can't fully account for why I feel so drawn to her. Mebbe it's my maternal instincts kicking in late. Mebbe it's just that…it takes a toll, you know? Having to abandon innocence to its fate time and again. When we don't go and trash it ourselves. Because it means surviving for another day of—surviving."

"I know that. I wish I had more to offer you. And the others. But the best I've got is, if we don't survive the next minute, the next hour doesn't matter a spent shell casing. When you're on the last train west, all bets are off."

For a moment they sat in silence. Something about their manner kept the rest of the gaudy-house staff and patrons steering well clear of them. Even the freckle-faced boy who'd brought them their now-neglected drinks.

She reached out and patted his hand.

"I know you do your best, lover," she said. "And no one else could do half as well. Just promise me that we're looking for something better."

His winter-sky eye fixed unwaveringly on hers.

"You know I can't promise happily-ever-after, Krysty."

"You can't promise a comet won't land on top of us either. Promise me that we're still *looking*."

He sighed again.

"There's got to be more than this, Krysty, something better that's staying just out of reach. If it comes our way, I wouldn't say no."

"Why are you really so reluctant to let her come along with us, lover?"

Ryan rubbed his chin. Even over the tinkling piano and loud gaudy joviality, she could hear the bristles rasp.

"I can't really put my finger on it," he said. "There's just something...weird about her, you know?"

For a moment she gazed at him with her emerald eyes. She knew what kind of a bewitching effect they had on him.

She gave her hair another twitch. Ever so slightly.

He laughed. "Point taken. I should know better than to try to get one past you, Krysty."

"You know," she said, sipping her beer, "you really should."

Ryan looked around. Their friends seemed occupied and as safe here and now as they ever were anywhere.

"You know," he said, "with what we got paid for that job from Hamarville, and what Baron Dugan's giving us for this next gig, we could spring for a private room, just for you and me. What do you say we go check it out?"

A third of her beer remained in her mug. She tossed

it back in a single swallow. Then she wiped her mouth, smiled and set the mug down with a decisive thump.

"I thought you'd never ask," she said, rising to her feet.

Chapter Eight

The companions hadn't traveled more than half a mile down the road that led east from Duganville, between broad fields with workers steering mule-drawn plows, before Krysty stopped dead and said, "Something very bad is about to begin."

The words sent a jolt of alarm blasting through Ryan's guts and tingling down the nerves of his arms and legs. None of his people were prone to crying wolf; Krysty had an advantage.

The flame-haired beauty had a touch of a psychic mutation that gave her a limited ability to snatch glimpses of the future. Almost invariably bad ones.

She rarely got those flashes of vision, but Ryan had no doubt she'd just had one of her bad premonitions.

Walking point, forty yards ahead down the crude but often-dragged road, Jak whirled with his white hair flying in the morning sun.

"Wags!" he shouted. "Coming fast!"

"Off the road!" Ryan rapped.

For just a moment, he thought about splitting the group out to either side of the road to prep an ambush, just in case. But he could hear the engine sounds now. There were a lot of them, mebbe not just four or five.

"Left! Into the field. Hit the ditch and get down fast."

Sweetwater Creek was the lifeblood of Duganville,

as well as its economy. It provided a reliable supply of water, enough for the ville's population of several hundred and for hundreds of acres of croplands stretching up and down the valley. A system of irrigation ditches conveyed it to their crops. The nearest happened to be the one that ran north of the track.

That was fortunate, because the mostly flat valley bottom didn't offer much else in the way of cover and concealment.

"What about those trees there?" Mildred called as they began to race for the nearest ditch. A couple hundred yards ahead and to the left rose a small stand of trees, an orchard.

"No time!" Ryan shouted back. His boots thudded on freshly plowed furrows. It was bad terrain to run on, soft and uneven, but he and his friends had motivation.

He heard whistles blowing. At first that surprised him, then he saw people racing west toward the shelter of the ville's walls, others unhitching their beasts from the plows before driving them in the same direction. He realized the whistling was a signal system among the various Duganville workers laboring to get their crops in the ground, now that the frosts were done for the year, telling them to run for cover.

Jak reached the nearest ditch that ran parallel to the road and plunged in, raising a splash of brown water. He had his Colt Python out and was aiming it back toward the east, along the ditch.

His Scout longblaster already in hand, Ryan jumped in after him. The water was almost knee-deep. He reckoned they were lucky it wasn't much deeper.

Ryan could see the approaching wags now, appearing out of an apparent depression at the edge of the fields half a mile or so farther on. If he'd had any doubts about the wisdom of treating the high-speed approach of a number of wags as hostile action, they were dispelled immediately.

There might be honest explanations for why a friendly caravan might be driving balls out for the ville, but there was no good reason for eight pickup wags to suddenly fan out left and right, leaving only one on the road, while the rest took off straightaway across the field. That made hostile intent plain even before Ryan made out that their beds were stuffed full of people. And blasters.

"Make yourself small, everybody," he barked. "Our best shot is if they cruise on by without noticing us. But have blasters up and ready to rock in case they do."

"Maybe they're not looking for trouble with us," Mildred said optimistically.

"Then they are intent on attacking the ville," Doc stated, "and likely to regard us as associated with them, hence foes."

"I'm not willing to take the risk they're all that picky about the people they chill," Ryan said. "You?"

"They do have the look of coldhearts," Krysty agreed. She was behind Ryan, since he'd made a point of steering to interpose himself between her and danger. She had her Glock blaster in one hand and another arm around a cowering Mariah.

Several laborers, caught by surprise at the far eastern fringe of the fields, were racing as fast as their bare sun-brown legs could carry them back, high stepping with vigor despite the difficulty of running on turned earth. One of the wags veered at speed to Ryan's right. It rolled right over one of the fleeing workers, male or female, Ryan couldn't tell at this range.

"I'd say that's a 'yes' on coldhearts," J.B. remarked.

The wag driver had veered so suddenly that the rear wheels broke loose. Plowing up tan soil, the wag careened clockwise. When it was broadside on to its original line of travel, it rolled.

Coldhearts dove out of the bed in all directions as the vehicle began to topple.

"Did Baron Dugan shoot their dog?" Ricky wondered. He was hunkered down a little closer to the wags than Ryan, huddled against the other ditch bank. "They seem triple pissed off."

"Maybe just psycho high spirits," Mildred suggested from behind Ryan.

"I think the kid's right," the one-eyed man said. "They're acting like something's stuck up their butts crosswise."

Coldhearts were bouncing up off the tilled dirt like predark rubber toys. Amazingly, they all seemed to have bailed out successfully, and the softened surface had cushioned their falls. Hooting audibly even over the multithroated engine roar, they ran back to the wag and, half a dozen or more strong, promptly rolled it over onto its wheels. If they left any of their number on the ground chilled or wounded, Ryan couldn't see them.

Even before the coldhearts clambered back in the bed, the driver collected his wits enough to start it rolling again, in an arc that would head it back for the ville.

The other wags had pulled way out ahead. They had halved the distance between them and Ryan's friends already.

"Dark night!" J.B. said. "They're not going to miss us."

It was true, Ryan saw. One wag, a sun-faded rebuilt

red Ford by the look of it, was practically riding the southern bank of the ditch—the side Ryan was on, nearer the Duganville road. It had pulled a couple lengths ahead of the other six vehicles that were charging full ahead without waiting for the last one to catch up.

"Stay low," Ryan commanded the others as he shouldered the Steyr. "I'm going to try to even the odds."

He half expected Mildred to offer some back talk about how they still didn't know for sure the onrushing intruders were hostile to *them*. She did not. After they'd gone out of their way to run down and chill some random, unarmed grain-grubber who was bent on nothing but getting the nuke away, it was hard to maintain any illusions about the general nature of their ill will.

Ryan pointed the longblaster along the ditch and right at the nearest wag. He had his eye well behind the Leupold scope, which was mounted deliberately far forward on the receiver to eliminate the risk of recoil blacking the shooter's eye. Not that Ryan had made *that* mistake since he was a youngster.

He laid the reticule on the Ford's front grille, then fired. The longblaster bucked and roared. Ryan worked the bolt as recoil kicked its short barrel up.

When Ryan had the sights on the wag again, he saw a cloud of steam shooting from under the hood. He'd holed the radiator, but the wag kept coming.

He aimed for the driver next. He couldn't make out any details through the windshield, even whether it was male or female. It might have been a stickie or a caribou, for all it mattered to Ryan. He let out half a deep breath, held it, then squeezed the trigger.

He'd tried to take into consideration the jouncing of the truck as it traveled along the plowed field. He'd aimed for the driver's head because it was the clearest target, small as it was.

The wag hit the crest of another furrow and jounced up. By sheer luck, Ryan's full-metal jacket 7.62 mm slug skimmed low across the hood, missed the rising dash, passed through the open space in the steering wheel and took out the driver. Ryan knew it as soon as he brought the weapon back to level. He could see the bullet hole in the windshield through his scope and the driver's head lolling on a dead neck as the wag slewed to his right.

He saw the coldheart in the passenger seat grabbing frantically at the wheel. Ryan lined up the sights quickly again and fired once more. Whether he hit that one he couldn't tell. When he recovered from the shot's recoil, the truck had gone full broadside to him and was rapidly slowing to a stop, bogged by the turned earth. He couldn't see movement or silhouettes through the passenger-side window, though whether it was because he'd dropped his second target, too, or just spooked that person into ducking, he had no way to know.

"Get down!" he heard J.B. yell. The fact the little man actually raised his voice would have clued him in to the immediacy of the danger even if the words hadn't. J.B. rarely shouted.

Ryan ducked promptly behind the ditch's bank. Cool water splashed him as several of his companions dove for the same side.

He heard a snarl of several blasters on full-auto. Bullets kicked up dirt along the top of the bank and thudded into the bare dirt of the far side. An engine whined by, no more than twenty yards away.

"Take care of that one!" J.B. cried. "I've got the rest!"

Holding on to his Steyr's forestock with his left hand,

Ryan let go with the right and quick-drew his SIG Sauer P226. As he did, he heard the roar of J.B.'s Mini Uzi, also full-auto, from his left. The Armorer was standing up, blasting at unseen bandit wags.

The wag that had performed the strafing run down the ditch apparently swung toward it, not far past Ryan's group. The black nose of a rugged pickup suddenly appeared, bouncing to a stop with its odd doubled headlights hanging perilously out over the water and clumps of dirt falling away from the tires.

Ryan wasn't clear about what the driver thought he was accomplishing by the stunt—likely trying to catch the embattled group in enfilade. He couldn't have expected what he got. Unless he was sick of breathing.

At once J.B. pivoted and fired two quick, short bursts at the newcomer. Ryan saw the near front tire burst, causing the wag's snout to sag. The second spray was followed by the sound of shattering glass. Nine millimeter slugs had knocked out the right side of the windshield and the passenger window.

The passenger door opened. A coldheart in a black vest with colorful bandannas tied around both arms tried to dive out. Krysty, closer to the wag than Ryan, stood and fired a burst from her Glock, holding the blaster in a two-hand combat grip. The coldheart yowled like a startled bobcat, fell to the ground and began rolling away from the ditch.

Mildred and Doc, strung farther down the ditch, also rose to open fire. Mariah cowered beside Krysty, sunk so far the water covered most of her, holding her hands over her ears. Ricky and Jak, on Ryan's eastern side, simultaneously started shooting across the ditch at a wag swinging in on the north side.

A female coldheart with black hair stood in the pickup's bed and was pointing an M16 at Krysty, who was just ducking into cover. These were some seriously heeled coldhearts, Ryan thought as he lined up the sights of his SIG on the black-haired woman's shirt and double-tapped her right below the grip of her longblaster. She folded out of sight into the wag bed. The longblaster toppled over the side, out of sight onto the ground.

Six—no seven—other wags were cruising up and down on both sides of the ditch. Ryan's heart sank as he saw their beds were filled with coldhearts waving blasters. There had to be thirty or even forty of them.

"Right," he called to his companions, firing a couple shots toward the cab of a passing truck and hunkering down. "Our one chance is to grab that wag with its nose hanging over the ditch and try to power out of here.

"First reload, then pop up and back the bastards off!"

He followed his own advice, gave a three count, then shouted, "Go!"

Ryan rose to find himself facing what looked like a field of bright yellow wildflowers, if viewed from above.

"Down!" he roared, following his own command as a lead shitstorm broke out right over his head.

The coldhearts already had backed up all on their lonesomes. Their wags now sat parked among the furrows, none closer than forty yards away. At the appearance of Ryan and his companions, or at least their heads and blasters, dozens of the bastards opened up with longblasters from the beds of the trucks.

Apparently the idea of establishing fire superiority was a triple-good one, he thought as he glanced around quickly to confirm that his companions had ducked, too. Too bad the coldhearts thought of it first. And have five times our firepower.

The one lucky thing was that, having apparently decided to put themselves out of ready handblaster range before stopping to provide more stable firing platforms for their blasters, the coldhearts had also moved out well past the point where they could angle shots down into the ditch low enough to endanger any of their intended targets.

"What now, lover?" Krysty yelled, leaning close to Ryan's ear to make herself heard above the thunder of blasters.

"Get ready to cover me when they all run dry."

Without even confirming that she'd heard and understood—trusting that she had, because she was Krysty—he scuttled up the ditch to the point where the blunt nose of the wag hung over the dirty water.

Not for these coldhearts were the more primitive, usually single-shot black-powder weapons that increasingly served the Deathlands' everyday population. They all seemed to have magazine-fed longblasters shooting smokeless powder—what Ryan and his friends thought of as "modern," even though the "modern" era that had produced them was itself well past a century dead.

But while they were showing surprising tactical shrewdness and discipline in acting together, the coldhearts were still a bandit gang. And fire discipline was one area they weren't ace in. If the sound was any judge.

Even as Ryan got in position, the storm of blasterfire began to let up as those magazines ran dry.

"Now! Cover me!" Ryan shouted.

He sprang up onto the bank. As expected, he saw

no one inside the truck's cab, from which most of the glass had been blasted out. The driver's door was open.

As his friends opened fire to either side of him, he also saw at least a dozen of the coldhearts rise from among the furrows between the ditch and their wags, longblasters in hand. They'd dismounted and begun creeping forward to storm the ditch under their own side's covering fire.

He saw a couple falter and go down. Though he still held his SIG, he didn't fire. He was focused on moving fast, getting into the cab—and jacking them all a ride to safety.

It wasn't a triple-good shot, but it was the best one he could see. They couldn't withstand this kind of odds from a half-assed defensive position like an irrigation ditch. Not when they could be outflanked so easily.

He dove into the truck—to see a bearded face flashing yellow teeth in an evil grin at him from below the level of the dashboard.

Then the steel-shod butt of a longblaster filled his vision.

Red stars appeared, then blackness.

Chapter Nine

"I don't think this'un's ever gonna wake up, Sully," said the tall, gangly coldheart kneeling over Ryan's supine body.

Krysty, on her knees with her hands behind her neck, surreptitiously watched him from beneath her scarlet bangs. The coldhearts had dragged Ryan, half his face a bruise, into the middle of the field. His companions, themselves sporting considerably more lumps and facial discoloration than they had woken up with, were on their knees in a line beside him. Several dozen coldhearts ringed them, with longblasters trained on them.

"He's just out cold," the chief raider said.

Or faking, Krysty thought. Please, Gaia, let him be faking. Or, at worst, out cold.

Her mate had unquestionably been knocked unconscious by a longblaster butt to the face moments before dismounted coldhearts had swarmed into the ditch and overpowered the rest. She knew with chilling certainty that that might mean he'd sustained a brain bleed, which would chill him just as well as having his head blown clean off. It would just take more time to do it.

"I dunno," the first man said, straightening. "He looks pretty far gone to me."

"He's breathing, Carlson," the leader said in exasperation. He was another tall man, and the wind was whipping his long brown hair around broad shoulders left bare by his black shirt with torn-off sleeves.

"Yeah. That don't mean he ain't in a coma."

From his belt Carlson drew a long, skinny blade like a filleting knife. Bending over, he plunged its tip an inch deep in the muscle of Ryan's right thigh.

"See," he said, pulling the blade. "Nary a twitch."

"For nuke's sake, Carlson," another raider grumbled. "Let it go."

"Quit screwing around," Sully said. "Don't go finishing him off trying to make a point. If he does wake up, I want him able to holler nice and loud, help us show those ville rats what's in store for them if they don't open up the gates and let us in to take what we want."

He turned to stare in the direction of Duganville, half a mile or so distant.

"Time to show these yokels the Buffalo Mob means business," he growled. "Otherwise we'll have every punk this side of the Platte thinking they can get lucky with us the way that taint Hammerhand did."

That roused a grumble of agreement that passed among many of the group surrounding Krysty and her friends. Evidently Sully had poked a still-raw wound to their egos.

The keenly analytical part of her mind—of course she had one, much as she preferred to rely on intuition—wondered what hurt this coldheart boss Hammerhand had managed to inflict on such a well-equipped crew. Especially since she gathered from scraps of conversation overheard as they were all dragged here and dumped that this was only a part of their total numbers. They'd heard rumors that he was a rising force in the North Plains.

Hands on hips, Sully surveyed the captives. He wasn't bad looking, but Krysty had learned long ago that beauty could be skin-deep at best. Even if ugliness sometimes went right down to the core.

"Ladies first," he declared, stepping up to Krysty and Mildred, who were kneeling in the middle of the line. "We'll have the boys show you a good time."

"What about us women?" a slight and unusually scruffy-looking black-haired woman asked.

"Well, Marcuse, I tell you what. You think you can get a rise out of any of these limp-dick-lookin' motherfuckers, knock yourself right on out. And when we're done havin' fun, we can make a nice bonfire out of all of them, right out here in the open. The way the wind's blowing, it should carry their howls all the way to the ville plain as day. That should make these kettle-boilers get their minds right."

He hunkered down in front of Krysty, grabbed the front of her red-plaid men's shirt and ripped it open.

"Nice rack," he said. "Let's see all the goods."

He drew a hunting knife from a beaded doeskin sheath. Its blade glinted in the sunlight as he brushed the red bangs away from Krysty's eyes.

She did not look up at him. She didn't want to concede that much.

With a grunt, he plunged the knife downward inside her scavvied purple sports bra, blade out. The tip raked a line of pain down her sternum as it cut her white skin.

Her breasts popped out.

"Nice," he said, straightening and putting the knife away. "Grab her arms and spread her out."

He began fumbling at the button-up fly of his canvas pants. "Rank has its privileges," he murmured.

"You leave her alone!"

The cry had come from the end of the line of captives to Krysty's left. Without turning her head, she glanced that way to see that Mariah had jumped to her feet and stood with fists clenched at the ends of arms stiffened down her sides. Her face was paler than normal from rage. It was almost as white as Jak's.

Sully continued to unfasten his trousers as a quartet of Buffaloes moved in to grab Krysty, first by the arms.

"Get away from her!" Mariah screamed.

"Somebody shut that skinny little bitch up," Sully said. "Rest of you snap it up."

Despite her own plight, Krysty couldn't help watching Mariah, even as she sagged her not-inconsiderable weight to make it harder for her captors to manhandle her to their leader's specifications. A chunky woman with a red cloth band wrapped around a shock of pale orange hair and a neon-green band wound around small breasts beneath a pair of dirty coveralls stepped up and slammed Mariah to the plowed ground with the steel-shod butt of her Marlin lever-action longblaster.

"Can we have a crack at her, too, Sully?" a man asked.

"Do what you bastards please! She's going on the fire with the rest of these taints. Now get some air on that fire-crotch triple-quick, you lazy mutie-suckers, or I'll start letting some air into you!"

Krysty was dragged onto her back. Rough hands grabbed her ankles and tried to pry her legs apart. Other than resisting with all her strength, frustrating their efforts if only for the moment, she did not overtly fight back.

She knew what the others were thinking. The same thing she was. The Buffalo Mob boss had made a triple-bad mistake in letting his captives know the hideous fate he had planned for them up front.

They knew they had nothing to lose, which meant that when the moment arrived—and it would soon—they would commence the serious business of chilling and mangling coldhearts until sheer self-preservation forced them into finishing them off, double-quick and on their feet. Krysty would not allow herself to be raped. She would call on Gaia and exact a terrible toll for the attempt.

A strange sound drew her eyes back to her left as hands fumbled at the fly of her jeans. It was half a shrill keening, half a guttural growl. And although it sounded like nothing human, it was clearly coming from where Mariah lay huddled on the busted-up ground.

The orange-haired coldheart took a look back. She turned her face toward her leader in apparent confused consternation. Her skin had a green tint beneath her pale freckles.

Sully had his dick in hand, but he was looking at the source of the weird noise, too. Krysty heard him choke out, "What the nuke?"

Krysty saw blackness gather above the fallen girl, like deep shadow—but in midair. She couldn't figure out where it came from, but it seemed to her almost as if it were being drawn out of Mariah. As if it were all the blackness in her tortured young soul.

For a moment she wondered it her adrenaline-pumped mind was playing tricks on her. Or even if she were perceiving something real but with some mutie sense the norms didn't share.

But the orange-haired woman was clearly seeing it, too. She gave a strangled cry of fear, falling back a step, almost stumbling on the yielding, uncertain surface. She raised her longblaster, not as if she meant to shoot the rapidly expanding shadow, but as if to ward it off.

The blackness was unquestionably spinning, though Krysty would be hard-pressed to say how she knew that. It began to drift away from Mariah toward the woman who had clubbed her down.

"Get away!" she screamed at it. "Back off."

"Knock that nonsense off, Patience," Sully said. His hard-on was starting to soften. The coldhearts who had been trying to strip Krysty were as frozen as the rest of them, watching the inexplicable drama unfold. "We got *business* here."

The cloud seemed to whirl faster. Patience jabbed at it with the butt of her longblaster.

The stock sank into the cloud and was suddenly yanked into it. The butt shattered, pieces whirling briefly in the cloud before seeming to dissolve.

Patience let go the weapon, but not before her right hand was drawn into the whirlwind of shadow.

She screamed. Krysty saw blood spray, caught in the cloud like water swirling down a drain, and pink shreds of skin.

Then the blackness sucked the coldheart woman in, tore her to pieces as she screamed, and consumed the fragments.

THOUGH HE HAD no idea why everybody was looking at Mariah, Ryan acted. He'd been playing possum and biding his time, and all that time he had kept his attention riveted on Krysty.

He launched himself at the coldheart boss who stood there with his prick in his hand, even as the man stared past him in something like horror. Not even the demonic shrieking could break Ryan's all-encompassing focus on his target. He planned to break that brown-haired bastard's neck, and if that meant he died with his fingers on his throat, well, he'd always known he wouldn't die in his sleep.

But something could break his concentration on rescue, or revenge, whichever it wound up being. Something heavy hit him behind the knees as he began his rush, wrapped itself around his legs and planted him on the ground so hard the breath was knocked out of him.

Fortunately the relative softness of the plowed-up earth meant he didn't bust his jaw or his neck. Or even concuss himself again.

"Ryan! No!"

To his amazement, he recognized the voice of the person who'd brought him down twenty feet short of Krysty, his goal. It belonged to none other than Mildred Wyeth.

But then he focused his eyes on the marauder chieftain once more, and his growl of rage at Mildred's betrayal died as stillborn as his determination to break free.

Something moved past him. He didn't see it. He didn't hear it. He didn't even smell it. But he *felt* it in his skin, which suddenly seemed to be trying to crawl off his body and escape in all directions. He felt it in the hair standing up on his nape and limbs and body.

It was a feeling of wrongness. Like something that didn't belong here. In this world.

From the corner of his eye he saw what looked like a black whirlwind half the size of one of the bandit wags spin past him. It was making a beeline for the Buffalo Mob boss.

Sully's brown eyes were standing out of his fear-bleached and strained face. But he stood his ground and fought. He whipped out the Ruger Blackhawk holstered at his side and began to fan it like somebody who'd watched too many cowboy vids.

Except unlike everyone Ryan had ever seen try that triple-stupe trick, he controlled the handblaster. Six shots cracked out with the head-splitting sharpness of full-on .357 Magnum loads that Ryan and the others knew so well from Jak's double-action Python.

He might as well have had his now-flaccid but still fully exposed dick in hand, pissing into the black cloud. The slugs vanished without a trace.

And then it took him. He shrieked as he was torn apart and sucked in. Or away. To somewhere.

Coldhearts scattered in all directions, like a big covey of quail that had just had a lynx drop from a tree branch right in its midst. But the black cloud caught the man who had stood closest to the now-vanished leader even as he turned to flee. His screams echoed his boss's.

Ryan felt Mildred roll off. He would thank her later for saving his life. Now he sprang back into action.

Somebody raced by on his right. Or tried to. Ryan pivoted clockwise, mostly on reflex, and flung out his arm.

It was pure luck that his forearm clotheslined Carlson, the coldheart who had stabbed him in his thigh to see if he was faking, right across the windpipe. The cartilage of his larynx imploded with a crackling pop. He fell down gagging and clutching at his throat. His face was already purple behind his handlebar mustache.

Dropping bloody unconsumed chunks of the coldheart it had swallowed, the terrible black whirlwind reversed course instantaneously. One of the four Buffaloes who had been holding Krysty spread-eagle on the ground ran into it full speed. He barely had a chance to shriek before he was ripped to pieces with such violence that blood exploded from his shredding body faster than the blackness could suck it down.

Ryan saw Jak land like a catamount on the back of a fleeing Buffalo built to justify the name. He plunged not one but two daggers into the coldheart's bull neck from either side. He had to have hit the carotid arteries on both sides, because blood shot out in violent sprays. The coldheart dropped to one knee and his momentum took him straight forward onto his face as Jak leaped nimbly free.

It didn't much surprise Ryan that the coldhearts hadn't found the knives. They had stripped off Jak's jacket with the razor-sharp shards of metal and busted glass sewn onto the collar and shoulders and tossed it with the rest of their captives' gear piled next to a blue pickup.

That was his target. The ratty woman he'd heard Sully call Marcuse was sprinting for the wag as fast as her legs could carry her. Unfortunately for her, her legs were short and Ryan's were long. Just as she reached out a clawed hand for the door handle, he caught her tangle of black hair from behind and yanked hard, back and sideways, as momentum carried him past her.

Her neck snapped with a sound like a blaster shot.

As she convulsed in her death throes, Ryan pulled near enough to jerk the handblaster out of her holster. It was a Glock, which turned out to have a round chambered, as he immediately found out when he turned to fire it into the face of a blocky Buffalo who was about to blunder full-speed into him, bawling like a frightened calf. Ryan wasn't even sure the man knew he was there.

Behind him he saw Ricky hit a blond, bearded coldheart in the knees from the left as Doc threw a body block into his torso from the right. Ryan heard at least one of the knees give way, and the three went down into a squalling, clawing tangle like a ball of angry alley cats.

Ryan didn't see what happened next because by reflex he looked to find his lover. The redhead was standing about where she had knelt, holding one of her former captors by the right arm and leg. Mildred had him by the left set of limbs, face downward. The two women pendulumed the coldheart to and fro three times as he howled and struggled to no avail.

Then they pitched him face-first right into the hungry black cloud that was advancing to claim him. His last screech seemed to linger on the air after the bloody rags of his body had disappeared.

Ryan held up the Glock in both hands. It was hefty—a .45 ACP Glock 30. He looked around for targets.

Several of the wags were peeling out of there as the whirlwind devoured another one of Krysty's former captors, who was rolling around on the ground clutching at a broken elbow. To Ryan's right, J.B. ducked a vicious attempt at buttstroking him in the head with a Mini-14. He pistoned a right hard into the coldheart's lean gut. Then he straightened, wrested the weapon from the taller man's hands and slammed him in the side of the head with the buttstock edge-on like an oiled-wood machete.

The Buffalo fighter fell onto the corrugated ground, cradling his split-open and blood-spurting head. J.B.

shouldered the carbine, pointed it down at the man's face and pulled the trigger. The Ruger's blast was double-loud, as a short-barreled .223 longblaster always was.

The coldheart kicked once at the dirt with the heels of his pointy-toed cowboy boots. Then he went limp.

J.B. nodded in satisfaction and, like Ryan, looked around for targets.

There were none. The Buffalo Mob raiding party was dead or running away as fast as the wags they'd managed to make off with would carry them. Only the stocky man Doc and Ricky wrestled with remained. And not even marksmen as triple keen of eye and steady of aim as Ryan and J.B. were willing to risk a shot under those circumstances.

Anyway, Ryan reckoned his two friends had control of the situation. Until both of them jumped away, Doc springing back like a startled heron on his long legs and Ricky rolling rapidly away in the other direction, bouncing off the low, mounded ridges to the field.

The coldheart was instantly on his bandy legs. His broad face was mostly hidden by a mask of blood and mud, except for wildly staring eyes and a mouth twisted in rage.

"Which one of you rad-suckers wants some?" he yelled. His long black pigtail whipped about his wide shoulders as he snapped his head left and right to look from one of his antagonists to the other. He held a knife with a short, triangular blade in one hand.

The black whirlwind came for him, skimming a foot above the furrows. Somehow he sensed the awful doom barreling down on him from behind. He spun, knife at the ready.

He screamed shrilly, then he slashed at the cloud of blackness with his knife.

He made contact. Whatever force lay within the swirl of shadow seized his knife and hand and tore off the front half of his forearm. His shrieks rose an octave, and he tried frantically to pull free.

But the cloud had him. It drew him in and whipped him into ragged shreds and threads of red fluid, which quickly disappeared into the shadow-swirl.

For a moment the cloud hung there. It seemed to Ryan to be waiting, searching.

No coldhearts remained. Was it their turn now? Ryan wondered.

The black cloud seemed to collapse in on itself. Ryan caught a fleeting impression of a few night-black strands, scarcely more than threads, flying back toward Mariah, who still stood staring with eyes like two holes pissed in snow and her fists clenched by her sides so hard, her rigid arms trembled. But that might have been his imagination, which was in high gear now and powering right along after the events of the last half hour or so.

As the perhaps-imaginary threads seemed to vanish into Mariah's body, she swayed slightly, as if dealt a blow.

Then she dropped to the tilled soil like an empty suit of clothes.

Ricky accepted the offer of Doc's extended hand to help him off the ground. He was pale and a bit green in the face.

"Now that's something you don't see every day."

Chapter Ten

"Stranger inbound!"

Hammerhand had just emerged, stretching and yawning, from his lodge when the cry went up. It was repeated by several voices among the other Bloods already awake to greet the gray dawn slowly spilling out across the scrub-dotted surge of the Plains.

He sipped his chicory, which he'd grown up with and enjoyed. He was not much concerned. He had well over a hundred effectives in his band now, with a dozen more coming aboard in the wake of the Buffalo Mob wag-raid's success of a week earlier. Had any serious threat been perceived, the message would have said so, and it would've been a lot louder.

Had his scouts and sentries missed a significant threat approaching, somebody was going to wind up staked out over an anthill before the sun now rising set. Hammerhand believed in being openhanded with his rewards and tightfisted with his punishments. But when he had to make a statement, he made it.

He had slept well. The lodge was a traditional tepee, like about half the several dozen lodges in camp, made up of tanned bison hides and long lodge poles—in his case four, in the traditional Blackfoot style, as opposed to three, as most of them had. Aside from the fact he'd also grown up in one, he found them most practical:

warm in winter, cool in summer and dry when it rained, along with being easy to lug along, assemble and take apart. Some of his growing tribe preferred white man–style tents, scavvied synthetic or present-day oiled canvas.

It was their choice; he insisted on loyalty, bravery and skill from his people. It wasn't his lookout to run their nuking lives.

"What've we got?" Mindy Farseer asked, walking up beside him.

As usual, he thought, she looked indecently chipper at this hour of the morning, not a hair, or a feather wound into it, out of place. She carried a Savage 110 bolt longblaster action in .270 Winchester, a common cartridge on the Plains, esteemed for its combination of good hitting power with long range and flat trajectory. The piece was mounted with a Swift variable power scope. She was lethal with it out to a thousand yards. She wasn't called *Farseer* for nothing.

"Intruder alert," he stated.

"Far out," she said, dialing the telescopic sight up to its full 12-power magnification. She wasn't bloodthirsty, but she did love to use her skills.

Hammerhand called for his own telescope to be brought to him. The tepee flap opened, and Maia, one of his love partners from the night before, came padding out carrying his old-school folding spyglass in its blue velvet bag. She was buck naked as she approached Hammerhand, opened the drawstring, removed the telescope from the bag and handed both to her lover. Then with a cool smile to Mindy's disapproving glower, she turned and walked back. Hammerhand watched her briefly, appreciating the added swing she gave her hips and buttocks.

"Let's go check it out," he said, striding forward as he expanded the scope.

A KNOT OF BLOODS gathered on the eastern edge of the low hill they'd made camp on outside the laagered wags. They had added several to the stock they'd taken off the Buffalo Mob's hands, although Hammerhand had found other things that needed doing and had yet to go back and collect the rest of the Buffaloes' rolling stock.

The Bloods were pointing down the slope to a figure about a quarter mile off, stumbling through the knee-high grass toward them. The dishing of the land meant it was clearly visible, not whited out in the dazzle of the rising sun. But details weren't easy to come by with the naked eye.

That was why Hammerhand had his spyglass. He held it up to his eye and adjusted the focus. Mindy unsnapped the lens covers from her own scope and shouldered her blaster.

He heard her suck in a sharp breath. "Whitecoat," she whispered. "Can I drop the hammer on the nuke-sucker?"

"No," Hammerhand said, studying the ragged figure. The man seemed to be on his last legs but still found the energy to adjust his eyeglasses at every single step. "It's a whitecoat."

"That's why," she said.

"Whitecoats're evil," Joe Takes-Blasters said between yawns as he walked up scratching the back of his neck.

"Whitecoats are frauds," Mindy said. "Rad-dust-eating, crazy cultists pretending to know the ancient 'wisdom' that burned the world, which I judge makes them evil, too, now I think on it. Say the word and he's history."

"The word is, 'no.'"

"What?" his two lieutenants exclaimed, half a beat apart.

"Boss, it's a whitecoat," Joe said, as if he thought mebbe Hammerhand had missed that part. Then, with a noticeably brighter tone he went on, "Unless you wanna save him for something special?"

"We don't do that," Hammerhand said. "Without good reason."

"And being a whitecoat isn't?" Mindy asked. That showed how powerful her loathing—or fear—for them was. As a rule, she was strongly opposed to any death that was dealt out any way but swiftly with minimal suffering. Especially when *she* dealt it out by blowing apart somebody's head at a couple hundred yards.

"I had a vision," Hammerhand reminded them in tones of rapidly tiring patience. "In it I was told that a mystic adviser would stagger out of the wastelands to guide me. This was foretold. He lives."

He folded up the spyglass.

"Go fetch him. Alive and uninjured. You, Joe. Take whatever backup you need."

Joe looked doubtful. "Backup? For one scrawny, tore-up-ass-looking whitecoat?"

"Take two Bloods with you, just in case," Hammerhand directed. His aide had a tendency to overestimate his own abilities, considerable as they were. Especially when brute force was concerned. He didn't assess the whitecoat as posing any more threat than Joe did—on the surface. But he was a man who kept his eye on the fine and wavering line between triple bold and triple stupe.

Joe nodded. "What if he resists?"

"Then thump him some and restrain him. But nothing broken. No internal bleeding. Understood?"

"Understood." Joe set off bawling at the others—who were mostly sipping chicory and waiting for their breakfast stew of beans and Pronghorn to get hot—for one of them to volunteer.

Half a dozen hands shot up. When he explained no chilling or hurting would be involved, the number of hands went abruptly down to two.

"That's the problem with us," Hammerhand said. "We're still not motherfucking subtle."

"I don't like it," Mindy told him, as Joe and his helpers, one male, one female, went trotting down the slope toward the figure. The intruder had collapsed and was crawling toward the camp on hands and knees.

"I don't like it," Mindy said.

"That's your job," Hammerhand stated. "Not to like shit. Noted. Now your job is not to say any more about it."

"I hear ya," she said grumpily. But she did not sling her Savage longblaster.

Hammerhand took up his spyglass and watched as the trio fanned out to approach the crawling man. He paid no attention to them, even as they surrounded him with handblasters drawn.

"Keep your fingers off the nuke-withered triggers," he murmured to his distant warriors. "You, too, Mindy."

"Rad-blast."

Joe had to have said something to the man, because he looked up. He had a dark beard and eyeglasses with heavy, dark frames, along with the whitecoat, which looked as if he'd wrestled a bobcat in it and lost.

Whatever he said either satisfied Joe or got his mind right about his own boss's firm commands. He and his helpers holstered their weapons, then Joe and the woman, Serena, who was powerfully built, hauled him to his feet.

"Pat him down, Joe," Hammerhand said. Of course the burly man couldn't hear him at that distance. But saying the words made him feel better. "Just because he ain't much of a snake, don't mean he's not packing venom."

To his relief his lieutenant did so, running his big hands up and down the whitecoat's body and limbs to look for unpleasant surprises. To Hammerhand's surprise, he came up dry.

Joe handed the man off to Red-Eye, the male Blood, and he and Serena marched the captive toward the camp, although they seemed to be aiding the whitecoat rather than dragging him. Joe followed close behind, fingering the hatchet holstered at his side in a way that Hammerhand did not favor, under the circumstances. Orders or not, his lieutenant was a man who greatly preferred splitting skulls to splitting hairs.

Hammerhand folded the scope, stuck it back in its bag and hung it from his web belt.

The group of Bloods standing around watching the little drama unfold had grown to twenty or so. Hammerhand heard a joint intake of breath as they saw the intruder was indeed a hated whitecoat. As he was half carried up to where Hammerhand stood waiting, blasters left holsters and longblasters were unslung.

"Back up off the triggers, everybody," Hammerhand said almost conversationally. "If any one of you really believes a lone whitecoat, let alone one who looks like it'd be all he could do to crawl into his own open grave without help, can take your leader down, feel free to walk away now. No comebacks."

He meant it, too. When he gave his word, he stood by it, no matter what. Of course, there were times when, if a body *thought* he was giving his word—well, that was his or her own lookout. He was a leader, after all, and that implied things.

"Okay, boss?" Joe asked as Serena and Red-Eye brought the man staggering to a stop in front of Hammerhand. "I didn't need any thumping at all."

"Good job. And try not to sound so disappointed. Can you stand on your own, whitecoat?"

The man straightened his glasses on his nose and nodded. Then he straightened the specs again.

"I—can," he said in a voice that sounded like a rusty hinge. "W-water?"

"Water," Hammerhand commanded. A kid named Little Wolf obliged, holding up a skin bag for the stranger. He was too small a fry for Hammerhand to consider accepting into the band under usual circumstances, but the boy's aunt, Shyanna, had vouched for him, and she was a warrior of merit.

At a nod from Hammerhand, the two Bloods released the whitecoat's arms. He lurched but managed to keep to his feet—barely. He seized on the uncapped bag with both hands and upended it. His Adam's apple, covered with a thinner layer of dark stubble than his chin and cheeks, bobbed up and down.

Water overflowed his mouth and ran down the sides of his face. Hammerhand made no comment. Water, clean water, was plentiful here. It was why they'd picked the site to bivouac in for a spell.

At last the stranger finished. He handed the bag, now mostly empty, back to Little Wolf. Then he adjusted his eyeglasses again and peered through them with dark eyes at Hammerhand.

"Are you—" He coughed into his grimy fist. "Are you Hammerhand?"

"I am. Who the nuke are you?"

"I am Dr. Alvin Trager," the whitecoat said.

"You got business with the boss?" Mindy asked. "Why were you sneaking up on our camp?"

"I was not…sneaking. I was making my way here as best I could. I met with…mishaps on the way."

"Looks like it," Joe muttered. The man wore filthy rags of a once-white shirt and black pants beneath the white coat. They were in better condition than the lab coat but still in sorry shape. There were red streaks of scabbed-over cuts visible through some of those tears.

"What is that business?" Hammerhand asked. "Time's blood. By which I mean, yours."

"Yes." Trager nodded, then fiddled with the glasses again.

If Hammerhand didn't chill the bastard, he was either going to have to get used to that tic, or Trager was going to have to get that hand lopped off.

"I was sent here to offer my assistance to the mighty Hammerhand."

"Glowing night shit," Mindy said. "Who sent you?"

"I have...associates," Trager said. "Others like me. We keep alive the old-days science."

"So mebbe if you tell us where to find this nest of rattlers so we can rub it out, we'll feel a mite better about letting you live," Mindy said.

"But—but we offer you our help! We can be of great service to you. It's why I was sent."

"Before we talk about the service your buddies can do for us," Hammerhand said, "first you gotta show us you can be more use to us breathing than with dirt hitting you in the eyes. Just because I'm not gonna let Mindy or anybody else chill you right now doesn't mean the sun has set on that idea. *Comprende?*"

The man nodded so vigorously he almost nodded his glasses off his nose. "Oh, yes. Oh, yes, indeed."

"So what's this about these other whitecoats 'sending' you?" Mindy asked.

"They—we—know that Hammerhand is destined for greatness," he said. "His is the strong hand that can unite the Plains. And perhaps the Deathlands."

"Whitecoats? Don't tell me they had a vision, too," Mindy said.

Hammerhand frowned at her. Don't talk about that outside the family, he signed to her. Though the signs were widely understood across the Plains, and not just by Indians, he felt fairly confident a whitecoat out of some weird hermit lab wouldn't know them. And the beady eyes never flickered away from his face, behind the thick lenses that magnified and distorted them.

Mindy's eyes widened, and her face went slightly pale. She nodded.

"Don't think you can flatter me either," Hammerhand told Trager, although the whitecoat had, and Hammerhand did not feel bad about it. “What good are you to me? To us?”

“I can tell you things.”

“Things are good,” Hammerhand said. He clapped a hand on the man’s stooped shoulder. Even though it was a light touch, the whitecoat almost collapsed beneath it.

“Come back with me to my lodge and you can be a little bit more specific about ‘things.’”

Chapter Eleven

"Dr. Sandler!" the tech cried out in obvious alarm. "Dr. Oates!"

Frowning at the man's tone, which was altogether unprofessional regardless of what had occasioned it, Dr. Sandler turned to look at the man where he sat in the cool darkness, pierced by myriad flickering lights in green, yellow, orange and red, before a console in Lab Central.

"What is it, Shaughnessy?"

"It's a Level 5 spatiotemporal disturbance in our target zone."

"Impossible!" Dr. Oates exclaimed.

Dr. Sandler felt his mouth tighten slightly. Such an outburst, muted as it had been, was also thoroughly unscientific. Dr. Oates had a keen mind, no question. Otherwise Dr. Sandler would have disposed of her long ago. But he had to remind himself she was still just a woman and subject to the vagaries of her hormones.

After all, that was why he was in charge, even if some in Overproject Whisper might harbor evolutionarily unsound notions of women's complete equality with men. They were all in perfect agreement that most people were fit to follow orders, and only a scientifically selected and trained few were fit to give them, of course. But some fools nonetheless remained willfully blind to certain details of nature's innate hierarchy.

"Perhaps," he said to his colleague. "Perhaps not. Are your detectors in proper working order, Shaughnessy?"

"They're all perfectly calibrated, Dr. Sandler," the tech answered. "I'd stake my life on it!"

"You have." Dr. Sandler stepped up close behind the tech's swivel chair and peered at the indicator lights. "What do we have?"

Shaughnessy was a young man with a red crew cut that made his unfortunately prominent ears stand out even more. Dr. Sandler considered them a sign of genetic imperfection, but the man had proved himself good enough at his job to warrant his continued tenure. There was no point in expecting a technician to be the equal of a scientist. That was *why* they were technicians. Nature's hierarchy was as iron in its castes as the distinction between genders or races.

Despite his coolly rational reserve, Dr. Sandler felt his eyes widen when he looked at Shaughnessy's screen. He, too, would have called the reading impossible had he been as lax in his control of his emotions as his female associate.

"That is indeed anomalous," he said, allowing himself a micrometrically precise nod. "What are its coordinates?"

Shaughnessy worked his keyboards. Latitude and longitude numbers appeared in the upper-right corner of the display, overlaid where they would not interfere with the visual representation of data.

"Fifty-one kilometers west of the confluence of the White River with the Missouri and five point three kilometers north of the course of the former Interstate Highway 90, Dr. Sandler, Dr. Oates."

"How shall we respond?" Dr. Oates asked. She had stepped up beside him.

Anger was welling within Dr. Sandler, a purely understandable response to unreasonable interference in their work. Even if it was kept secret from the rest of Overproject Whisper. And even more imperatively so from the umbrella project, the Totality Concept.

"It is those genetic misprints Doctors Hamlin and Stone!" he snarled. "Those Operation Chronos bunglers will disrupt everything. Everything!"

Dr. Oates reached out a pale, precision-manicured hand and almost, but not quite, touched the sleeve of Dr. Sandler's immaculate white coat.

"May I speak to you privately, Dr. Sandler?" she asked.

"Yes."

They withdrew to a space along the bulkhead of the compartment. Dr. Sandler felt the stirring in the airs on his eyebrows and arms as he stepped into the hush-field.

"May I remind the senior scientist that even if this timeline is contaminated by anomalous events, at least four others nearby in the multiverse will still continue with satisfactory to near-mathematically certain chances of success of the introduction of the next phase?"

"But the Baronial America Endgame is key," he said. "Especially to our success. And may I remind the junior scientist that, by undertaking to bring it to fruition on our own, the only possible outcome that can preserve us from purgation is complete success?"

Wisely, she nodded her narrow, close-cropped head.

"Of course, Dr. Sandler. But let us consider alternate

possibilities. What if this unprecedented disturbance is *not* due to the Operation Chronos renegades impinging on our timeline?"

He scoffed. "You disappoint me, Dr. Oates. What else could it be?"

"As scientists," shc answered coolly, "is it not our duty to find out? To gather evidence before coming to a conclusion?"

He scowled; she did not flinch.

And then he realized, *She's right. If she seeks to use this to her future advantage, she will discover, also, how very wrong she is.*

Aloud, he said, "You are correct, Dr. Oates. We shall dispatch our asset to the scene. I trust our operative continues to foster close relationship with the Primary?"

"His reports indicate success, in exact alignment to your own predictions, Dr. Sandler."

He nodded, feeling gratified—and mollified—at her acknowledgment of his prowess.

"Most satisfactory," Dr. Sandler said.

He turned away to study the interrupted Goode homolosine projection that glowed on a gigantic display above the instrument consoles at the front of Lab Central. There the map of the current target timeline of twenty-second century Earth showed a wealth of information: environmental, population, economic and political indices. As well, a few red dots indicated potentially serious disruption of their ultimate secret offshoot project to achieve a key step in the realization of Totality decades in advance of even the most optimistic projections of Concept Central Authority. A new red dot, brighter than the rest, would soon be added.

"But make no mistake, Dr. Oates," he said, unable

to keep a note of harshness out of his voice. "This is far and away the ripest timeline for our plan. And should it suffer significant disruption—even, or perhaps especially, absent interference by our subcompetent rivals—we could lose it utterly."

"But the parallel timelines—"

"Remain suboptimal, Dr. Oates. Given the stakes, we can simply not afford anything but the highest probability of success. The very survival of our genetic lines depends upon it."

"WHAT CAN I tell you?" Mariah asked. She sat with her back propped against the side of a pickup grille. The vehicle's shadow stretched far off to the east, cast by the low blood-red sun.

In spite of everything, Krysty's heart went out to her. The two of them had grown close in a surprisingly short time. How—why—even Krysty wasn't sure.

"The truth might do for a start," Ryan said harshly.

He stood a bit apart from the rest of the companions, who slumped in various postures of near exhaustion. The exception was Jak, who had recovered his weapons and jacket and headed off on his usual lonesome patrol, keeping a watchful eye over his friends.

Krysty shot Ryan a reproachful look. He didn't pay her any mind. He was fixated on what he saw as his duty. To her no less than the rest.

"That big cat didn't mysteriously vanish," Ryan said to the girl. "You made it go away. That was that nuke-awful screech we heard."

Mariah hung her head. Her pigtails hung limp to her shoulders.

"Yes."

And she didn't tell *me* the truth either, Krysty thought. Even though—as a secret mutie herself—she could understand the girl's reticence, she still felt betrayed.

"And the stickies back at that farm where we found you. You knew why they left you alone, and you knew why thcy looked like they exploded. Because you made them explode. You sicced that—that cloud on them, and it tore them apart like ripping up so many sheets of paper."

"Yes," she said.

They were still where they'd been dragged as captives, in plain sight of Duganville—them and the four wags the Buffalo Mob had abandoned in their panic flight. Three of the four ran fine, even the one that had gotten hung up right on the brink of the ditch bank. Only the truck whose radiator Ryan had punched a hole in with a shot from his Scout longblaster refused to start.

At some point the residents of the barony were going to venture back out into their crop lands to find out what had happened out there. Ryan seemed content to leave that for when it happened—if they were even still here when the locals nerved themselves up enough. Clearly, he needed this matter settled, and settled now.

"Why didn't you tell us?" he asked.

"I was afraid."

"Ryan, get real," Krysty said. "What if she had told us what happened? Would you have even believed her?"

He frowned, then nodded. That was one thing out of so many Krysty admired about him: his intellectual honesty, as relentless in its way as everything else about him.

"Mebbe after the thing with the tiger," he admitted. "But not the first time. No way."

"I thought you'd get scared of me," Mariah said.

"I'm sure the hell scared of you now. That's just with what we've seen. I'm not taking account of any other world-shattering secrets you might be hiding from us."

Mariah just shook her head wearily. "You want me to go away. I'm a monster. That's all right. People always send me away when they find out."

"We're not sending her away!" Krysty said. Ryan was startled to hear genuine anger in her tone.

"It sounds like a double-good idea to me," J.B. stated. "Or should I just keep my trap shut?"

"That second thing," Mildred said dangerously.

"Fireblast, Krysty," Ryan said, "what's gotten into you? The girl's as dangerous as old dynamite that's sweated nitroglycerin all over. She could chill us all at any time."

"Yeah," Mildred agreed. "And exactly who among us couldn't? Isn't that the reason we've all stuck together—because we're all deadly? And that it takes a passel of us working together to stay alive in this bad old world?"

Ryan looked at her. For one of the rare times in his life, the one-eyed man found nothing to say.

"She does make a persuasive point," Doc said gently.

J.B. sighed.

"Well, since now you go and put it that way, Mildred," he said, "I'm minded what Trader's old pal Abe always used to say about dangerous folk… I'd rather they be on the inside pissing out than on the outside pissing in."

"And there you have it," Mildred told them.

"Ryan, she's right," Krysty said.

"She did save us all when the coldhearts were—" Ricky began. Then his words choked off as if he'd had his gullet slit. His cheeks turned pink and his dark eyes grew as round as predark silver dollars. He was mortified at the fear he'd spoken out of turn—and humiliated at the very thought of what the Buffalo Mob boss, and by his order much of the rest of the gang, had been about to do to Krysty.

"You're right, Ricky," Krysty said hastily. "No need to be ashamed. She didn't hurt us. She didn't leave us to our fate and hope to sneak away unnoticed in the commotion. She helped us."

It was Ryan's turn to heave a massive sigh. "Yeah," he said. "Reckon she did."

"You have wondered aloud on more than one occasion, Ryan, why we let her tag along if she was not of any use in a fight," Doc said. "Well, it would certainly appear that she can be powerfully useful in battle, indeed."

"True."

"But we don't want you using that power more than you absolutely have to," Krysty told Mariah, going to the girl's side and placing a gentle hand on her shoulder.

"I don't," Mariah said to the furrowed gray ground. "It…scares me."

Krysty threw her arms about her. For a moment the girl held herself as rigid still as a rigored chill. Then she melted to turn and throw her arms around Krysty, lower her head and sob against the redhead's bosom as her own skinny body was fixing to tear itself apart.

Krysty cradled Mariah and murmured soothing sounds at her. They didn't make sense, but they didn't need to. Her black hair, tightly parted in the middle, smelled of the lilac soap, another product, somehow, of Baron Dugan's distilling operation.

The girl's tears soaked into Krysty's shirt.

The shirt had been hastily repaired. Not so much because of modesty, which was a commodity they could afford a limited amount of, the way they traveled and generally stuck together, but because Krysty felt vulnerable with her breasts exposed.

Ryan grunted, loudly enough for Krysty to know he wanted her attention. She looked up at him.

"Time's blood," he reminded her. "We need to do something about all these wags, weapons and other gear that have fallen into our hands, before the ville folk come out and decide to make some kind of issue about it."

"Where shall we go?" Doc asked. His voice sounded muzzy. Krysty realized his mind, damaged by his captivity at the cold and soulless hands of the Operation Chronos whitecoats, had begun to wander. Doc's mind focused to razor sharpness at times, especially when it was most sorely needed, such as in fighting for their lives. But when the inevitable adrenaline-depletion slump set in after combat, he sometimes drifted away.

To Krysty's surprise, Ryan chuckled.

"Right straight back to the ville," he said. "If we say we're entitled to this loot by right of conquest, who's going to contradict us? They had to have seen what happened here."

"How do you plan to explain—" J.B. tipped his head toward the still weeping Mariah "—you know?"

"Well, we hope they didn't see it in that much detail," Ryan said.

"Even if they saw the scary parts," Mildred added, "I don't think there's any way they can accept it. It was too freaking strange. I bet all Ryan has to do is flash that devilish smile of his and spin them some of his vintage bullshit."

"Reckon I can do that," Ryan said, grinning.

Krysty stroked Mariah's head. The girl seemed to be trying to unload all at once a weight of grief that had built up over a long time. Perhaps her whole life.

"What about her?" Krysty asked Ryan.

"She can help with the chores. Plus, who knows? We might find ourselves in another tight place, where that...talent of hers could prove a big help."

"She can come with us?"

"For now," Ryan said. "As long as she doesn't slow us down, same as before. So what do you say you get her bundled into one of the wags so we can load up and shake the dust of the rad-blasted field off our boots?"

Chapter Twelve

"I'd rather die than tell you anything!" the captured Buffalo Mob underboss exclaimed. Spittle flew from his bearded mouth, striking Hammerhand's buckskin pants.

"Suit yourself," Hammerhand said. He pointed his .44 Magnum Smith & Wesson Model 29 blaster point-blank at the coldheart's head and fired.

The blaster had heavy recoil and a wicked muzzle blast. But Hammerhand had strong wrists, and he liked a weapon that could make a statement.

The captive's head split down the middle, like a melon hit by a machete. Handfuls of gray brains slopped out, and his right eyeball burst from the socket to flap from the nerve as he fell forward.

"Right," Hammerhand said, tipping the revolver's muzzle to the sky. It was still barely stained with pink in the west, the attack had happened so quickly. "Anybody else want to go in for any macho posturing? You might've noticed I'm in a literal frame of mind today."

He was walking in front of their fifty-odd Buffalo Mob captives. Most knelt in the long grass of what had been until a very few minutes ago their camp. Others tended to the dozen or so wounded, all under the blasters of their watchful Blood captors.

Their fifteen chills still lay where they had fallen—

except for the ones being unceremoniously dumped out of their wags by Bloods instructed to secure the rolling booty and make sure they were all ready to shift out of there at Hammerhand's command.

"That detailed information you gave us on the Buffalo encampment was spot-on," he said over his shoulder to Trager, who followed a pace or two behind.

The scruffy little whitecoat had not taken part in the attack but had waited behind with a small sec team until Hammerhand sent for him. The leader of the Bloods did not want his magical-mystical superadviser getting in the line of fire. If he came across—and so far, he sure had—then his value was beyond price. If he didn't in future, Hammerhand favored chilling the man himself for wasting his nuking time and making him look like a dick.

"Our powers are great," Trager said smugly.

"Better than average, certainly."

Hammerhand stopped and turned to face the prisoners. He struck a contemplative pose, with his blaster hand tipped back almost to his shoulder. Then, as if coming to some decision, he lowered his arm. At the same time he rolled the weapon in his hand, cocking it with his thumb as he returned it to a firing grip.

It wasn't necessary. He was an ace shot, his aim hardly less true when he fired the revolver double action despite the far lighter and quicker trigger-pull needed to shoot single-action. But the distinctive metallic clacking, he had noticed, tended to make an impression.

"So," he said, pointing the handblaster first at one and then another prisoner at random, "who wants to talk to me about what happened outside Duganville last week, where you got your asses handed to you by half a dozen ragged-ass outlanders you had the drop on?"

"That's it?" demanded a brown-haired woman with a dirty green bandanna tied at a slant around her head to bandage a scalp cut. "That's why you took us down? To ask us some nuking questions?"

The blaster shot was very loud. It echoed among the low grassy ridges surrounding the one, slightly higher and flatter than its kin, the late Buffalo Mob supremo Bull had picked for his bivouac. Long before the reverberations had chased each other away down the shallow draws, the woman was lying on her back, folded straight back with her knees still on the ground and her eyes staring at the sky. A darker, wetter stain was spreading across the sternum of her faded black cotton T-shirt, in the hollow between her breasts.

"My tribal elders always taught me there were no such thing as stupe questions," Hammerhand said, rolling the blaster back in his hand again. "They were wrong again, as you can see. They knew nothing of the real world, really, obsessed instead with maintaining some kind of pure Plains tradition, when not one of our band has as much as half the old Blackfoot blood rolling in our veins. Including me.

"So, some ground rules before we continue. You can answer a question with a question if, and only if, you really do need more info before you can give me a proper nuke-sucking answer. Everybody got that? I have a lesson plan all prepped for slow learners."

Heads nodded vigorously.

Using the info Trager had supplied, courtesy of his shadowy "associates," Hammerhand had carefully mapped out his predawn attack to complete his destruction of the Buffalo Mob. The Buffaloes had about eighty souls in their camp and six wags, three of which were big cargo trucks.

To ensure victory, Hammerhand had brought more than twice their number. Heroic battles against desperate odds were all good and well—warriors loved to sing about them, especially around the campfires late at night when the Towse Lightning flowed like the blood that all too likely would soon follow. But he had early learned that in the real world, if there was one thing warriors loved, it was a winner.

His scouts had watched the camp all night and done reconnaissance right up to the now-thinner line of wags they surrounded themselves with. The Buffaloes still weren't up to spotting skilled Plains sneakers. They had confirmed that the info Trager gave Hammerhand about their dispositions and security was righteous.

Then it was time to use some of the other gifts Trager had given them: four modified M4 carbines with sound suppressors and third-generation night-vision scopes. In the hands of four of the best Blood longblaster shots, naturally including Mindy Farseer, they had taken down four key armed and alert sentries spaced around the perimeter.

Meanwhile Hammerhand and Joe Takes-Blasters had led two forces of Blood warriors creeping up on two sides of the camp—not opposite, but about sixty degrees apart.

The reason they had picked the last half hour before dawn to make their final stealthy advance and then attack was that the human body hit a lower ebb at about that time—and visibility was especially tricky. Though Joe led sixty fighters, and Hammerhand almost a hundred, they had achieved their objectives unseen.

Night-bird calls from the snipers confirmed they had downed their targets. Joe had the honor of leading the first attack, suddenly jumping up screaming and opening fire from close range on the sleeping camp.

It had not—quite—been a feint. When the Buffalo Mob began to fight back, fixing their attention on the yelling, blasting assault, Hammerhand had led his unit in from the flank.

Being caught from their left-hand rear utterly demoralized the Buffaloes. Such resistance as they offered was quickly blasted or hacked down. A few escaped into the weeds; Hammerhand was content to let them go. Most of the opposition surrendered within minutes.

The cost to the Bloods had been three chilled and five wounded. Only two of the wounded were badly hurt and they were expected to get better. Especially if Trager delivered on his promise of unknown med tech, which was more valuable than any amount of scavvy.

Now, still elated by his one-sided triumph on what was still a powerful and formidable foe—even if one outgunned and outfought—Hammerhand was working on doing the thing Trager had asked of him. As well as satisfying his own growing curiosity.

"Do I need to shoot somebody else, just to get the ball rolling?" he asked. "Do you really want to take it there?"

"You're not gonna believe it," said an older Buffalo, a man with straw-blond hair and a face that looked to consist mainly of seams. "We're afraid you'll chill us for lying."

Then he set and jutted his jaw. "You gonna chill me for saying that?"

"No. I'm saying I'll chill people for jacking me around.

But I'll let you in on a little secret. I've already heard some triple-crazy-sounding tales about what went down."

And so he had. Trager had asked—in a way that made it clear it was really a demand—that they go check out something that happened at Duganville. The demand part didn't please Hammerhand, but he was starting to see how the country lay in his relationship with the "prophesied" wanderer from the wastelands. And since the whitecoat had come across with some heavyweight goodies, he was willing to suck down his pride and play along.

For now.

So he and Mindy, the sharpest-witted Blood after Hammerhand himself, had paid a visit quite openly to the distillers' ville. Dependent as his wealth and power were on trade, Baron Dugan welcomed people of reasonably honest intent. Or at least those who weren't stupe enough to show their ill intent. And who were pretty utterly outnumbered.

He had quickly learned that whatever happened had started with their old friends, the Buffalo Mob, making an appearance that pretty much pinned the needle on the gauge on the stupe side. The baron had made enough jack to acquire an actual machine gun, an M248 whose crew could swiftly run up the watchtower that gave the best field of fire on any kind of threat. What the Buffalo Mob would really have gotten if they pressed the attack was their wags and themselves shot to shit with powerful 7.62 mm rounds before they got in a good handblaster shot of the wire.

Hammerhand was glad they hadn't done so, since that fact had sweetened his haul of plundered wags today. But what interested him was *why* they hadn't.

The problem was, the details he got were as muddy

as spring runoff creek water, and even contradictory. All that was plain was that the Buffalo raiding party got chewed up bad, leaving the seemingly normal if well-armed pack of outlanders they'd messed with in possession not only of some of their lives but with half their rad-blasted vehicles. They had promptly driven back to the ville and sold two, a working truck and a broke-ass one, plus a load of plunder, to the ville folk for a stiff price.

Which they got, he and his lieutenant gathered, not so much out of gratitude at running off a major cold-heart attack, as severe disinclination to piss off the outlanders, married to a desire to see the last of them as rapidly as was decently possible. And once they loaded themselves and their new-bought supplies aboard the pair of wags they were keeping for themselves, the mysterious outlanders obliged that desire.

What had happened in between and put such a scare up the ville rats? Well, Trager had mentioned that his whitecoat "associates" had told him via their secret commo technique that they wanted an "anomaly" checked out, and they had not steered him wrong that an anomaly there had been.

"I know that plenty of people who were there survived," Hammerhand now told his captive audience. "So I reckon either that's some of you, or that some of you heard the stories. So now tell *me*. And while I give my word I won't chill you just because you tell me something hard to believe, if I catch you lying—"

He held the handblaster briefly side-on to his audience, as if he were explaining to children what it was.

The dude with the badlands face nodded. "I was there. And I didn't cotton to what was going on."

"I don't care about that part," Hammerhand said. "Just tell me straight."

"Yeah. We were gonna hit Duganville. It's a rich target. but it turned out to be better defended than we heard. Before we even got there, we ran up against this bunch of people leaving the ville, and they laid some serious hurt on us as we ran down on them.

"Well, Sully—he was straw-bossing the raid—he wasn't gonna take that drek. Would've been bad for our rep, you know? We outnumbered them a power, and we managed to take them down even though it cost us plenty. Ace so far?"

"Ace. Keep talking."

"So Sully got the notion to make an example of them. Try to put a scare up the people in the ville. A negotiating tactic, you know? We was half a mile out, but we reckoned they had binocs on us. So he decided we'd gang-fuck them and then give them an extrahard send-off."

"Women *and* men?" Hammerhand asked. "Never mind. What happened next?"

The rugged-featured man looked doubtful, but he went on.

"All of a sudden there was this, like, black dust devil. Dunno what else to call it. Never seen nothing like it. It tore people apart and ate them right down like some kind of big mutie animal!"

"It *was* just mutie monsters, like as not," a female voice growled from behind the speaker.

"Interesting," Hammerhand said, ignoring the interjection. "Anybody else see that black dust-devil thing?"

After a moment of hesitation, a hand went up from among the huddled prisoners. Then two more. Hammerhand interrogated them, too. They backed up the first Buffalo's tale, although nobody could provide any further detail.

Three others who had been on that ill-fated raid agreed with the skeptical woman that it had to have been an animal of some kind. Just one that was black and that nobody got a double-good look at.

Because all that agreed, roughly, with what the people of Duganville had told him they saw through their field glasses, he did not reward any of the speakers with extra holes in their body. Everybody seemed to be telling him the truth. Just the truth the way they saw it.

"Now," he said, "see how easy that was? If anybody remembers anything more they want to tell me about that little adventure, you come talk to me in private later.

"In the meantime—as it happens, I am recruiting. So let's see a show of hands. Who wants to join a winner?"

"I STILL SAY it smacks of slavery," Mildred said, pulling her head back inside the wag.

"How you reckon that, Millie?" J.B. asked. He was driving the black pickup wag up a dirt road winding into the Black Hills, west of the hot-spot Rapid City ruins. The hills here weren't high, but they were surprisingly steep in this section. Right now the track ran around the side of an inclined slope with exposed granite standing out here and there among the tall spruce and ponderosa pines on the left, with another fairly steep drop to a stream thirty or so feet below on the right. It was slow going for the two-wag convoy, more because of concern about getting into trouble too fast than about road conditions.

"We're delivering a young woman to marry some older dude, whom she's never laid eyes on her whole life," she said. "All arranged long distance. She's a mail-order bride! Bought and paid for."

It was a bright and beautiful morning, with only a few feather clouds visible up beyond the tall treetops. The Armorer frowned as if having trouble fitting his head around his lady love's arguments. He was neither stupe nor slow—the opposite of each, in fact—but he was so intensely practical that he found it difficult, sometimes, to come to terms with abstract arguments.

Especially where people were concerned, with their messy, irregular, tangled-up balls of emotion. So different from the well-ordered and basically predictable machines he loved to tinker with.

"Well, she did say she was fine with it when her Maw Dombrowski paid us to deliver her to this Borodin dude."

"What else did you expect her to say?"

"No?"

"Maybe she didn't feel as if she could. Her mother's a pretty formidable type. Wealthy and powerful, even if she does call herself a rancher and not a baron."

"If this Pearl is a slave, why doesn't she try to run away?"

"She's afraid we'll track her down and return her."

J.B. shook his head doubtfully. "Any case, while I'm not exactly known for being particular in the looks department where it comes to women, she does have a face on her kind of like the south end of a northbound mule."

Mildred fixed him with a withering glare. When he failed to wither, she sighed theatrically.

"John," she said. "You are *so* tone-deaf."

He looked at her in confusion. "What?"

By now she knew his apparent confusion was genuine. He honestly had no clue he'd as good as called Mildred homely. Not that she considered herself in the same category as Krysty—because she wasn't totally unrealistic. But she also had *some* vanity.

She opted to let it go. For now.

"What's that got to do with her being a slave or not?"

"Well, I mean, this Borodin fella, he's supposed to be pretty well-off himself, with his logging and his mill. Wouldn't he go for something a mite prettier if he was able to *buy* a wife?"

"Why would he go for her, then?"

"You'll have to ask him. Ryan tells about how arranged marriages are common among baron families back East, though. Way to cement alliances, even resolve disputes. That kind of thing. Nothing tends to draw rival clans closer quicker than having a common grandkid or two, I guess."

"It didn't seem to work that way for my married friends' in-laws," she said. "But I suppose barons are different."

"You can say that again."

Chapter Thirteen

"So, Trager," Hammerhand said, "did you get what you wanted?"

He deliberately didn't say the title *Doctor*, because omitting it visibly needled the whitecoat.

The little man looked thoughtful and fingered his patchy-bearded chin. Hammerhand thought that up close the man looked mostly like a big old black rat with the mange, dressed up in a predark lab coat.

"While it was regrettably short on concrete details," he said, "I believe so. At least a relatively consistent account of what happened emerged. That should be of use to my associates."

"Ace," Hammerhand said.

It was noon. The sky had mostly cleared, although the wind had risen and was whistling over rolling land just showing spots of green. The new recruits, which was most of the captured Buffalo Mob, had all been duly sworn in as members of the New Blood Nation, as Hammerhand had taken to calling his outfit. He had ordered their weapons returned, which got him disapproving looks from both his lieutenants. But because the prisoners signed on of their own free will, he took them at their word. And if any were trying to pull a fast one, Hammerhand would be happy to make an example of them.

That worked, too.

Now the wags that had dropped Hammerhand's assault teams a mile from the camp the previous night had driven up to collect the new recruits. The freshly minted Bloods were stowing their own equipment plus everybody else's into their former transport.

Joe Takes-Blasters frowned at Trager, but more in confusion than anger.

Unperturbed by the scrutiny, the whitecoat took a fresh red apple from a pocket of his coat and bit into it. Hammerhand had no clue where he'd gotten it. Or rather, where his associates had. He'd also given one to Hammerhand, so the Blood boss took no offense now.

"You gave us some straight skinny on that Buffalo camp," Joe said to the little man.

"Of course I did," Trager replied, unconcerned by chunks of pale yellow apple flesh falling from his lips.

He seemed to be waiting for the rest of it. Joe just stood there and looked at him. Hammerhand understood that, having said his piece, his lieutenant was done speaking. He was a man who preferred to let his fists, his blasters and his one-piece steel hatchets do his talking for him.

The youngster Little Wolf trotted to his side. "Aunt—I mean, Shyanna—says to tell you we're ready to roll, boss!"

"Thanks," Hammerhand said. The kid went bouncing off like a pup who'd just been petted.

"What about the holdouts?" Mindy asked. Ten or twelve of the intact Buffalo prisoners had refused to swear allegiance to Hammerhand and his cause. So had several of the wounded ones. Additionally there were some Buffalo wounded who didn't seem likely to recover. They had been too wrapped up in their own misery to say yes or no.

"Chill them."

Mindy raised an eyebrow. "You sure? That doesn't sound like the deal you offered."

"But it was," he said. "Did you hear me say anything about what would happen if they didn't join? No, you didn't, because I never did say that. I wanted actual, willing volunteers. Okay, mostly willing. And I wanted to show how generous I was to those who earned it. The rest—"

He shrugged. Trager, paying the whole exchange no mind, took another noisy bite from his apple.

"Let's just say I also want to show the world that those who stand against me fall. They had their chance. They made their choice. That ends it. And them."

Joe's heavy brow furrowed more deeply. "How do you want it done, boss?"

He didn't care for torture. No more than Mindy did. But he was loyal as a dog, both to his old friend and to his sworn chieftain. He would do as he was told, like it or not.

"Quick and clean," Hammerhand said. "I want them killed, not hurt."

Trager scoffed.

"I hadn't expected you to be so sentimental."

Hammerhand frowned. At some point there would have to be an adjustment of the terms between him and this disgusting little man, prophesied guide or not, and a reckoning. But for now, he was useful, as even Mindy had been forced to acknowledge, still skeptical though she was.

"I'm not a sadist," he said. "I'll hurt you. Make no

mistake about that. Hurt you bad. But only if you give me good reason to. An honest enemy gets an honorable death. That's part of the message, too. You wouldn't understand."

"FIREBLAST!" RYAN EXCLAIMED as the brake lights lit up on the wag ahead of his and Mildred waved her hand out the passenger window to signal trouble ahead.

Krysty, behind the wheel of the pickup in whose bed he rode, had already stopped the wag.

Despite her lightning reflexes, and the slow speed at which they were grinding up the twisty road, the trailing wag almost rode up onto the leading vehicle's bumper before it stopped. That was far enough for Ryan to catch a glimpse of what the problem was: a makeshift barrier of gray boulders and dead trees blocking their advance. Bearded faces and longblaster barrels were visible behind it between bare skeletal branches.

"Roadblock!" he shouted to the open driver's window. "Back it up, Krysty!"

Even as he shouted Ryan felt the wag jolt into reverse motion. She was ahead of him.

He turned to look back the way they were going as his lover stuck her head out the window to better see to steer. He knelt for stability, holding an M16 they'd kept out of their coldheart trove. In case of ambush, putting a lot of lead in the air in a hurry could actually be a help instead of just a way to waste ammo, shooting holes in the air. The longblaster's full-auto capacity had a way of being useful in such circumstances.

With a terrible grinding sound and slapping of boughs, a hundred-foot ponderosa pine toppled downward from among the trees upslope to crash across the road behind them. It had obviously been cut or weakened in advance.

They were truly caught in a well-prepared ambush. The only question now was their ambushers' intent.

"Give us the girl an' we'll let you off with your lives!" a voice bellowed from behind the front roadblock.

Ryan had already guessed the intent was to get hold of their apparently valuable cargo, alive and unpunctured—by virtue of the fact they weren't all dead already. They had gotten caught in the killing zone of a classic fire-sack ambush. A hail of bullets would have ended them at once, but nothing more than rocks, big and small, rolled down on them from above would have been enough to lay them all staring at the sky. Just in a slower, more agonizing fashion.

So their attackers' lack of desire to chill them—at least, before they got what they wanted—was obvious. And so was the response.

"Forward or back?" Jak yelled from the vehicle's bed.

"¡Adelante!" Ryan responded. He was betting ambushers in these parts would not likely understand the Spanish word.

But he knew Jak did. Ryan had barely started to blow the word out of his mouth before the young albino leaped out of the pickup bed and raced into the scrub to the left, uphill side of the road. He vanished at once, with scarcely a disturbance of the branches.

"Ricky!" Ryan yelled. "Get the package down! Krysty, cover behind." Then he also sprang from the back of the trapped wag as Ricky piled over the back of his seat to shove a very surprised Pearl Dombrowski to the backseat floorboards.

The one-eyed man made his way up the steep hill, with considerably less grace and a lot more noise than Jak had. It didn't matter under the circumstances. Things were about to get a lot louder.

Behind him he heard Krysty open and slam her vehicle's driver's door as the redhead obeyed his order. He hated putting her in the more exposed bed of the pickup truck, but it was only slightly less safe than the cab. If the thin-gauge metal of the tailgate would do little to stop high-velocity fire, adding the equally paltry protection of the bed's front and cabin's rear would do little more than slow the bullets a bit. Only the big four-cylinder block of the 150-horsepower 2.7-liter engine would stand up against those. The soft lead slugs belched out by most black-powder blasters could be warded off more easily, but Ryan wasn't going to bank on them being lucky enough to be facing those.

He and his companions, well-practiced—and seasoned—in ambush busting, didn't plan on giving the coldhearts first crack. J.B.'s Mini UZI began chattering from the lead wag's driver's-side rear window, followed a heartbeat later by bursts from Doc's longblaster, an M4 carbine with a fore pistol grip, also on full-auto. At the same instant Krysty opened up, blazing bursts at the ambushers with her Glock 18.

Ryan half expected to be met with a withering volley from the scrub as he headed upslope. If the ambushers had a party placed in cover there, they could pour flanking fire on the wags stalled on the road and wipe out their occupants. But nothing happened. Indeed it took a handful of seconds before shots began to crack from both barriers. They sounded to Ryan like black-powder weapons, not the higher, sharper reports of smokeless cartridges.

Meeting no opposition nor any sign at all of the enemy, he curved to his left, hoping that his path would take him to a point overlooking the ambushers behind the rear barricade.

Chapter Fourteen

Huddled behind their crude but effective roadblocks, the dozen ambushers were popping up between reloads to fire away with mostly single-shot black-powder weapons. When they shot, the barrels of their longblasters were unmistakably pointed high. They weren't actively aiming to hit the two-wag convoy they had so neatly trapped.

Jak was not surprised. It was clear they'd expected their targets to surrender meekly when they so totally and unexpectedly got the drop on them and that they still didn't want to damage the merchandise, in the form of Pearl Dombrowski. They intended to intimidate.

Exactly what made the young woman such precious cargo, Jak had no idea. He cared less. All that mattered was his job.

He licked his lips as he leveled his Colt Python between the budding branches of a holly bush, snuggled close along the hip of a granite outcrop. He was barely ten yards from the nearest ambusher, not more than twenty-five from the farthest. They were a scabby-assed lot, he thought, even by the standards of someone who grew up waging a guerrilla war in the Gulf Coast bayous. They wore rags and scraps of poorly made homespun clothes, which seemed to be held together mostly by man grease and filth, as their heads seemed mostly held together by matted hair and beards. The albino could still smell their body funk over the rampaging sulfurous stink of their blaster powder.

Two of them looked a bit less scabrous and rat-chewed than the rest: a tall man in a mostly intact green plaid shirt and jeans, who was blasting away sporadically with a mismatched pair of black-powder cartridge revolvers, and a shorter, wider black man with a lever-action carbine. Along with their better weapons, both of them had clearly visible features instead of masks of fur and filth.

They were obviously the command element, which the brown-bearded tall dude confirmed when, during a break where his accomplices were reloading, shouted, "You all best surrender now, while you got the chance! We still promise we won't hurt you!"

Right, Jak thought. His mind made up, he thumb-cocked his big blaster, took care along its vented rib and squeezed the trigger.

Although Jak's first love was knives, he could shoot a blaster well, especially at short range. The high-velocity .357 Magnum hollow-point round planted itself in the long semigroomed brown hair behind partially visible hair.

The two-blaster shooter's head came apart as if hit with a twelve-pound sledgehammer.

For a heartbeat or two no one on the barricade even noticed. Their attention was focused on their targets, who continued to pump brisk fire in their direction. Then the stocky guy with the lever-blaster jumped and turned his head when his apparent boss's half-decapitated body brushed against his shoulder on its slump to the ground. He turned, his body language shouting confusion.

One thing Jak had learned fighting his bayou guerrilla war was to cut off the head first. He sighted on the black guy and fired his second shot. He aimed for the head, but an unpredictable hitch in his target's motion sent the slug blasting through his right shoulder instead. Over the lingering echoes of his own blaster shot, Jak could hear the coldheart squall as a spray of flesh and blood was knocked out the exit wound.

This time that triple-loud noise of .357 Magnum handblaster going off caught the ambushers' attention. Heads turned toward Jak's hiding place.

He had already left it, sprinting down the short distance to the road, still using the concealment offered by dense brush and straight tree boles. As he ran, he drew his trench knife with his left hand.

Though freshly reloaded longblasters, as well as astonished if grubby faces, were turning his way, Jak was grinning ear to ear as he burst into the open behind the barrier.

It was time for some fun.

LOOKING FOR IT, with a rough notion of where it would come from, J.B. saw the yellow muzzle flash from Jak's Colt Python as the albino fired his first shot from concealment above and behind the ambushers.

Even as the report slapped his ears, he stuck his head out the wag's driver's window. "Hang on, Doc!" he shouted.

He floored it even as he called his warning.

"Wait!" Mildred exclaimed as the big pickup truck

shot forward—right toward the barricade. "What are you—"

The heavy pipe-work cage covering the wag's nose hit the barrier. The dead trees were backed by enough heavy boulders not to budge far. The coldhearts had to have worked like jolt-walking beavers to build the thing. J.B., who admired little more than a job well done, would have to tip his fedora to them…after he took care of business.

He put the wag into Neutral, pressed his hat firmly onto his head, let go of the Mini UZI and yanked the door open. As he stepped out of the cab, his heavy machine pistol fell to the extent of the sling looped across his shoulder. He pulled his M-4000 shotgun out of the foot well and pumped it open enough of a crack to confirm it had a 12-gauge shell with tarnished brass base and red plastic hull nicely chambered.

Then in his standard manner—not visibly hurrying, yet moving with enough purpose that it worked out to be fast after all—he clambered up on the hood of the stopped wag.

Jak had fallen upon the ambushers from behind their backs like a white wolf on a fold of sheep. J.B. saw eight or ten defenders looking around in apparent confusion as the albino charged. He slashed a man a head taller across a bearded face—or what the Armorer presumed was a face, though he saw more hair and dirt than skin—and as that man fell over, clutching at a fount of spurting blood, Jak unloaded a round from his handblaster into the rib cage of a second coldheart as that one turned to try to aim a muzzle-loading longblaster at him.

From behind, J.B. heard the boom of Ryan's Scout

longblaster echo away between the steep, short hills. The Armorer had not worried about getting back-shot by the ambushers behind the pine they'd felled, but that was mostly because he never saw any amount of worry keep a bullet out of anybody's hide. He'd be lying if he said the fact that his friend was giving that gang of bastards something else to put their minds to gave him no comfort, though.

Almost in front of J.B.'s perch, a wide-shouldered black man was trying to raise a replica Winchester 1873 carbine to take Jak down. Most of what J.B. could make out behind the chunk of granite he sheltered behind was his head. So the Armorer took quick aim and blew it mushy with a tight column of Number 4 buckshot.

Another coldheart, this one to J.B.'s right, swung a single-shot shotgun toward him. The Armorer loosed another roaring blast from his Smith & Wesson scattergun. The charge cut through a bushy gray-shot beard to take the bandit where his gullet met his upper chest.

As the ambusher toppled backward in an arterial spray of gore, J.B. raised his bespectacled eyes to look for more targets. And found none. He saw nothing but backsides and elbows as the surviving ambushers rabbited away up the narrow dirt road or bounced and tumbled down the slope to the rocky creek bed like so many spastic jackrabbits.

His pounce reflex engaged by the sight of fleeing prey, Jak stuck his Python back in its holster and started hounding after the fleeing coldhearts. J.B.'s shrill whistle brought the albino up short.

"Don't chase them," he called. "We need you close. Might be more."

He felt a certain apprehension that Jak wouldn't listen. The small, pale scout was as much wolf as man. He didn't yield readily to authority at the best of times, especially when authority's voice was delivered by someone other than Ryan. He did respect the Armorer, as a comrade and a killer, but that didn't mean he felt any compulsion to obey him on nothing more than J.B.'s say-so.

But Jak's overriding compulsion was to keep the others safe. By framing his words as the voice of reason rather than command, J.B. won a quick nod, accompanied by free-flying long white hair, and then compliance, in the form of Jak vanishing into the scrub to the left of the road, as swiftly as if he'd teleported out of there via mat-trans.

"Ace on the line," J.B. said as he heard Ryan's longblaster speak again. He knew Ryan was likely outnumbered worse than Jak, and the Armorer had been taking on the front ambush. But even though he didn't have a lot of insight about what made people tick, J.B. had ground into him years ago that the easiest and best thing to attack in any fight was your enemy's morale. Once you convinced him he couldn't win—he couldn't. And very little convinced anyone of that as quickly and effectively as a sudden attack from behind. That was what had sent this bunch skedaddling.

The group behind the second barrier would have been confident that even if their intended victims didn't roll over and show their throats when they found themselves stuck in the coldhearts' trap, they were still safe and secure—and it was their targets who were caught between two fires. To be met first by Krysty and Ricky opening up on them, and then finding themselves sniped by Ryan—who knew how to take his shot and shift to a new location without being spotted almost as skillfully as Jak could—would turn that confidence with its bare ass in the air.

But just to be sure, he jumped back down to the roadside before he started stuffing fresh shells in his scattergun.

Chapter Fifteen

Ryan felt a thrill of cruel amusement at the jacklit-deer expressions of the ten ambushers crouching behind the brown branches of the rear barricade as they tried to process the spectacle of one of their number thrashed on the dusty brown ruts with the back of his head blasted clean off.

But the one-eyed man did not hang around to congratulate himself. While the sound of his first shot was still reverberating in the little valley, he was already shifting to a new vantage point. Because there was a kind of granite-knee outcrop a hundred feet or so up the slope from the road, offering a number of ideal points to snipe at the road from excellent cover, he had picked a less advantageous hide in some scrub twenty feet away from it, in the direction they had been traveling, for his first shot.

Now he shifted to the closest niche among the folds and bulges of the hard, rough rock. He had to expose himself to view, briefly crossing an open patch of slope. But the ambushers were still looking around in consternation, trying to figure out where the chill-shot had come from.

As usual, folks had a tendency to look anywhere but up.

The one-eyed man lined up another target, a scrawny

guy with a blond neck beard. But either something made the coldheart duck, or one of his buddies jostled him. Ryan saw the matted head vanish clean out of his scope's field of vision at the exact instant the trigger broke to the gentle, inexorable pressure of his finger.

After he'd ridden out the recoil and let the Steyr fall back online with a fresh 7.62 mm cartridge chambered, Ryan tracked along the fallen tree that blocked the road. He saw a face mostly covered by a black beard that seemed to sprout from directly under the eyes, which, like the mouth, were black circles of surprise and looked right at Ryan, staring up from between the dry triple clusters of long, curved pine needles.

He shot the bandit right through the shouting mouth. A dark cloud with wet red highlights glinting in the sun fanned out behind the bushy head, and he collapsed.

As Ryan pulled back to shift to another firing point, a little higher up and ten feet to his right, he saw the blond guy with the neck beard sprinting straight back down the road.

A couple of the ambushers popped off shots at Ryan as he moved; none came close. And then as some scattered cheers from the small but enthusiastic contingent of Ryan's companions announced that the coldhearts manning the front barricade had been routed, the surviving attackers gave it up and lit out, following the man Ryan had missed.

Though they were currently pretty flush with ammo, with plenty of the stuff recovered from their erstwhile Buffalo Mob captors still stowed in the wags, Ryan had a deeply ground-in prejudice against wasting his relatively rare and expensive longblaster cartridges. Instead he drew the SIG and sent a few quick 9 mm shots after the running bandits to keep them headed the right way.

When the last man was out of sight, still running strong, Ryan holstered the handblaster and made his way quickly down the slope. Rather than fight his way through the prickly dead branches of the ponderosa pine, he moved back around the hill as he descended so he could come out on the road next to Krysty's wag.

"Great job," he called to Krysty and Ricky. "Krysty, you get back in the wag and keep tabs on our passenger. Ricky—"

"We're fine." Mariah's voice came out of the cab. She'd started sounding a lot more self-assured since it had become clear in the wake of the brush with the Buffaloes that her companions didn't mean to run her off anytime soon. What with her saving all their asses and all.

Ryan for his part was only willing to let gratitude carry him so far when it came to those outside their tight little circle. But she *had* proved useful, no doubt about it.

"I can look out for Pearl," Mariah said.

Ryan looked at Krysty, who gave him back a cool green gaze, apparently neutral. But he knew her well enough to know that she wanted to go where the action was, or might be—and that she trusted her new little friend with the black pigtails to do what she said she'd do. And truth to tell, he'd rather have her along. Ricky would have served as well to ride herd on their cargo, but Ryan had other needs for him.

"Ace," he called back to Mariah. "You do that. Krysty, come with me. Ricky, I want you on the other side of that tree, keeping careful watch down the road. Stay in cover, and sing out if you see anything you don't like."

"Right!" the kid answered. Slinging his DeLisle carbine, he slipped down the lower slope far enough to work his way below the jutting dead crown of the big tree.

"Shouldn't we try clearing that?" Krysty asked with a wave at the pine.

"That's a negative," Ryan said. "If something comes up that road that might not like us, I'd rather have it between them and us."

She nodded, then accompanied him in a swinging, long-legged walk to where the other wag was nosed up against the first barrier. J.B., Doc and Mildred were gathered on this side of the roadblock, looking it over with weapons slung or holstered. Jak was nowhere to be seen, which was no surprise. He was somewhere past the barrier, keeping a lookout. Ryan and company would never spot him unless he meant them to, but neither would the bad guys.

"Can we bulldoze it out of the way?" Ryan asked.

"Don't reckon so," J.B. said. "Unless you're willing to risk messing up the wag."

"No."

J.B. sighed, pushed his hat up on his head and mopped his brow with an olive-drab handkerchief.

"Then we're going to have to clear a bunch of it by hand, although we can probably rig some ropes and drag some of this deadwood at least mostly out of the way with the wag. It'll take time, though."

Ryan looked at the sky. It wasn't even noon yet.

"We're not on a tight schedule here," he said. "So let's get to doing it."

They had barely begun to work on tying a thick rope around one of the dead trees' boles when Ricky came running up the road behind them.

"Wags coming!" he shouted. "And there's at least thirty men with blasters with them!"

"CALM DOWN, SON," J.B. said, straightening from the roadblock and pushing his hat back on his head. "Just tell us what you saw."

"Three wags, coming up the road slow," Ricky said. His temples seemed to be about to burst. "They're full of coldhearts with blasters. Plus more walking beside them."

"Do you think they're coming after us?" Mildred asked. Her brown face was sheened with sweat from exertion, although the day wasn't hot.

"I don't want to bet my life they aren't," Ryan said grimly.

"Are you certain about the numbers?" Doc asked. He had taken off his long black frock coat and rolled up his shirtsleeves to work.

"I couldn't tell exactly how many there are," Ricky said. "Lot more than twenty. I counted that many and then decided I couldn't hang around any longer."

"That's probably a wise choice, Ricky," Krysty said.

"How long do you reckon we've got?" Ryan asked.

"Mebbe ten minutes if we're lucky," Ricky said. "If we aren't—five."

Ryan grunted. He looked to J.B.

"Even using both trucks together, we couldn't bull a way through the roadblock by then," the Armorer said matter-of-factly. "Bastards did a good job. I'll give them that."

"What about ambushing them?"

Ricky bit his lip. He knew how deadly his friends could be. But some odds were just too great. Even for the likes of Ryan and his hard-core crew.

But he also found he couldn't say that. Not to Ryan's face and one bleak blue eye.

The one-eyed man nodded abruptly, once.

"Right. Look on your face tells me everything I need to know."

J.B. clapped his young apprentice on the shoulder. "Friendly advice? Stay away from the poker table."

"So what now?" Ryan asked. He was always the man in charge, and though he seldom pressed the point, there was never any doubt of that. But he was also not afraid to ask his companions for suggestions or advice. "Ditch the wags and press on afoot?"

"If they've got too many people for us to take on," Krysty asked, "won't they mebbe be able to clear a path through the roadblock double fast? And then they'll still have wags, and we'll be walking."

"That's true," Ryan said.

"What I cannot fathom," Doc stated, "is why, if they commanded such numbers and resources, they did not bring them to bear upon us from the very outset."

Ryan shook his head in disgust. "Who knows how coldhearts' minds work? Much less these crazy coldhearts. Anyway, knowing won't load us any blasters, to say nothing of giving us twice as many hands to shoot them."

He looked back at the big dropped tree still blocking the way behind the wag. Ricky knew full well it would provide far less of a hindrance to the pursuit he had seen coming up the track after them than the prepared roadblock would.

"We can head up the hill," Ryan said. "We know where we're going. Mebbe we can slip them that way."

"But the wags, Ryan!" Krysty protested.

He shook his head. "Not worth dying for. Grab your gear, everybody. We've got climbing to do."

"I can do it," a quiet voice said.

Though there was nothing sinister in her voice, the girl's words iced Ricky's blood.

"Mariah," Krysty said, half-hushed. Her face was even paler than normal beneath its sheen of sweat. Her sentient hair had coiled into a tight red cap of curls of its own accord to help the slight mountain breeze cool her sun-heated skin.

"I can," Mariah said in a tone that suggested she needed to affirm it to someone. "You need me to. *I* need to."

Krysty cut her eyes to her lover. "Ryan—"

"Do it," he told the girl. "Ricky, get our guest to safety."

"Why me?" he started to ask. Fortunately he choked it back. Leaving aside the possibly compelling reasons, and the this and the that, the real reason was because Ryan said to.

"Yes, sir," he said as he grabbed Pearl by the shoulder and hustled her to the still-open passenger door of the wag.

"Wait," she said. She resisted slightly, briefly, but gave in to Ricky's insistence. "But I want to s—"

"Sorry!" He pushed her headfirst into the foot well as politely as he could.

Or he hoped it was polite. There was no time for more. Even as she squawked like a chicken with a thunder mug dumped on her head, he piled right in and sat on top of her.

"Sorry!"

He of course stayed sitting upright. He swiveled his head forward as soon as he could without risking breaking his ankle or her neck. He wasn't about to miss this, sphincter-clenching terror notwithstanding.

This time the cloud seemed to unreel right out of the slight, black-clad body like black spider silk. As it did, it spun into a blacker and blacker cloud, like a dust devil in a coal-dust heap.

"Getting close!"

It was Jak. Ricky knew, or anyway had guessed, that he was keeping watch on the road ahead, which led toward their destination—and their payday. But his urgent cry now came from behind them.

The approach of known, definite danger had clearly overridden the press of potential danger in his albino friend's mind.

"We've got it," Ryan called back. "If they get too close, discourage them. Everybody else, keep clear!"

"Like you need to tell us," Mildred replied. She had scuttled around to put the snout of the wag, which J.B. had backed away from the barricade to allow his companions to work, between her and the eerie girl.

The cloud had become a swirling shadow so dark it almost concealed her. Then it swept forward, away from her, toward the heavy logs and heavier granite chunks piled behind them.

To Ricky it seemed the whirlwind paused ever so slightly, as if reluctant to break contact with its creator. He thought it had to be his imagination.

Then the cloud swept straight toward the roadblock. And into it. It simply dug in a good six inches without any sign it was meeting resistance.

Suddenly long splinters and yellow dust were whipped around the cloud, followed quickly by chunks of rough gray rock. It all frayed into threads, then nothing as he watched.

It was quickly replaced by more scraps of debris as the cloud swept left along the length of the barrier. It disintegrated wood and stone in a stretch several feet wider than the wags.

Then the black whirlwind simply winked out, if it had never been.

"Lemme up!" The muffled command came from beneath Ricky's buttocks. He more sensed the request by its buzzing through his skeleton than actually heard it.

"Oh! Sorry," he said to Pearl. He jumped back out of the open door. The young woman popped up like a prairie dog.

And gasped. Directly in front of the wag, a major portion of the roadblock was gone. Vanished.

"Ace on the line," Ryan said, sounding unimpressed. "Mount up and ride, people! Time really is blood here. Let's get Pearl to where she needs to be."

Mariah's eyes closed, then she slumped. Krysty, standing right behind her, caught her under the arms. The girl's face and hands—all the skin her severe garments left visible—were paler than usual. But unfamiliar pink spots glowed on her paper-white cheeks, and it seemed to Ricky that her mouth was set in an equally unfamiliar, if slight, smile.

But Krysty's brows were pressed together in a look of almost painful concern.

Chapter Sixteen

"But you have to!" Trager exclaimed. "My associates demand it of you!"

Rage burst like a bomb, red and black behind Hammerhand's eyes. How dare the cretin order me around! he thought. This whitecoat dog lacks respect.

The two of them stood on a lone low mesa, west of the bigger one his contingent had camped on for the night, with their wags laagered on the gentle slope surrounding it, above the reach of flash floods. The sun had almost dropped behind the Black Hills, miles away to the west. The evening wind whispered and moaned between the low badlands buttes that surrounded them.

Hammerhand stood with his arms folded across his bare chest, gazing south toward the Pine Ridge country. Lakota lands.

He kept his hand from his hatchet and forced the bile back down his throat. He knew how Trager dared: the power of his vision and the Glowing Man. And the power shown by Trager's "associates" in all the gifts they had granted, information and material alike. Hammerhand understood what that giving implied: the power to produce or even possess such marvels in such abundance as to pass them out. The power to withhold that generosity. And, no doubt, great power to compel.

He had made a bargain with himself, once Trager had

appeared, as promised, out of the wasteland, and their relationship had taken form. He needed Trager and what his associates could provide. But they needed him, too. So he would take what was available and give in return no more than he felt he had to. And only so long as he saw the benefit to himself and his people.

"What I have to do," he made himself say calmly, "remains for us to see."

"My associates—"

"Aren't here." So far as I know, Hammerhand thought, and so far as Dr. Trager feels compelled to at least pretend.

To his satisfaction he saw the whitecoat's face pale slightly in the golden slanting light, even behind its perpetual coat of grime. Whitecoat or not, crazed monk of lost world-burning science or…something even more sinister, or not, he could see a threat if it were veiled thinly enough.

"But, Hammerhand," Trager said as the strain showed in his voice and in the depth of the lines on his perpetually stubbled face, "be reasonable. We have done much for you. And we ask but little."

So far, Hammerhand thought again.

"What you're asking for now isn't little," he said.

"A simple reconnaissance. No more. A mere investigation."

"You're asking me to invade the turf of a bunch of surly inbreds. On ground where we'd give up almost every advantage we have as riders and raiders, while they'd have all of theirs. No, thanks."

"But you got information out of Duganville easily enough, just by asking for it diplomatically. No threats or violence involved."

"Barons like Dugan are plump and bourgeois, bound to their prosperity. They've got to keep up appearances, if nothing else. Back in the Black Hills, the barons don't have those kinds of limits. So the difference between them and coldhearts isn't always easy to see. I'm not sticking my dick in that scorpion nest just on your say-so."

"Are you afraid, then?"

Hammerhand let his voice drop dangerously low. "Are you calling me a coward?"

"No! Never, mighty Hammerhand! I wouldn't dare even think such a thing!"

"Thought not. Then again, I'm not stupe enough to risk getting this nation I've been working so hard to build—this nation that's so important to *you* that you're helping me build it—busted up bad on a bullshit high-risk, low-reward gig like this."

"But something big is happening," Trager said, openly pleading now. "Something important. It's already happened at least twice that we know of. We don't know what it is, and it is vital that we understand it. It could be a far bigger threat to you than to us."

"Mebbe. But if it's happened twice that your tribe noticed, it'll happen again. Mebbe this time it'll happen some place it makes sense for me to take a look. Not to pull back from the middle of doing a job you yourself advised us to do."

HAMMERHAND'S ORIGINAL VISION had been conquest, pure and simple. He and his roaring men and women would by fire and blood force the North Plains to their will, which was of course his will.

But Trager had planted different seeds in his mind.

Or just cultivated them, helped them germinate and grow. Not even Hammerhand himself knew which it was. And that fact made him wary.

Hammerhand's grandma, Doe Legs, had been his sole ally in his birth-band, after his mother, Ranita, was killed in a freak giant hailstorm, and his father, Thunder Face, turned his even-more-angry eyes away from his oldest son to pursue greater rank within the clan and nation.

Doe Legs had a saying: "You catch more flies with honey than with vinegar." He'd dismissed that as just more oldie-traditionalist crap, ritual gibberish she said because her mother and grandmother and so on back to skydark had said it. Another incantation that meant nothing—brought no rain, nor game, nor warded off mutie attacks or wildfire.

After she died in her sleep he had been all alone, rejected by his father and his father's relatives. And that had sent him on the path that led to hatred and exile from his birth people. He never had taken that saying seriously.

Until Mindy Farseer had strode boldly with him into Duganville. Posing as traveling traders, who were common as dirt in the turpentine-stinking ville, they had readily learned how the wanderers who had chilled a number of their Buffalo Mob captors and driven off the rest in pants-shitting terror had gotten the best of the ville's shrewd inhabitants when it came time to sell their plunder. Even Baron Dugan, who prided himself on driving hard bargains, gave up too much jack and goods.

The ville rats seemed *proud* of the fact they'd let themselves be fleeced. In their eyes, the nameless wanderers, the lean and dangerous one-eyed man, his flame-haired woman, and the rest were stone heroes. They had thwarted a raid, which, even if it had never been double likely to penetrate Duganville's razor-wire perimeter, would at the very least have been bad for commerce.

And, maybe, a worse precedent. Successive assaults of drought and acid rain had turned the Central Plains, which like these lands seemed to be recovering at last, back toward its old, desperate state as hard-core Deathlands. Life was getting hard—harder than it usually was—for the sod-busters and ville rats and for the coldhearts who preyed on them. The Buffaloes weren't the first nor the biggest nomad band to decide to try its luck in the literally greener pastures of the Northern Plains.

They weren't even the *worst*. Refugees were streaming north and west, too, not always to the happiness of those already there. And some of the fleeing coldheart bands took preying on the weak literally and turned cannie.

So Duganville had gone so weak-kneed in relief at their deliverance that they paid the outlanders top jack for their wags and other loot and hardly overcharged them at all for the additional supplies they'd stocked up on and loaded into the pair of wags they kept.

That got Hammerhand to remembering his grandma's words. And then Trager began to suggest that, rather than having to batter the whole Plains into submission, he could actually get large swathes of it to submit to him not just voluntarily, but eagerly. Just by offering the promise of safety.

There would still be a lot of fighting to do, the whitecoat explained, enough for him and the hottest blooded of his Bloods, and then some. Especially with the original holders of that name sure to take the warpath against him, to wreak vengeance for his humiliating murder of some of their elders. Although, of course, being traditionalist to the bone, they were still endlessly debating their campaign against him around the council fires.

So now, with Trager's guidance, Hammerhand was putting himself in position to be perceived, not as a scourge, but as a savior.

"Boss," a man's voice came from behind. Twenty or more feet behind. No one wanted to be accused of trying to sneak up on their warlord. And much less wanted to pay the price of a hunter's defensive reflex should they somehow actually succeed in doing so.

"You bring me news, Eagle Claw?" Hammerhand asked without turning.

Like Hammerhand, his two main lieutenants, Mindy and Joe Takes-Blasters, had charge of chunks of his ever-growing band, spread out north of the Pine Ridge country.

"Scouts just brought word," his current second-in-command told him. "Party of Lakota warriors are heading north through the Badlands. Twenty or so, riding horses with remounts."

"Horses," Hammerhand said. "How quaint."

Then he laughed. It hadn't been so long that horses were pretty much the only option he and his little band of straggly tailed outcasts could muster for transport—aside from walking, which was almost as distasteful to the Plains nomad way of looking at life as going off to take a wage-slave job in a Duganville turpentine still. And even now what the whitecoat would term his "human assets"—showing that for Trager, being a whitecoat wasn't something that he took off the way he could the actual lab garment—were growing faster than the number of wags and motorcycles they had to ride. Plenty of his Bloods still rode horseback.

"Right," Hammerhand said. "Have scouts shadow them while you start getting the clan ready to roll."

"What about the other bands?"

Hammerhand faced him. Eagle Claw Bateman was a skinny kid with black hair tied up in a complicated braid with an eagle feather stuck at the nape. He looked painfully young, although his age was actually just a few months shy of Hammerhand's own. An Oglala of the very band of the far-flung Great Sioux Nation they were all here to keep an eye on now, Eagle Claw might very well have been one of the supposed strays they were about to hunt, had he not gotten caught painting satirical caricatures on the tepee of a particularly moss-backed clan elder a couple seasons back.

While Eagle Claw was promising enough on his own, Hammerhand had chosen to keep him close in part to see if he would decide to revert to his blood ties. But he seemed to accept the Bloods wholeheartedly as his new kin, as well as nation. Now he was coming off mostly as excited on the verge of hyper. And if some of his former playmates happened to wind up on the wrong side of his blaster sights—well, that was just the game they all played.

"Leave them lie for now. If the Lakota got wind that we're up here somehow, this could be a feint. Send messengers to bring them up to speed, and tell them to stay where they are and keep their eyes peeled."

And we will all pray to the Spirits that this is yet another "unofficial" raid by unblooded youngsters looking to count coup off some unlucky trade caravan, he thought, and not a sign their elders have decided to make a hard move north.

This particular branch of the Lakota was frankly more than he cared to take on as a whole. That was why he had kept his people firmly on their side of the line, rather than boldly rolling into the Pine Ridge territory to put a more direct stop to the raids that had been increasing while the Oglala elders looked the other way.

"You don't want reinforcements?" Trager asked.

Hammerhand laughed. It wasn't forced or faked. "The Lakota are some hard motherfuckers," he said. "But the day I need more than eighty of my Bloods to take down twenty of their teenyboppers will be a good day to die. And you're still here, Eagle Claw?"

The young man gulped, turned around and hustled back toward camp.

"One job at a time, whitecoat," Hammerhand told Trager without glancing his way. "We're going to take care of this one now. Then we'll wait and see where this 'anomaly' of yours crops up next, if it does. And if it doesn't, it wasn't that important, was it?"

He turned and started walking at a leisurely pace toward the sound of revving engines.

"And believe me. If this 'anomaly' of yours has anything to do with those outlanders turning the tables on a whole Buffalo raiding party that had them on their knees, I want a piece of it every bit as bad as you do!"

Chapter Seventeen

"I got to say," J.B. stated as he squinted through Ryan's big binocs and fiddled with the focus, "these are not exactly the farm pests I pictured in my mind when we hired on with those sod-busters."

"They're not what I expected either," Ryan said, grunting. He lay next to J.B. in the shade of a stand of smallish cottonwood trees, clearly planted as a windbreak a generation before along an irrigation ditch that ran along the west side of a broad-bean field. The ditch ran with water from a tributary of the Belle Fourche in the watershed northeast of the Black Hills, maybe thirty miles north of the old Ellsworth Air Force Base crater farm and hot spot. Ryan watched their targets through the Leupold scope of his Steyr Scout longblaster. "I was thinking more—I dunno. Prairie dogs? Mutie prairie dogs? That size anyway."

"You think they're worse than armored coyotes?" Ricky asked from directly behind them.

Their two wags were parked on the far side of the windbreak, just beyond the morning shadow they cast on an expanse of prairie. The rest of the group stood behind the two men prone in the grass that grew around the base of the trees. Except Jak, who perched on the hood of the wag with his Python in hand, pointedly scanning the rolling land and slowly rising hills to the southwest and generally every direction except due east.

"Definitely," Ryan answered Ricky's question. "Armored coyotes you can still discourage by giving them a swift kick. And if they do go for your throat, you can chill them the way you would a feral dog—grab the forelegs and spread 'em hard and fast. These things..."

He shook his head.

"I don't have a clue what'll even faze these monsters."

J.B. had to admit his best friend's characterization of the creatures was no overstatement. Instead of mutie varmints the size of prairie dogs, these things were the size of timber wolves, easy. And they even looked like some kind of canines if you squinted triple hard.

But the arrangement ran to little more than the fact they had snouts, heads, high-shouldered bodies, tails and four legs.

To start with, their backs were covered in thick spines. Not thin needle-y ones, like a porcupine, but thicker, backward curved and tapering, a bit like a hedgehog. And blue, or maybe blue green, which was not like any hedgehog of J.B.'s experience.

Although the feet looked doglike enough, with strong, hooked talons of black or dark blue, the head was like nothing J.B. could call to mind, not even from his nightmares. They started out wolflike at the back, with pointed and possibly armored ears that swiveled or pressed back against their skulls, and black eyes. But instead of fang-loaded jaws, the snouts were long tubes that tapered to what at this range looked like a sucker, not unlike the kind stickies carried at the ends of their fingers. Except as bad as stickie fingers were, those didn't have holes in them for active sucking. These rad-blasted things had to have *some* kind of mouth, to judge by the way they ran around kind of hoovering in the flowering bean plants right off the stakes up those narrow funnel snouts.

"What I want to know," Mildred said, "is what kind of animal those spiny blue horrors could conceivably have mutated from?"

"No clue," Ryan said. He didn't say anything about abstract knowledge not loading any blasters. Once again they were in a situation where what they didn't know might just chill them.

"They do still bear, as Ryan has observed, at least a passing resemblance to the canids," Doc said. He sounded more fascinated than horrified. "Although what genetic leaps and bounds could have brought any such into shapes like these lie beyond my ability to encompass."

"Mebbe they're not carnivorous," Krysty suggested hopefully. She stood with Mariah at her side. The girl stuck as close as a second skin to the redhead, although the rest were gradually warming to her. Or thawing anyway—as J.B. himself was. "I mean, if all they eat are these bean plants—"

The blue horrors had apparently been settled in a spell. The sod-busters had allowed weeds to sprout around their precious crops, for reasons which J.B. now judged amply clear. A jackrabbit started from a clump of green grass growing at the base of a bean plant that one of the muties had just begun to nibble.

Instantly four of the spiny creatures pounced on it from all directions. They didn't seem to move noticeably slower than the jackrabbit. One caught it from behind before it took three long, frantic bounds. The hare actually screamed as it was hoisted into the air by a back leg.

The other muties closed in with their weird sucker-tipped snouts. The jackrabbit simply came apart in a spray of bright red blood. The dismembered chunks vanished up the skinny funnel noses without any more signs of chewing or swallowing motions than there were of jaws.

"Or not," Krysty said.

"Do they really just suck things apart?" Ricky asked. "Because it sure looks as if they just suck things apart."

"It does," Mildred said. She sounded sick.

"What was that predark saying?" Ryan asked. "'The only easy day was yesterday.' Right."

He snugged the Scout's butt plate against his shoulder and thumbed off the safety.

"Blasters up, everybody," he said. "We still don't get paid until we clear these ugly bastards out of the beans. So—"

The longblaster spit yellow flame, bucked and roared.

From long experience of working closely with his friend and following his lead, J.B. had managed to pick up on which blue horror Ryan had targeted. He had glass on it when the copper-jacketed 7.62 mm slug hit it broadside in the right front shoulder. It was a classic takedown shot for hunting big four-legged game, meant to shatter the shoulder joint and render the beast incapable of fleeing even if the damage done by the still fast-moving bullet—and the knocked-out bone fragments—to its lungs and heart failed to chill it instantly.

Whereas those wicked thick spikes might have enabled it to shrug off a handblaster bullet, at least from certain angles, it clearly didn't shed Ryan's 147-grain full-metal-jacket round. Venting a steam-whistle squeal of agony, the creature reared up in the air. Its head flew back, shooting a stream of black-looking blood from its sucker-tipped muzzle. Then it fell over on its side, kicking at the yellow dirt furrows with its hind feet.

"Ace on the line," Ryan said grimly. "They're triple ugly. But they die, just like everyth—"

The ground erupted two feet to his left, on the far side of him from J.B., as a big blue blur surged toward him.

DIRT FLYING UP out of the ground between the trees alerted Ryan to the fact he was about to die.

He barely had time to note it, much less react to it. The blue horror that had suddenly surfaced was already in midspring while he was still lying prone with the stock of his longblaster welded to his cheek. The creature was leaping from his blind side.

Something whipped right to left above his head. It caught the mutie midjump in what would have been its lower jaw if it had jaws. The head snapped back. The creature was knocked onto its spiked haunches, wailing in pain and surprise.

A burst of full-auto blasterfire ripped above Ryan's head shatteringly loud. The wail turned into a glass-breaking shriek that knifed right through the sound of a second short burst roping the mutie. Black blood flew from multiple impacts.

As it flopped to the ground, Ryan reared up onto his knees. The mutie began to move with visible purpose despite its pain, rocking on its side and then starting to get its taloned feet under it. Ryan shouldered his longblaster, pointed and fired.

The creature's head shattered as if it had been struck with an ax. It went limp.

"Nice roundhouse kick, Krysty," Mildred said approvingly.

Ryan chambered another round from the 10-round box magazine and bounced onto his feet. His lover stood right behind him, loading a fresh magazine of her own—an extended one—into the well of her Glock handblaster.

"Thanks," he told her.

And then a dozen of the horrors boiled out of the earth all around them.

"Fireblast!" Ryan exclaimed. "They can't possibly dig that fast."

Fortunately these new monsters surfaced too far away to spring instantly on any of the group. Instead they seemed to have some inkling what had befallen their cooling-down comrade. They began to stalk around the embattled group, staring them down with eyes like bottomless black pits.

"I think they're already under the ground," Mildred said slowly. She had shouldered a looted M16 in preference to her ZKR 551, whose soft-lead .38-caliber slugs might not pierce the muties' unnatural armor, and was warily tracking whichever mutie happened to be nearest with her blaster and her wide eyes. The entire party stood in a shoulder-to-shoulder circle, facing outward. Except Jak, who now crouched on the wag's hood with his Python in one hand and his trench knife in the other. For the moment, the muties ignored him.

"Which would mean—" Doc had drawn both his slim sword and his absurdly outsized 9-shot .44 LeMat with the short-barrel shotgun beneath the longer main one.

"That they're all over this whole area," Krysty finished grimly.

"You've got that right," Ryan said. He might also have opted for a blade-and-handblaster combo, but he still hung on to his Scout. He felt as if its power gave him a far better chance of stopping one of the muties than his 9 mm SIG, after the way the one that had tried to jump him absorbed nine rounds at powder-burn range and showed signs of still being fit to fight.

The muties continued to orbit them. Their numbers had at least doubled and continued to grow. Some marched in a counter direction to those closest to the embattled group. All gazing unblinkingly at them with their uncanny black eyes.

"It's like they're coordinating," Mildred muttered from behind the sights of her weapon.

"Wolves and feral dogs hunt cooperatively," Doc said.

"This is worse."

For once, Ryan found himself agreeing with the stocky woman. The way these creatures acted seemed wrong in a way that wasn't simply explained by their outlandish mutated appearance.

Jak caught Ryan's eye above the hunched blue backs. Ryan gave his head a slight shake. He didn't want the albino launching a one-man attack, from the rear or not.

"I don't know if you're keeping up with current events, there, Ryan," Mildred said tautly, "but they're starting to close in."

"Yeah," Ryan started. "On three. One, two—"

Six blasters began barking at once. They still had three selective-fire longblasters liberated from their erstwhile captors and still had ammo stores of 5.56 mm, because they seldom shot them full-auto. They did now, Doc with his M4 carbine and Krysty, like Mildred, with a full-size M16, ripping 3-round bursts into the muties. J.B. joined in with his Mini UZI.

Ryan's Steyr Scout came equipped with ghost-ring iron combat sights as well as the Leupold scope. He used that to blast powerful shots into the nearest horrors. He wasn't sure whether the full-auto longblasters could punch through those thick coats of spines, but he knew the Scout could.

Weird ululations filled the air in an unearthly harmony of pain. For a moment the circling monsters melted back. Ryan heard Jak's handblaster crack out from behind. He hoped the albino remembered to shoot either low or wide of his friends. He wasn't triple eager to stop a high-speed jacketed hollow-point round.

Or, more likely, just slow one down.

Then more muties boiled up through the small craters the first eruption had left.

"Not good!" Mildred said, during a momentary lull in the shooting. "We don't have that much ammo!"

Ryan was already feeding a fresh magazine into the well of his Scout, which, unlike most bolt-actions, had been built specifically to fire from detachable box feed devices—like the M16s, but in a burlier caliber. He was in little danger of running dry, but he wasn't shooting bursts.

And there seemed little danger of them running out of snouted blue spiny things either, even though at last ten were lying on the ground around them, keening in their weird fluting voices or lying still, bleeding inky black into the grass or over the tree roots. But the numbers of the horrible things were getting larger.

"Looks like they're nerving themselves to come again," J.B. said.

He was swapping his machine pistol for his slung M-4000. Ryan suspected the Armorer was less concerned about the relative stopping power of the different blasters on well-protected enemies and more about the fact that, unlike the Mini UZI, his Smith & Wesson scattergun was designed to be effective at whaling on many foes up close and personal. He intended to be prepared for when the muties got on top of them.

Ryan wasn't waiting. He raised his carbine, took flash aim and put a slug through a black, soulless left eye. At twenty feet the full-jacketed bullet had scarcely slowed from the muzzle. It splashed black ichor, turned whatever the horror used for a brain into blood pudding and continued on the length of its horizontal body. Or a good proportion of it anyway.

The monster fell without so much as a twitch.

The others lunged forward as one.

"Get away from me!" Ryan heard Mariah scream.

Chapter Eighteen

The girl's scream ripped at Krysty's heart like the strong digging talons the muties carried on their forelegs.

Though she knew it wasn't safe, she took her eyes away from the open sights of her blaster to flash a quick glance over her shoulder. She wished she could assure Mariah that she and her companions would keep the monsters and their horrible sucking snouts away from her, but their chances of keeping the muties away from *any* of them weren't looking good.

Mariah's face, though dead pale, didn't show the wide eyes and strained mouth of terror. Her brows were rammed together hard in the middle, and sheer fury flashed in her dark eyes. Her fists were knotted at her sides.

And blackness began to spool outward from her very pores.

"Ryan!" Krysty shouted. "Get clear! *Now!*"

Even though breaking their defensive circle was about the last thing in all the Deathlands any of them wanted to do in the face of an all-directions rush from monsters, the tall man reacted without a flicker of hesitation. He tucked his blaster across his chest almost in port-arms position and threw himself into a roll, forward and right.

The other person standing more or less directly in line with Mariah's raging gaze was Krysty herself. She did the same as her man had, except angling to her left. There was no point in evading the whirling black death that was gathering around the child to hurl herself into a point-blank blaster shot from one of her friends.

She came up on one knee, with her left hand to the ground to arrest her forward progress. Ryan had come out of his roll in a near-perfect kneeling aim, with his Scout longblaster shouldered and ready to roar. As of course he would.

She was triple-graceful. *He* was a killing machine.

But before she could raise her M16, Mariah stalked past her. Her furious face and rod-stiff figure were barely visible within the whirling darkness.

The onrushing horrors froze in place. It seemed to Krysty that their bottomless black eyes went wide as they saw the girl—or more accurately, a black whirlwind with black-and-white stockinged pipe-stem legs—marching toward them.

They set up a wailing chorus in a new banshee key. It was shriller than their pain-piping but eerie in a way that would have raised the hair on Krysty's nape even if it hadn't been alive and capable of moving on its own.

Then the muties charged again. At Mariah.

Even the monster that seemed to materialize right in front of Krysty's muzzle brake turned its tubular face away from her to hone in on the girl.

Mariah stopped. The whirlwind expanded to cover her completely.

The muties began running right into it. Krysty's heart jumped into her throat for fear they would prove magically immune to its mysterious power, that they would suck her charge to pieces before her horrified eyes, then turn their attention back to Krysty's friends—and to her.

But when the first mutie in Krysty's line of vision sprang toward the cloud, the devil's vortex simply unspooled it into rags and tatters and threads of green and black.

A dozen vanished without a sound—and without turning away.

"Dark night!" J.B. exclaimed.

Still the blue-green muties came on. "It's like they're attacking the cloud, not her," Ricky said in wondering tones.

"Reload and stay frosty," Ryan commanded. He didn't call for a cease-fire, because nobody was still shooting.

Other muties came up from the ground through existing holes. Apparently the first wave to burst out had come from all the tunnels the creatures had dug for themselves. Eight or ten more appeared, one at a time. All hurled themselves to disintegration by the shortest possible path.

"What the nuke's wrong with the things?" Ryan demanded in a hoarse voice.

"Perhaps they sense some kind of vibration from the…manifestation," Doc said dubiously. "It seems to drive them into a frenzy."

"Good an explanation as any," Ryan said.

He signaled them to gather, then whistled for Jak. After the briefest hesitation, the albino hopped down. He wiped the big blade of his trench knife on a dead mutie lying by the wag, then trotted over to take his place with the rest. He looked matter-of-fact, but Krysty could tell by the lingering dilation of the pupils of his ruby eyes that he was more than a little freaked out by the attack.

The black wind continued to whirl on for half a minute after the last mutie appeared to dash itself to destruction in it. Then it collapsed into Mariah and was gone.

Krysty broke ranks to run to her and catch her in a hug. "Mariah! Thank you. Are you all right, honey?"

The girl's slight figure trembled within her arms, but she nodded. And when she raised her face to look up at Krysty, her eyes were bright and her cheeks were flushed.

"Mebbe there are more of them," she said. Her pigtails bobbed across Krysty's arm as she turned her head to nod at the middle of the bean field. "Let me get them for you."

RYAN RUBBED HIS chin bristles meditatively.

"You dig with that power of yours?"

The bean field around them was littered with the chills of blue-green muties. As the party had approached the mound where they had first seen the monsters, cautiously following a dozen paces behind Mariah and her deadly vortex, they had come erupting out from between the furrows in such numbers that the companions had been forced to blast them. If nothing else, to avoid being trampled beneath the muties' talons in their frenzy to get at the girl.

Mariah looked at him. She swayed.

Krysty rushed to her side and put an arm around her thin shoulders. "It's all right," she told the girl. "You've done enough."

But Mariah shook her head and smilingly pushed off from the tall redhead. "No, thank you, Krysty. I'm fine. Really."

Despite the fatigue that clearly dragged at every word

as it left her mouth, there was a force to her voice Ryan hadn't heard there before.

Reluctantly, Krysty stepped back.

"I can try, Mr. Cawdor," Mariah said. "Tell me where you want it."

Mr. Cawdor? he thought. It's Krysty, but Mr. Cawdor.

Aloud, he said, "How about right down that oversized anthill there?"

"Okay."

She held out her hands as if sowing seeds. Shadow unfurled from her palms and knit itself into a spinning skein of blackness. She gestured as if urging it to go, palms up. Obediently it moved forward, mounting to the top of the low dirt mound.

"I'd be lyin' if I said that didn't give me a touch of the willies," J.B. said softly.

"You and me both," Ryan agreed.

The rest of the group was spread in a rough semicircle twenty yards to the ditch side of the mound. They had blasters in their hands but not pointed. Just in case.

Once at the top of the mound, the whirlwind promptly began to settle down into it. "It's like a screw going into wood!" Ricky said.

"Yeah," Ryan stated. "What do you say we don't startle her, just in case?"

But Mariah had her face set in white concentration, willing the apparition into the earth. Without sound or apparent resistance, it settled down and out of sight.

Mariah tramped up the brief slope to peer down. Following Ryan's lead, the others joined her.

The cloud was whirling a couple feet beneath the rim of the hole it had made. Expanded, really, Ryan reckoned, because the muties had already had a hole they were using to go in and out of. Mariah looked at Krysty, who looked to Ryan.

He nodded. The girl made patting-down motions. The whirlwind began to drill deeper.

He saw the mouths of other tunnels laid visible to his eye. The cloud continued to bore downward. The girl had to have limits to her ability to project the vortex and control it. But she hadn't reached them yet.

Suddenly around the cloud he saw the surrounding walls open out.

"Can you cut that off for a moment?" he asked Mariah. He remembered that she'd said it hurt her to unleash the phenomenon. But then, she hadn't seemed reluctant to trot it out here today. He needed to be sure he was seeing what he thought he'd seen around the fringes of the black mandala.

The cloud winked out. "Are those rocks of some kind?" Ricky asked.

Ryan saw them, too. They were hard to miss; they were strewed, huddled against each other, all across an area of earthen floor the whirlwind bore had revealed, which lay a good dozen feet below the deepest point the cloud had yet penetrated. Green ovals, about a foot long and six inches wide.

"Eggs," J.B. said.

It was true. Not just because some lay split open, with some pale yellowish-green ooze slopping out if the fragments, but because he could see at least four tiny gray squirming figures. Even without the blue-green spines, those weird tube snouts made it clear what they were.

"Baby monsters," Mildred said. "Doesn't that beat all to shit?"

"I never would have guessed such beings were oviparous," Doc said. "Perhaps they are some variety of monotreme, akin to the duck-billed platypus."

"Well," Ryan said, "we've found what the muties were so rad-blasted set on protecting. Can you clean them out, Mariah?"

"Are you sure, Ryan?" Mildred protested. "They're just babies."

"Baby monsters. I hate to say 'nits make lice,' because that's just a bullshit excuse barons trot out to justify acting more like coldheart pricks than usual, but it applies."

"But what if they're, like, some kind of endangered species?"

"Fireblast, Mildred! Can you hear yourself? I only hope we're endangering them enough."

"These are no natural creatures," Krysty said in a somewhat hollow voice. "Expunging them would be doing the Earth a favor."

Ryan guessed she was treading on uncertain ground, emotionally speaking. She felt a connection to the Earth and to nature—almost to an obsessive degree, with how she personified the Earth as Gaia and all. At the same time, as a mutie of bizarre and unprecedented powers, her little friend Mariah wasn't truly *of* nature.

And Krysty wasn't either.

"I wouldn't lose sleep over cleaning out a nest of baby stickies," Ryan said, "if we ever came across any. Anyway, our job was to clean out this field. That's what I mean to do."

He looked to Mariah. Krysty was hovering over her like a mama bear, which was nothing new although still far from his favorite thing to see, considering. Mariah was standing upright, held her head high, and looked fit to fight. Fit as he'd ever recalled seeing.

Doing this black dust-devil stuff might hurt her, but it sure did seem to agree with her.

"How about rubbing out those eggs?" he asked her. "Do you feel up to it?"

She nodded vigorously.

"Okay. Go to it."

She leaned over the widened hole her cloud had made and held her arms down into it. Blackness streamed from her palms. The vortex took form again at the bottom of the egg chamber. Like earth or stone or metal, the eggs and larvae vanished with neither sound nor trace.

"Good," Ryan said. "Now can you, say, root around? Clear out a wide enough space to make sure we got all the little monsters?"

She looked at him. In the corner of his eye he thought to see the whirlwind waver as her concentration split, but it didn't vanish.

After a moment, she nodded.

"Ryan—" Krysty began.

"I can do it," Mariah said. "I can!" And the whirlwind came climbing back up the bore again.

She backed away from it. So did Ryan and the rest. Useful as it was—lifesaving, even—nobody was triple eager to get any closer to the terrible, all-consuming funnel of blackness than necessary.

When it reached the top of the hole, Mariah backed away a few steps. The cloud obediently followed, eating a line through the mound.

"How far?" she asked.

"Ten feet or so," Ryan said. "That will do for a start."

She stopped at about that limit, then ran the cloud back toward the first hole to begin spiraling it around and around outward from the center, widening the hole from the top slowly down.

"Wow," Ricky said. "It's like she's routing it out."

"So it is," J.B. agreed.

"Old lady Dominguez and her kin aren't likely to be thrilled with what we're doing to her bean field," Mildred said.

"Nuke them," Ryan said. "We're doing what they hired us to do. If they don't want to pay, I'll tell them we'll just put the boogers back in their bean fields. Or mebbe their backyards."

"But we can't—"

Ryan gave her a look.

Chapter Nineteen

A yellow light winked from the top of the next low mesa south of where Hammerhand crouched with most of his war band beneath the pale arch of the Milky Way.

"Here they come," Hammerhand murmured in satisfaction to Eagle Claw. "Right on schedule. Right into our laps."

He felt additionally gratified that his people had done this all on their own, without the help of any of Trager's whitecoat magic, although now more of the whitecoat's high-tech gifts would be brought into play.

"Be ready," he said softly. Eagle Claw passed the word.

The twisty intertwining gulleys weren't deep in this part of the Badlands, maybe ten, fifteen feet, nor were their sides steep, which was strike.

Then again, thanks to the good scouting his people had put in this night, they'd had some leeway to pick their engagement ground. Hammerhand knew from experience, both his own and that of warriors who, when they talked, he listened to. He might have had trouble as a kid listening to his elders and his parents, but then, they so seldom said stuff he wanted to hear…

He pulled the pin from the gren he held in his right hand.

"Got your piece ready?" he asked Eagle Claw.

"Yes."

The first horse came into view. It was ridden by a bare-chested young man, who carried a spear hung with eagle feathers that bobbed to his mount's trotting gait. Like most Plains ponies, these were unshod. Shoes were unnecessary on this soft sand anyway.

The warrior had dark streaks painted down his cheeks like tear tracks from his eyes. That signified aggression. So did the butt of what looked to Hammerhand to be a lever-action longblaster jutting over his right shoulder for easy access. There were some dark patterns painted on his buckskin, as well, but the raiding party was down where even the starlight had trouble reaching, and Hammerhand could make none out.

A second horse, dark in color, trotted behind his. The seventeen young men and a few women who followed him, single file toward Hammerhand's hidden vantage point, all led a single remount. The single-file thing meant they'd paid *some* attention in warrior class; it was intended to make it hard for even a skilled tracker to figure out their actual numbers. And from what little Hammerhand could see from the darkness and the angle, none sported a hand painted on their face to signify they'd beaten a foe in melee combat. Or wanted to claim such.

It might have had any number of explanations, but it suggested strongly to Hammerhand that they were all good little traditionalist weenies, eager to show their allegiance to the ancient ways, even those that dated years before skydark.

Yeah, he thought. The Oglala elders don't know about this raid.

That made things tricky. But then, Hammerhand was triple tricky himself.

The silent procession approached the mesa on which Hammerhand and his main group waited. The enemy showed no sign of seeing anything amiss. They'd have had to have an eye in the sky to have much chance of doing so, because only Hammerhand was even the least bit visible from below, and that was only as much of his head as he had to poke up to watch them come through a long clump of grass. The leader moved to his left, indicating they intended to pass that way when the gulleys forked around Hammerhand's minimesa.

But they weren't going to pass. Not if he and his Bloods had anything to say about it.

"Fire," he ordered without turning his head.

He heard the pop and waited until the red flare reached the height of its arc, almost directly above the little marauder column. Then he pitched the gren right in front of the lead rider.

The flare's red glare illuminated surprised, upturned faces. And then the horses began to rear and whinny in fear as grens rained down from the surrounding heights, to both sides of them, as well as directly behind.

It was already too late for them.

"MAY I TALK with you for a bit, Mariah?"

The girl put down the bundle of dried scrub brush she had gathered for the morning cook-fire. "Sure, Krysty," she said. "What about?"

The redhead glanced at the others. They sat around the bonfire conversing in low voices. They had bought some fine smoked-elk haunch that afternoon with the grudging yet complete payment they got for purging the bean field of monsters—if purging it of many bean plants, as well. For people who lived as they did, a fine, full meal was a celebration—and something to celebrate.

She reached for Mariah's hand. "Walk with me a bit."

After a moment's hesitation, Mariah put her hand in Krysty's. It was cool and dry.

"Where to?" the girl asked.

"Outside camp a ways." Krysty laughed softly. "I guess we don't have much to be afraid of, do we?"

"We've got Jak on guard," Mariah said seriously.

"That's true."

They were camped out in a low draw near a streambed, with cottonwood trees on both banks. It had rained in the afternoon, after they'd finished their unexpectedly bizarre extermination job. Now the air was fresh and cool, the grass was damp slick underfoot and the sky had begun to show patches of stars, bright through cloud.

A wolf howled. Other voices joined it. From somewhere down the small stream rose a derisive chorus of coyote yips, as if challenging their bigger, more formidable cousins.

Krysty led the girl to the top of a low rise and sat on a fallen tree. The branches were bare and the dirt and clumps of sod had fallen away from the roots, leaving them bare, like a frozen tangle of worms. She patted the bole. Mariah sat beside her.

"Thank you for what you did today," Krysty said, measuring her words as if they were a handful of flour from an almost-empty bin. "You were a big help to us. We wouldn't have been able to clear out that nest without you doing what you did."

Even in the darkness it seemed the girl's eyes gleamed with happy excitement. She nodded vigorously, making her pigtails bob.

"I'm so happy I can help," she said.

"I'm surprised, though. I thought you were reluctant to use your power. That it hurt to do so."

Ryan had not put her up to this. She was asking out of her own genuine concern for the girl. She cared about Mariah…more than was probably good for her. But she had seen the troubled way her mate had looked at Mariah, off and on since the bean-field fight.

Krysty's lover was a man who seldom felt conflicted. To him, survival was both an imperative and its own justification. At least in most ways. And Mariah had greatly enhanced his and his companions' chances of survival on several occasions during their brief time together, when she hadn't outright saved their lives.

Mariah bit her lip thoughtfully. "Well, yeah. I was. I didn't like it. It scared me…that I scared other people. And it still hurts.

"But then I was able to help you. And I felt better about using it, in spite of the pain. It made me feel good. It made me feel as if I was worth something."

"I see."

"But it isn't just that. When I was able to burst through that roadblock, I felt powerful. It was the first time in my life that I felt anything like it. I wasn't hurting anybody with my power, or even anything. But then today—"

She sighed and shuddered. "It felt wonderful to do that. Even though I was chilling creatures. Even babies. They were wrong, just like you said. They don't belong here. And mebbe that's not their fault. But they had to go."

"That's how I size it up, too."

"So are you scared of me?"

"A little."

Instead of looking downcast the girl smiled and hugged her. "I like you, Krysty. You're always honest with me."

"I try to be."

"So tell me something else. Honest."

"You sure you want to ask it?" Krysty asked.

For a moment her smooth brow furrowed in puzzlement. "Oh. You're thinking I won't like the answer. But I want to hear it anyway. I promise I've heard worse."

Krysty had to smile. "Fair enough. Ask away."

"Why do you want me with you? Why are you so nice to me? I mean, the others aren't mean. Even the ones who still think I may be a danger to you, like Mr. Dix and Jak. They don't call me bad names and try to hurt me. So that's better than most people. But you—you seem to really like me."

"I do, Mariah." She reached up to stroke the girl's hair. Her heart broke at the way she at first flinched.

"So, why?"

"Well, first, I like you because you're, well, likable, I guess. You have a good heart despite your hard life. I admire you for that."

But still, I wonder—does the dark cloud reflect something within your soul? But not even a person as open as Krysty thought being honest was the same as saying *everything* she thought.

"But it's as if I look at you and see hope. It's your innocence. If you can keep that in spite of everything—well, mebbe it means the world isn't doomed to just sink deeper and deeper into ruin and misery until it just dies. And mebbe there's hope for *us*."

"What do you mean?"

"Sometimes I feel as if we're just doomed to wander aimlessly forever, doing whatever it takes to survive."

"But you do a lot of good! You help people. You helped me."

Krysty exhaled, making a sound that was half sigh, half moan. "It's largely by accident. I have to be honest. I guess that by not deliberately preying on people, we wind up…kind of better than average for the Deathlands."

Smiling, Mariah shook her head. Krysty found the girl's shift from her former perpetual gloom almost disconcerting.

"Well, we'd better get back to the others," Mariah said, hopping to her feet. "We don't want them to freak out when they find out we're gone."

Krysty laughed. "Oh, they know, for double sure," she said, standing up. "You don't think that much gets by Ryan or J.B., do you?"

"I guess not."

Suddenly she wrapped both arms around Krysty's waist and pressed her cheek between Krysty's breasts in a fervent hug.

"Thank you so much," the girl said. "You've helped me change the way I look at myself. And—everything!"

"I'm glad, honey," Krysty murmured, stroking the back of the child's head and feeling actually kind of awkward. The pigtailed, black-clad girl—whom she had settled on believing was about twelve or thirteen—might have been tweaking her maternal instincts, as Ryan had more than half hinted at on more than one occasion. That didn't mean Krysty felt comfortable playing the *role* of mother. Even a little.

But that wasn't what made her frown pensively as she gazed over the top of Mariah's head at her lover and friends gathered laughing around the little fire.

She was thinking, But have we done you any favors by making you see things differently?

And have we done *us* any favors?

HAMMERHAND STOPPED THE buckskin mare thirty yards short of the outskirts of the Lakota camp.

"What do you want here, Blackfoot?" challenged the chief, who stood waiting for him with his senior warriors flanking him. All cradled longblasters and looked grim.

The tall, spare man with the gray braids hanging down to either side of a breastplate made of linked bones was Marion, chief of an important Oglala band. He had clearly gotten word of the young renegade Blood's approach, as Hammerhand had known he would. His own scouts had enabled him and the small group he had led into the Pine Ridge area to evade observation most of the way, but the last couple miles he had known that wouldn't work.

You told me what I want to know by being here and ready, old man, Hammerhand thought.

Marion's black eyes bored into his. His posse was openly staring at the decorated horse. They might not know the name of every kid in the cluster of tepees on the low, sloping hilltop behind them—kids who were notably absent from view, as were the normal late-morning activities of the women—but they nuking well knew every horse claimed by their band on sight. Plains-riding nomads were all the same.

"I've got something that belongs to you," he called back.

"And what is that?"

For answer Hammerhand half turned on the horse's bare back, lifting the stubby-barreled blaster he'd stuffed under his camo-clad right buttock before riding into view of the camp and thrusting it skyward with a fluid motion and firing a flare into the sky.

Before turning back he ostentatiously stuck the empty break-action flare pistol back between the bare skin of his side and the waistband of his trousers.

"Now we wait," he said with a smile.

He let the buckskin drop her head to grass in the long grass of the natural ramp up the side of the hill. Then he crossed his hands on the point of his horse's neck where it met its back and sat there smiling at the Lakota elders.

The stoic act was a sham, mostly. He knew that; he was a Plains warrior himself. The people of the nations could be as outgoing as any random bunch of white-eyes, but they never wanted to give anything away in dealing with outlanders. Even ones with whom they nominally had no beef—the way the Oglala had none with Hammerhand's bunch, wild men and women though they were.

Ah, but you were looking, Hammerhand thought as the elder warriors behind Marion began to surreptitiously fidget. The big boss stayed a statue. *It's why you're here.*

Patience was not a core element of Hammerhand's nature. In large part that was why he was here, instead of being a good little warrior drone back among the Blood Nation of his elders. But it was a skill he had learned, being brought up a hunter. It served him well, too.

Gradually a crowd began to gather, respectfully ten yards or more back from the senior delegation. They were mostly fighters, men and women, none too young to carry a blaster, none too old. They had been told to expect shooting to happen once Hammerhand's approach was signaled by their pickets. Now curiosity was getting the better of them: why wasn't anybody blasting this upstart renegade?

It took ten whole minutes to find out, during much of which Hammerhand was laughing inside. Sometimes deferring gratification was totally worth it.

Then here they came, stumbling around the blunt nose of the Badlands mesa Hammerhand had ridden past not long before: the remnants of the "renegade" raiding party, hands tied in front of them with buckskin thongs, led by a pair of Bloods on their very own captured horses.

A gasp ran through the now-crowd, and one or two titters.

The "remnants" were every last one of the youngsters who had set out. Although they were bruised up some, and one or two sported broken arms in slings, they were all breathing and—by Plains fighter standards—intact. They had been so disoriented by the sudden hailstorm of flash-bang grens launched by Hammerhand's ambush from all sides of them that for most, even controlling their freaked-out horses was impossible. All had put up some sort of a fight and had been quickly and efficiently beaten down.

Now here they were, a sorry line of captives being brought home to their kin. Every one was birth naked, and every one had face, genitals and asses—and breasts, in the case of the four young women—painted a bright pink.

Marion's eyes stood out from his impassive stone face at that sight, and a couple of the prisoners' less old compatriots broke into outright laughter at their plight.

"I rounded up these strays and brought them back for you," Hammerhand called. The chief's expression went from surprise to thunderhead fury. "All safe and accounted for. You can thank us later."

I wonder if these stupe kids even realize yet that they were set up and sent out to die? he thought. *Tripwire*, my grandma said they called it in the old days. An excuse to start a fight—or get stuck into one that wasn't rightly yours.

His grandma was different from the rest of his band in a lot of ways, not least that she wanted to teach young Hammerhand about the past mistakes the white-eyes made, not just the People. Of course, her skin was as black as crow's wing, and the long, near-white braids were frizzy and thick. Since skydark the Plains nations had defined themselves as who was willing to ride with whom and what tribal ways they chose to live by. And "pure blood" meant lacking the mutie taint.

Another pair of Blood riders appeared, herding the shuffling, nude captives from behind. They held captured repeaters, a Marlin .44 Mag lever longblaster and a Ruger Mini-14. Nice blasters.

"Better ride closer herd on them till the wet dries out from behind their ears," Hammerhand said. "And best make sure they know what they're doing before you let them get their hands on weapons and good mounts again. Mighta got their stupe selves chilled."

The Blood escorts dropped their leashes and turned to ride back the way they had come.

"You all have yourselves a nice day," Hammerhand said. He turned his buckskin's head about and followed them at a leisurely walk.

He half expected to feel the impact of a bullet from Marion's big M14 longblaster hitting him right between the bare shoulder blades. He stayed riding slow and tall.

And then he heard the old man start to laugh, until his guffaw outshouted the wind that whistled through the narrow, twisted gulleys.

Chapter Twenty

"Dr. Sandler, I must protest!"

Not bothering to conceal his scowl, Dr. Sandler turned away from the large digital map, which had its yellow crosshairs centered and was zooming in on a point in what, for convenience's sake, was delineated as the state of South Dakota. The target lay in the fertile central portion of the now-defunct state, several miles east of the James River.

Dr. Sandler did not reply to his associate's unseemly outburst. Instead he nodded toward the hush field.

"What do you protest, Dr. Oates?" he asked once they were screened from the prying ears of techs, who, regardless of clearance, belonged to the lower orders. Consequently they could not be expected to have the mental equipment to deal with deeper truths. Even in a shadowy section of a shadow organization.

"I understand it is your intent to examine the scene of the latest anomalous incident directly, Dr. Sandler," she said.

"You heard it as well as I did, Dr. Oates. Our instruments did not deceive us as to its magnitude. If anything, to judge by Dr. Trager's reports, they may have understated its severity. And of course only we are in position to assess the possible ramifications of it."

"But the risks entailed," the woman protested. She actually allowed her voice to rise.

How like a woman, Dr. Sandler thought.

"Isn't that why we choose to deal with our current prime subject indirectly, by means of Dr. Trager? That we need to minimize our own exposure to reactionary elements within Overproject Whisper?" she queried.

"To be sure," he said. "But these are extraordinary circumstances. Perhaps you don't understand the possible ramifications of power such as our instruments detect—or at least appear to?"

"I do," she said, and sadly it surprised him very little that she sounded a touch sulky. "It could disrupt everything we're trying to achieve. Even force us to abandon this timeline altogether."

That's part of it, yes, he thought. He said nothing to enlighten her as to the new trend his thoughts were taking. Information was power, after all, and even with his ostensible partner in this clandestine work, he was reluctant to share that.

"But we already have the report Dr. Trager garnered from our prime subject's reconnaissance," Dr. Oates persisted.

"And even though the prime subject devoted relatively scant time to his investigation, being impatient to embark upon the active conquest phase of his plans to dominate the Plains—" *exactly according to our projected timeline*, he did not find it necessary to say "—do the details of that report not alarm you, Dr. Oates?"

"Will it alarm you any less if we see for ourselves what the prime subject describes?"

"I do not presume to know that, Dr. Oates. That is

why we do science, after all, is it not? In order to find out what is true?"

She frowned as deeply as she dared. Granted they were partners, but she was at least perceptive enough to know that this was not an equal partnership, nor could it ever be; evolution itself dictated the facts, not he or she.

"Yes," she finally said.

"Very well. Let's have no more of this nonsense, then, shall we?"

Without awaiting her response, which could only be redundant at this point anyway, he stepped out of the hush field, feeling a slight prickle on his skin as he broke through its invisible electromagnetic membrane.

"Are we locked on to the target location?" he demanded of the techs.

"We are, Doctor," one replied.

"Open the portal, then."

Dr. Oates walked to stand beside him as the techs duly manipulated their controls. He waited a few heartbeats before glancing at his colleague to confirm that she had regained her poise. He had no wish to be seen by Dr. Oates as validating her emotionalism. Fortunately, she had once again assumed a demeanor of scientific detachment.

An oval two meters in height shimmered into being between the two scientists and the main board. When it had fully resolved itself, its mirror effect vanished, to be replaced by a ground-level view of a furrowed field full of broken stakes and trampled green plants. Small craters dotted the target area, as if it had been subjected to light artillery bombardment.

The bodies of the anomalous creatures of which their prime subject's informants had spoken had been removed. Dr. Sandler felt a certain regret; he was confident they were either deliberate releases or, better, inadvertent escapees from some other secret division of Overproject Whisper. Had he been able to obtain a specimen, or at least photographic evidence, it could very well have translated into leverage he could use to improve their status and funding at the expense of someone else.

That he might be victimizing a project that posed no direct threat to his and Dr. Oates's joint venture, and which was more than possibly working on some aspect of the Overproject's greater aims, troubled him not at all. Nothing could be more vital than the work he and Dr. Oates were engaged in. Anything that hindered them was intolerable and had to be removed; anything that advanced their aims was not simply justified but necessary, in the interests of science and, of course, the greater good.

But if he had to settle for achieving their primary objective—it was, after all, the prime objective. And most imperative.

"Life signs?" he said.

"No life form larger than a meadowlark detected within a radius of one hundred meters, Dr. Sandler," a tech reported.

"It would appear the primevals are reluctant to return to work their fields," Dr. Oates observed, "even though they have disposed of the carrion."

"So much is obvious. We shall now pass through the portal."

"Would you care to have us summon a security team, Dr. Sandler?" asked a senior tech. "Either to accompany you into the target zone, or to stand by?"

"Not necessary," he said curtly. "We shall not venture far from the aperture."

"Understood, Dr. Sandler."

He stepped forward. Unlike leaving the hush field, there was no physical sensation at all to the transition. The matter-transfer units scattered about the globe, many of which remained operational, were ridiculously primitive by comparison to the portal—scarcely more advanced than the hand tools the primeval agriculturalists who worked these field were forced to rely upon to scratch their subsistence out of the dirt. They had been scarcely less outmoded at the time of their inspiration. After all, they had been meant to facilitate the work of the Overproject's servitors in the outer world, who knew a very great deal less of the truth than they convinced themselves they did—and to help to both buy their loyalty and discretion, and to overawe them.

Dr. Oates stepped through with him. She was unable to stop herself wrinkling her nose at the assault of the many stinks of the exterior surface world.

"I can still smell the decomposition," she complained. "And it would appear the primevals use animal excrement as fertilizer."

Dr. Sandler did not deign to respond. If she was worried about filth adhering to her shoes, she was displaying her susceptibility to female hormones yet again. Of course the portal would permit only themselves and such garments and appurtenances as they had originally transitioned with to pass back through. Everything that might have adhered to them, down to the atomic level—even inhaled impurities in their nasal passages and lungs—would remain here. Unless they invoked certain override procedures to allow them to bring samples back with them.

Instead he began to walk forward with measured paces toward what appeared to be a hole in the soil, fifteen feet from their entry point. The two of them reached the lip of the pit and peered within.

"Great Teller's Ghost!" he exclaimed.

The face Dr. Oates turned toward his was strained and pallid even by the standards of her icy northern European perfection.

"You were right to insist on seeing this ourselves, Dr. Sandler," she said. "If I hadn't seen it with my own eyes, I would never have conceived how momentous this is!"

He nodded, allowing himself to savor a moment of triumph at her capitulation. Only briefly, of course. Because he was a scientist, and the soul of science was objectivity.

"Clearly," he declared, "we must take action on this directly."

"I concur, Dr. Sandler," Dr. Oates said.

"Satisfactory," he said. "Let us return. We have work to do. And a specimen to obtain."

Chapter Twenty-One

"That doesn't look good," Mildred said from the passenger seat of the wag.

Ryan braked the vehicle.

"Fireblast!" he said, staring with his one eye at the mirrorlike ellipse that had suddenly appeared forty yards ahead of them. It lay on its side, fully as wide as the badly frost-heavy, two-lane blacktop road they were driving along through slow-rolling, spring-green prairie.

He felt a rare instant of indecision: Better to get out of the wags? Or keep everyone inside and ready for a full-throttle bug out?

He hit his palm against the steering wheel hub three times quickly. The trio of short horn blasts was the agreed-upon signal for everybody to exit the vehicles in a hurry.

"This is some serious whitecoat shit," he said, yanking his own door open. "If they cut loose on us with some kind of energy weapon, we don't want to be sitting on top of ten gallons of fuel."

Jak already had his right-hand rear door open and was gone. Behind Ryan, Ricky made an unhappy sound as he fumbled with the door handle. He got it open before Ryan felt obliged to intervene.

Ryan brought his longblaster with him. Ricky and Mildred emerged with handblasters at the ready. Behind him Ryan heard J.B., Krysty, Doc and Mariah climbing out of their wag.

It was late afternoon. Clouds were rushing overhead from the southwest with a speed that would have set off alarm bells in Ryan's head about an acid-rain storm coming on, except these were slate gray, not orange green. Precipitation was coming—he could feel and smell it in the breeze—but it was likely to come in the form of regular rain, if likely in double-heavy doses, with mebbe a violent electric storm thrown in.

Cautiously, Scout held leveled before him, Ryan advanced to the nose of the pickup wag. Across the black hood he saw Jak vanish into the tall grass in the ditch on the right side of the road with barely a rustle. Ryan knew the albino would keep watch from there and be ready to flank any enemies if they appeared, as the one-eyed man expected they would directly.

And so they did. Two lines of men filed out of the mirror at opposite ends of the ellipse. They had helmets with black face shields, gray and shiny black body armor that looked to Ryan to be some kind of plastic, and black weapons like long, skinny black eggs with a sort of notch scooped in the bottom where the handgrip was. They formed up eight men strong on either side of the road, weapons ready, with a six- or seven-foot gap in the middle.

Meanwhile Ryan's friends, apart from Jak, came up to stand with him, keeping close to the wag in case they had to dive for cover.

A pair of people stepped out. Both were tall, thin and dressed in gleaming white in no doubt deliberate contrast to the faceless black-armored sec troops. One was male, one female. The woman sported blond hair cropped so close to her head it looked almost silver in the waning daylight. The man's head was shaved bald.

A strange sound like a whistling scream came out of Doc. It sounded almost like a hurt or frightened child.

"It is them!" he shrieked in horror. "The whitecoats! They have come to take me back!"

He fell down next to the cab of the wag, curling into a fetal ball of fear and sobbing.

"Are you with Operation Chronos?" Krysty asked the white-clad pair.

"You know about those amateurs?" the man asked curiously. "No, we are not. And we have no interest in this demented old man. Now, lay down your weapons."

Ryan laughed harshly. "Not likely. A person might construe an entry like the one you just made as downright unfriendly."

The bald, skinny dude laughed. "Do you actually believe your primitive firearms can harm us?"

"Yeah, I do, as a matter of fact," Ryan said. "We banged heads against your kind before, once or twice. We're willing to take our chances."

"You may take for granted," the gaunt woman said, "that if we need to summon further resources in order to destroy you, that lies within our capabilities."

"But it is not you we are interested in," the man said. "Which fact you have to thank for being alive at this moment."

He turned his pale blue gaze toward Mariah, who stood beside Krysty, holding her hand.

"You, child," he said, in what Ryan reckoned he thought was a reassuring voice. A quick glance sideways told him it hadn't worked any better on the girl than it had on him. "Come with us."

"No," Mariah said.

"But we can give you—opportunity."

"I want to stay with my friends."

"You can help build a world of peace and order for everyone—not over the course of a century more of suffering, as our projections say it will take now. But in a matter of mere decades. Or even a handful of years!"

"I don't trust you. You're whitecoats."

"Forget the silly superstitions you've been taught by those around you," the woman said. "We represent science, order and hope. Look around at these people you're with. They represent filth, decay and random violence. What do you expect the likes of them to think of us? They are incapable of understanding us, with their dim and rudimentary minds."

"They're my *friends*," Mariah insisted. "They're not like you say at all. I don't think I like you much."

"But you belong with us, child," the woman said, dropping her voice low, into what Ryan reckoned she had to think were persuasive tones. To his ears it just made her sound like a different kind of threat. "Where do you think you come from, if not our laboratories? Do you remember who your mother was? Your father? Somehow you came to be abandoned in this dirty, dangerous world, all alone. Now we have come to take you home."

As she extended a pallid hand toward the now openly trembling Mariah, the woman seemed unaware of the snake-eyed side look her male companion shot her.

"But I know who my friends are! And I'll never go with you!"

The man uttered a sharp, hard yip of laughter, like a crazy fox. "What makes you think you have a choice? Security, secure the girl—unharmed—and dispose of the rest. I had imagined some of them might have possible value, as objects of study if nothing else, but I see that they are nothing but defective specimens in need of culling."

Ryan caught the gist of what the skinny baldhead bastard was saying. "Blast them!" he ordered, raising his Scout longblaster.

Taking quick aim at the male whitecoat through the ghost ring sight, he squeezed off a shot. But even as he shouldered the weapon, the pair in the long, white coats stepped backward through the mirror-like surface.

Ryan actually saw the bullet squash itself against that surface, as if it had struck the vanadium-steel wall of a redoubt.

From the other side of the wag's hood he heard J.B.'s shotgun boom. The helmet of a sec man on that side of the road suddenly snapped back. Ryan could hear its occupant's neck break.

"Take cover!" he shouted as more shots cracked out from among his companions.

The sec men had their weapons pointed at the group. Seemingly, all they had to do was pull the triggers, or depress the firing studs, or whatever, to blast the companions, which, physically, was true. But in actuality things weren't so simple.

In fact the sec team was at a disadvantage: they were in a state of *not firing*, and Ryan knew well the human mind needed time to work. The sec men had to perceive that they needed to shoot, make the decision to shoot, and their brains had to transmit the impulse to shoot to the muscles of their hands. Each step at time, even if only a fraction of a second. And if those delays added up to a second, that could make the difference between death and life.

But in this case it might only serve to delay the inevitable, by not many seconds more. Even as he hurled himself left toward the ditch, Ryan heard a peremptory buzz and the sound of a headlight shattering.

He put a shoulder down as he landed and rolled and saw to his horror that Krysty was still standing by the wag, apparently urging Mariah to seek cover with her. The sec men hadn't blasted her for fear of hitting the girl—yet.

"Drag her or leave her, Krysty!" Ryan shouted.

He pointed the Steyr, found a fast target and fired prone from the bank of the round-bottomed, weed-choked ditch. The sec men had their heads down over their long egg-shaped blasters, making them harder targets. His bullet instead struck the side of an armored shin of a kneeling trooper. The leg crumpled, dropping the sec man on his face plate in the road ruts.

Ricky and Doc had vaulted into the wag's bed and were blasting through the glassless cabin, sheltering from whatever it was the sec men were shooting behind the mass of its big six-cylinder engine. Ricky was firing his DeLisle, while Doc, who had recovered from his near-paralyzing fear of the whitecoats, was taking shots with his M4 carbine. Ryan heard the brief snarl of Mildred's M16 from the far side of the track and caught a glimpse of J.B. milking short bursts from his Mini UZI as he dashed for the cover of the grass to the right of the wag.

Something made Ryan's ears ring, the short hairs on his neck and arms rise, and his skin prickle as if with beginning sunburn. One of the sec men had shot his ovoid at him. He shot the man in the top of the breast-plate, just left of where his clavicle notch would be.

The bullet had to have deflected upward and punched through whatever kind of armor protected the sec man's throat. He dropped to his side and lay still.

But most of the sec men were still up and firing. Ryan and his people were in a tough spot. Their blasters could only hurt the faceless black-armored figures by accident. He gathered himself for a rush for the wag. If he could make it without having his insides pulped by near-soundless blasters that made dents like metal fists in the wag's hood and frame where they hit, he could ram them with it. See how they liked that.

Krysty was bent over, pleading with Mariah to flee. Ryan wondered where the redhead's own survival reflexes had gone. Then she jerked, her eyes rolled up and she dropped to her face on the road.

Ryan's heart seemed to stop. Blackness welled up within his eye. He tensed to jump to his feet, charge the faceless, black-clad bastards, do whatever damage he could lashing out with blaster butt and panga and boots and fists and rage before they sent him to join the love of his life.

But Mariah was faster.

"You monsters!" she screamed, throwing out her hands before her. Blackness streamed from her palms. It spun itself into a whirlwind of blackness between the fallen Krysty and the sec men, tall as Ryan and three times as broad in the wink of an eye.

Ryan heard muffled outcries of consternation from the sec men. His own people had stopped shooting when the cloud appeared. Now he could also make out strange, dry buzzes as the ovoid blasters shot.

The intruders were shooting at the black whirlwind. It grew without showing signs of being affected until it was high as a house and wide as the road.

Then it advanced.

Ricky and Doc had pulled out of the wag bed and were dragging Krysty's limp form to the open driver's door. As Ryan hopped up to help, he saw the sec men break, turn in panic and begin jostling one another in their fear-fueled frenzy to get back through that strange mirrored aperture before the black cloud took them. He heard horrific screams as at least one man failed and was torn apart.

Chapter Twenty-Two

"Pull back!" Dr. Sandler ordered. The communications net relayed the command from the microphone worked into the fabric of the collar of his white coat and broadcast it through the portal for a short distance, enough to be heard through the helmet sets of his security contingent.

They were already stumbling over one another in their terror-stricken eagerness to do just that, though. A second man waved his arms and legs wildly as he was drawn into the encroaching black whirlwind. Dr. Sandler made a mental note to mark the survivors as culls. They might, on review, be found still useful enough to serve as blunt instruments. But they would never be allowed to pass on their obviously defective genes. He would see to that.

"It's fantastic!" Dr. Oates breathed, staring in wonder at the whirling black cloud. She ignored the black-armored figures stumbling into the staging area around them, even when one thoughtlessly jostled her. "Such power."

The blackness spun straight up to the aperture. "Close portal," Dr. Sandler commanded. Obediently, the techs in the central control room—the aperture device was so calibrated as to operate at several key locations within the sealed facility—broke the connection.

The dark vortex winked out, leaving only a blank white bulkhead.

"But our wounded!" one sec man exclaimed.

Dr. Sandler took note of the number stenciled in gray on the man's breastplate, then of those on the chests of the pair of operators who flanked him. "Numbers 10 and 51," he rapped, "take 23 to Subbasement Zed-Two and dispose of him."

The two grabbed Number 23's arms. Number 10 yanked the sonic projector from his right gauntlet. He protested as they frog-marched him out the door.

"They were dead anyway," Dr. Sandler said, turning back to the rest, "as any fool could see. And we don't want fools among our ranks as brave soldiers of the Totality Concept, do we, men?"

They all braced and saluted, except the injured operator being supported by the two comrades who had dragged him through the portal. He dropped with a clatter to the nonskid flooring.

"No, sir, Dr. Sandler!" they sang out as one. Six of them were all that remained standing of the group of sixteen who had trotted out minutes before.

Considering, Dr. Sandler decided that no further punishment than revocation of breeding privileges was required. Although their disgraceful cowardice in allowing themselves to be routed completely was unpardonable weakness, they could not be blamed for being unable to stand up against the bizarre manifestation of the genetically altered girl's power.

He doubted anything material could withstand it.

"We are lucky you ordered the aperture sealed when you did, Dr. Sandler," Dr. Oates said.

"Luck had nothing to do with it, Dr. Oates. Merely

cool judgment. Although had you been more observant, you might have noted that the manifestation did reach the portal and was unable to pass through. As I knew it would be."

She dropped her gaze. "You are correct, Dr. Sandler. I failed to notice that. I was caught up in the moment, I admit."

"Obviously. Why did you feel compelled to blurt out your surmise as to the girl's origins in front of those primitive people, Dr. Oates?"

"I felt it to be the best way to appeal to a child of her age," Dr. Oates said, looking him in the eye. "To offer her a chance to rejoin her real family, as it were, instead of continuing to wander with a gang of violent and obviously unfit strangers."

"You *felt*," Dr. Sandler said, his voice lambent with contempt. He did not add, *How like a woman*, because it seemed unnecessary; Dr. Oates was intelligent enough, in her way. She would perceive the core evolutionary truth as well as he.

"I did not believe it necessary to explain that we ourselves played no role in her conception or engineering, although it seemed clear to me that some branch of the Overproject must be responsible. She is, after all, herself no more than a specimen. But what a specimen! Dr. Sandler, we must secure her, secure that power for our own glorious dream!"

Deplore her emotionalism as he had to, and did, Dr. Sandler could not fault its direction.

"In that, at least, you are thinking like a scientist, Dr. Oates," he said. "We must. And we shall."

She looked at the remaining sec men. The wounded one had drawn himself to a position of sitting at attention among his fellows. He still seemed unable to stand on his own.

If he could not economically be returned to full service in a reasonable span of time, he would be recycled. Just as the weak-minded Operator Number 23 had been. But that was down to Major Applewhite, their director of security, to see to.

"Shall we order out a full platoon of operators, Dr. Sandler?" she asked. "If they act expeditiously, they can in all probability stun the girl before she can deploy her enhanced abilities against them."

"We shall not, Dr. Oates. Have you forgotten your own initial reluctance to enter the target continuum to survey the effects of the manifestation? We have expended energy and caused spatiotemporal distortions far in excess of safe levels. To do any more at this time would be tantamount to manually triggering alarms within the Overproject—or among our rivals, such as Operation Chronos."

He turned his face toward the sec men. "You are dismissed. See 17 to the infirmary."

"Yes, sir, Dr. Sandler!" Two operators helped the crippled man to his feet, and they marched out the door.

"We have assets on the ground, Dr. Oates," Dr. Sandler said. "It's time to put them to use. Our prime subject must be made to see that now is an opportunity to offer some slight repayment for the aid we have provided him."

"But communicating with Dr. Trager—" Dr. Oates began.

"Your concern does you credit, Dr. Oates," he interrupted. He had regained his equilibrium. After all, he was not only a scientist; he was the senior scientist. In the present context, the patriarch, as it were. "Yet it is not entirely well-founded. As you know, our communications link to Dr. Trager draws such infinitesimal amounts of power and entails such a microscopic interpenetration that it remains intrinsically undetectable unless sensors are focused at its exact locus in space-time."

He turned away. "Enough talk. Further action is required. And now is the proper time to apply it!"

KRYSTY'S EYELIDS FLUTTERED, then her brilliant green eyes looked up into Mildred's as the doctor bent over her, where she lay stretched out across the wag's bench-style front seats.

"I'm fit to fight, Mildred," Krysty said, though the weakness of her voice belied her words. "Why are you upside down?"

Mildred reached down to briefly pat her friend's cheek. "It's a long story. I'm glad to have you back with us."

Krysty started to sit up. Mildred helped her.

"Krysty," Ryan said.

"Ryan," Krysty breathed. "Sorry for worrying you."

"I wasn't worried," the tall one-eyed man said, "once Doc and Ricky told me you were breathing. You're a tough one to chill."

"Why, thank you." Mildred could hear the smile in her friend's voice, even though her face was turned directly away. "I'm pretty sure that's the nicest thing anyone's said to me all day!"

"Play your cards right, somebody might even top it," Ryan said. His lips twitched in the ghost of a smile.

"Is she concussed?" J.B. asked. He had moved around the wag to stand at his best friend's side.

Mildred shook her head. "Nope. No pupil dilation. *Something* knocked her out, but it wasn't like getting a whack on the head."

"Judging from the sounds they emitted, and the effects produced by near misses, I surmisc those ovoid devices projected some manner of tightly focused sound beam. Possibly analogous to a laser."

"They called those things 'masers,' I think, Doc," Mildred said. "Like, 'microwave amplification of stimulated emission of radiation.' Or something like that."

He cocked a brow. "Did they? Indeed. I should further surmise that such weapons might be tunable. At higher levels of output, they could damage metal and inflict potential lethal wounds on flesh and bone. At lower levels, they might be used to disrupt the target's nervous system, stunning him. Or, well, her."

"A sonic blaster! I read about them in old predark books that my uncle had," Ricky said. "Cool."

J.B. nodded. The others laughed at the boy's enthusiasm.

"I wouldn't mind getting my hands on one or two of them," Ryan said. "But our girl swept them up clean, along with the wounded and the chills. Not that I'm complaining."

Krysty stood up. She swayed. Ryan caught her in his arms.

"Krysty—" he began.

"Shut up and kiss me," she said. He did.

Mildred walked around the nose of the wag. It looked as if somebody had taken a twelve-pound sledge to the bumper and grillwork.

Whatever those guns were, she thought, they pack a hell of a punch.

Disengaging, Ryan looked ahead to where Jak and Ricky were examining the road where the mirrorlike thing had appeared.

"Anything?"

Gently Krysty pushed away from Ryan. "Thanks. I can stand on my own now."

"No," Jak called.

"Didn't leave any kind of mark we can see," Ricky said. "I bet it didn't touch the ground. But there's nothing here but scuff marks, some blood and seven spent bullets that seem to have bounced off the gateway. Or whatever it was."

"It would seem the portal, whatever its nature, was selectively permeable," Doc said.

"I tried to push my whirlwind through it," Mariah said. "It wouldn't go in either."

She frowned. "I'd probably have to go through myself to get it to...wherever they are."

"But you're not going to do that, are you?" Krysty asked.

"Oh, no." Mariah's black pigtails swung as she shook her head furiously.

Krysty knelt beside her so that she was looking up into the pale face.

"Thank you," she told Mariah. "You saved us all."

"When they shot you, Krysty, I almost lost it. I couldn't let them do that to you!" She threw her arms around Krysty's shoulders in a fervent hug and burst into tears.

Mildred felt her jaw set. She looked past the pair to where Ryan and J.B. stood.

Almost lost it, she mouthed. Ryan shrugged.

He said nothing. It wasn't as if Mildred could think

of anything for him to say. But the inevitable speculation of what might make the girl "lose it," and just what exactly might happen next, hung over them like a cloud far darker and more ominous than the dense black cloud cover that had closed in overhead.

A droplet hit her cheek.

"Best we break this up and head out of here," Ryan called, as thunder rolled in from the southwest. "It looks as if the cloud's fixing to open up on us big time. We've got a roof to put over our heads, for once. Let's not waste it."

Chapter Twenty-Three

"Hello, people of Lone Calf. What's happening?"

Ryan's eye popped open at the words. After only a moment's free-wheeling, his mind snapped into focus. He realized they were being broadcast through a loudspeaker, and not from close by.

"This is Hammerhand, and the New Blood Nation. We have come to embrace you as our own. You'd be triple smart to embrace us back with open arms."

He went to the window of the second-story room he shared with Krysty. The redhead sat bolt upright in bed, the thin sheets falling from her pale, bare breasts.

Outside people were spilling into the narrow, crooked streets of the little ville in the predawn gray light. Although "ville" might be too grand a term for the little straggle of not upward of twenty structures, none too firmly nailed together out of crudely cut planks and random bits of scrap.

"I thought people didn't bother this place," Krysty said from the bed. "What with who the Spotted Elks are related to and all."

Ryan frowned out the window, which was open to allow in cool night breezes. The weather was warming up as summer came on.

"Wherever he's talking from," he said, "it's not where I can see."

"It's from the west," Krysty said. Their room faced east.

He glanced back. She was on her feet, bent over by the bed and just pulling her jeans up over incongruously purple scavvied panties. He did not fail to appreciate the sway of those heavy, beautiful, pink-tipped breasts.

Never know when might be the last time I see them, he thought. Could be today.

That was how they lived: it could *always* be that day.

"Looks like mebbe Hammerhand's decided he's big enough not to have to play by the old rules," he said, turning back to the window.

The amplified voice continued speaking, describing the glories of peace and prosperity—plus the prospect of adventure, for those who felt inclined—to be had by joining his growing nation.

"That's the carrot," Ryan muttered. "Where's the nuking stick?"

Lone Calf had started out as a crossing-spot of trade routes, from north to south and east to west, about thirty miles northeast of the mutie-haunted Pierre rubble. It had good water in the form of Bodacious Creek, along whose southern bank it stood. Then when shifting weather patterns had brought more rain of the water sort and less of the acid sort to this segment of the Plains a couple generations back, it had formed the informal center of a region of small-holder farms. Over the years it had grown to twenty or thirty buildings, none more than a single story save the big house, holding a hair over two hundred residents.

It was still held and largely occupied by the Spotted Elk clan, which, despite being named for a legendary Minneconjou Lakota hero, was more closely affiliated with the Northern Cheyenne. They had made it a point to intermarry as broadly as possible, which was considerably aided by its growing commercial importance, to the point the present scion, and proprietor of the Bodacious Creek Trading Post and Hostelry where the companions had passed the night, was a stout blond-braided woman named Helga Spotted Elk.

They made sure to maintain close family ties inside both the Lakota and Cheyenne nations, though, which meant that in spite of the fact they did fairly well for themselves, coldheart bands tended to give them a wide berth. Both those nations were always full of young warriors, male and female, who were young, dumb and lusting to make a kill or two and start their own reps, as the occasional raider found, usually right at the time they thought they had gotten away with a heist.

But apparently Hammerhand had decided he had enough coldhearts under his command that he longer need be afraid of retribution.

"So I'm waiting for your submission," Hammerhand's voice boomed. *"Just fly a white flag from the top of that fine hostelry at the center of town, there. That'll do fine."*

"There they are," Ryan said.

"What's that?" Krysty said, coming up behind him. She had her plundered M16 in one hand and was checking the magazine in the other.

Ryan pointed. "The stick."

The countryside around about the ville was the common rolling prairie. The flatter spots of low ground showed the deeper green of cultivation, and passing over the top of a hill, five hundred yards or so east, drove a trio of open-topped wags, stuffed with armed fighters. The sun rising red into a low black band of cloud made him blink.

"But there's something else I need to ask you for, Lone Calf."

Someone knocked at the door. Without even thinking about it, Ryan had picked up his P226 SIG handblaster from beside the bed as he rose. Now he pinched back the slide just far enough for a glimpse of dull silver to confirm a 9 mm round was chambered.

"Come in."

The door opened far enough for J.B. to poke his hatless head inside the room.

"Not going to shoot me, are you?"

"You'd already be a chill if I had a notion to shoot you, J.B.," Ryan said dryly. "What's happening?"

"Jak's up on the roof already. He says the voice is coming from a wag atop a hill, out five hundred yards or so west."

"That's a nuke of a long way to carry."

"Our boy Hammerhand found himself a big set of speakers and a generator to power the amp, looks like," J.B. said. "Plus the breeze is from that way."

"Wonder if we float a white flag if he'll let us drive right out of here?" Krysty asked.

"There's a group of outlanders put up in your hotel. Got a little girl with pigtails with them. I need you all to send her out to us. Just to show your good will and your good faith and all that happy horseshit."

"Sounds like that'd be a *no*," Mildred said, bustling in the open door with Doc and a frightened-looking Mariah following right after.

Ryan exhaled forcefully. "Fireblast. I reckoned we'd run across Hammerhand one of these days, what with him being the next big thing in this part of the Deathlands and all. I did *not* reckon on him looking for us in particular."

"There are more of them, off to the east," Krysty reported from the window. "Looks as if they're patrolling out there. Probably to keep us from trying to slip out that way."

She looked back at Ryan. Her green eyes were wide. "How many men does this Hammerhand have?"

"Anywhere between a hundred and a hundred thousand, to hear people tell it," J.B. said. "What with people's inclination to exaggerate, and one thing or another, right around a couple hundred seems right."

"If he brought them all," Mildred said.

"No response?" Hammerhand asked. *"Now, that's not good. I'm afraid I've got to insist.*

"I'll sweeten the pot. There's fifty horses waiting for whoever brings this girl to me. That applies to the one-eyed coldheart, the flame-haired woman and the rest of that bunch, too. I've got no beef with you. But if somebody *doesn't trot her out, I'm going to have to take back my invitation and just flat chill all of you in the entire ville. Your choice."*

"Speaking of *not good,*" J.B. said. He glanced out the window. Faces were turned toward the hotel in the streets surrounding. Even as he watched, a man pointed right to him.

Mariah had walked over to stand beside Krysty. Her dark eyes were huge and round in her snow-pale face.

"You won't give me to them, will you?"

"No way," Ryan said.

"Tell you what," the voice purred. *"Since I'm so generous, you've got half an hour. But then you've all*

signed your death warrants if I don't get the little girl. And if your consciences are getting all tender, no, the last *thing in the world I want is to hurt her."*

"You sure, Ryan?" Mildred asked. "I mean, sorry, Mariah—Krysty. But if there's hundreds of them, and they won't harm her..."

"You trust him that much?" Ryan asked. "A man who's trying to make himself baron of the whole North Plains?"

"Well—no." Mildred shook her head. "Sorry. Just forget I spoke."

"I have already, Mildred," Krysty said.

"Nobody move! I'll blast anyone who doesn't freeze!"

A SKINNY MAN in a stained linen shirt and baggy canvas trousers stood in the door with a double-barreled 12-gauge leveled at the companions.

J.B. was holding his Mini UZI, with his Smith & Wesson M-4000 shotgun slung. The machine pistol was muzzle down, but the block was locked open, ready to slam forward and open fire.

But J.B. was no more eager to commit suicide than anybody else in the room was. He made no move to put the blaster down, but he also didn't try to cut loose. The gaunt man with the prominent Adam's apple bobbing up and down to compulsive, nervous swallowing was on a hair trigger—unlike those black-armored sec men who had appeared from nowhere a couple weeks back. It'd be complete luck if the guy didn't blast any of them by accident.

"Give her to me," the man said, spewing spittle from a gob hole packed with crooked brown teeth. "I ain't gonna die for you taints. But I could surely use all them horses."

"Take it easy, Mr. Harkness," Krysty said.

"You know this dude?" Mildred asked.

"He introduced himself at dinner last night. You might want to point that blaster elsewhere, sir. You might hit the child, and then where would you be?"

"I ain't born yesterday, Flame Top. I know this here piece throws a tight shot column. I'll hit who I wanna hit and not her. So which of you wants to catch a charge of double aught?"

"Let's just calm down and talk about it," Krysty said soothingly.

"Ain't squat to jaw about," the intruder said. "Just give me the girl and we all get out al—"

His head jerked violently to his right—J.B.'s left—facing him. The words died in a gurgle. He folded straight down to the floorboards with a single jet of blood pulsing from his left temple.

Cat quick, Ryan was across the floor, grabbing the longblaster by both barrels and forcing the muzzle ceilingward. As the man completed his transition to a lump of bones and clothes and greasy flesh, Ryan twisted the weapon expertly from his relaxing grasp without setting it off.

Ricky's round face poked around the door from the right. "Everybody okay?"

"Better now," Mildred said. Ricky entered the room, stepping gingerly over the man he'd just shot.

Most "silenced" blasters were anything but. They produced a sound not triple quieter than an actual gunshot, but not so sharp and harder to pin down as to direction.

But Ricky's reproduction of a World War II DeLisle carbine, lovingly handmade with the help of his Uncle Benito, was an exception. Firing from a closed bolt action, shooting a subsonic round—the same .45 ACP cartridges a Colt 1911 used, as well as the rechambered Webley revolver Ricky carried—the weapon sound was only a little louder than a cough. In the excitement, J.B. hadn't even heard the longblaster go off just a few feet down the hall.

"So he's not part of the Spotted Elk family?" Ryan asked with a poke of his chin in the direction of the chill huddled in the doorway.

"No. He's a drummer for Old New San Antonio," Krysty said, "recruiting people to move to his ville."

"That was a long way to come to die."

"No doubt that fact played a role in his decision to act as he did," Doc stated.

"Got news for us, Ricky?" J.B. asked. He had left the boy on the top floor, keeping tabs on Jak.

Ricky nodded. "There's a whole bunch of wags, horses and people on foot in the hills west of town. Jak says they haven't gotten closer than fifty yards from the outskirts, but they're spread out and look ready to roll."

"Right," Ryan said. "Gather up your gear, people. We're—"

A figure loomed in the doorway. It was small and scrawny, like the late Mr. Harkness of Old New San Antonio. It held an ax over its head in both hands.

"Ahhh!" the newcomer shouted and leaped over the chill.

Ryan raised his handblaster and put two rapid shots through the center of his chest. Red blood stained the front of the canvas apron. The latest intruder fell back over the cooling body of the first.

"Anybody know who this was?" he asked.

J.B. stepped up and thrust the two bodies out into the corridor with his boot. Then he stationed himself just inside the doorway with his shotgun at the ready, keeping watch both ways to keep some other treasure hunter from running in on them unannounced.

"I saw him working in the kitchen," Mildred offered.

"Means he's related to Helga, most likely," Krysty said.

"She's not going to be happy with us, if that's the case."

"She and we both have to come through this without dirt hitting us in the eyes for that to matter," Ryan said. "Like I was saying, gather up your gear. We're going to secure the top floor and make our stand from there."

"We're not going to try to make our way covertly out of town?" Ricky asked.

"Even if we ditch the wags, which I'm willing to do, we'd never sneak out past a power of riled-up locals. To say nothing of the Blood patrols watching for us to try just that."

"The guests upstairs won't be happy about getting chased out," Krysty said. "Even if they don't decide to claim the reward themselves."

"We'll ask them nicely," Ryan said. "If that doesn't work, we'll ask them not so nicely. All right, people. We've got a purpose. Let's move like it!"

"But are you sure it's smart getting ourselves trapped on the top two floors?" Mildred asked. "What if they set the hotel on fire?"

"And risk roasting their prize?" J.B. said from the

door. “What do you think Hammerhand would do to them once he got here?”

“You’re right,” Mildred said. “That was stupid of me. Okay, let’s go play king of the hill.”

Chapter Twenty-Four

"Time's blood, people," Hammerhand's voice echoed across the prairie. *"Ten minutes and counting."*

The breeze from the west had freshened into a wind, and it was chill. This was not shaping up to be a warm day. But Ryan had been through worse. This was nothing to hinder him climbing up onto the pitched roof of the Bodacious Trading Post and Hostelry's top story, much less threaten to knock him off.

"Be reasonable, Cawdor," another voice boomed. This was louder, was feminine and came from the street directly below. "Try to see it from my perspective. Didn't you ever hear that the needs of the many outweigh the needs of the few?"

"Never did buy that line of shit," Ryan muttered. A shingle with dried old pine bark still on it came free right under his palm. He managed to hold on to the roof with the other as the loose shingle slid down and off the edge.

It was a long fall.

"What about your reputation for hospitality, Helga?" Krysty called from the room immediately below. It was on the east side, where they had spent the night, and happened to be the front of the establishment. That was the one side that didn't have one-story annexes built out from it. "You go giving up your guests to coldhearts who happen to ask, that might not help your business."

"Customers aren't much use to chills," the proprietor called back. "Anyway, I'm not asking you to turn yourselves over. Just give them that creepy little girl."

Truth to tell, Ryan would be lying to himself if he said he hadn't been tempted. She still put a chill up him, and although he was grateful to her for saving their hides on more than one occasion—he still didn't consider her one of them, and gratitude didn't load many magazines. They'd ditched helpful outsiders in the past and never looked back. Or scarcely did anyway. Of course, Krysty might never speak to him again. But he'd still rather that she *choose* not to talk to him nor forgive him, than to have her not be able to choose anything at all.

But he had no reason to trust Hammerhand. He might have already made himself a baron, and not an inconsequential one, by the force at his command, but Ryan knew full well that the thinking processes of barons and mere coldhearts weren't always that much different.

Or different at all.

"Don't you think you're giving this Hammerhand too much credit for keeping his word, Helga?" he called down.

Then, more quietly, "Morning, Jak. Situation change much?"

The albino shook his head. He was perched like a buzzard on the peak of the roof, right up against the smoking chimney.

"He's got a name for being hard but fair," he heard the trading-post owner call. "I'm not even worried about the reward. It's the 'burn down my hotel and chill everybody' part that occupies my thoughts."

Ryan hunched down on the other side of the chimney

from the albino. It felt like a solid enough platform. No more shingles wiggled under his boots.

"Fair enough," he called back down. "But no."

He looked around. The sun had cleared the horizon to the east. Below him, the lower floors of the big central structure were revealed in a crazy quilt of angled roofs: the gaudy, the kitchens, the blacksmith shop, various storage sheds.

Several dozen locals in the streets around the Bodacious all looked up at him. Some called entreaties or demands, which he ignored. If anyone had taken a shot at him—and risked hitting Mariah by accident—Helga had offered to stuff his or her offending blaster straight up her or his butt. And apparently the spectators took her at her word.

Ace on the line. It might not protect him forever but it didn't have to.

He settled his rump down on the roof. The shingles were rough and cold through his jeans. Then he looked out to the west, past the roof of the kitchen annex.

He could clearly see a distance-tiny human figure, standing next to a pickup with a pair of big speakers on its flat bed. A generator, presumably remodeled to burn alcohol for fuel the way most wag-engines were, stood discreetly behind him. Ryan's depth perception was not prime, what with the whole one-eyed thing and all. But he had learned to seat-of-pants estimate distance well enough through sheer experience that he was actually better at guessing range than most two-eyed folk. And it looked to him as if Jak's distance estimate was right.

He unslung his longblaster, stuck his left arm through the loop of the shooting sling and cinched it up tight to help support the weapon. Then he propped his elbows inside his knees, pulled the butt plate up tight against his shoulder and peered through the scope set to maximum four-power magnification.

That didn't bring much detail to his eye. It showed him a tall man with a dark face and long black hair hanging over the shoulders of an army jacket. He looked like a big bastard.

"Think what you're doing to us, Cawdor," Helga yelled. "There's children here. Babies."

"Not my people," Ryan muttered. He adjusted the scope to allow for approximated range. Then a couple of clicks to his left to allow for the rising wind. Finally, he centered the crosshairs on the middle of that broad chest. He sucked in a deep breath, released half of it, caught it, held it and fired.

The short longblaster kicked up. He rode the recoil with seasoned skill, working the bolt action as he did. It didn't come close to unseating him from his rooftop perch.

The longblaster came back down online while the noise of the shot still echoed among the ramshackle buildings and out across the low, grassy hills. At first he could see no sign of Hammerhand at all, meaning the bullet hadn't dropped him where he stood.

Then he saw something dark behind the flatbed wag's hood. He centered his scope on it and realized he was looking at the upper half of Hammerhand's head. The coldheart chieftain was looking right back at him, though he'd have had to have literal eagle eyes to make him out at this distance.

Missed him clean, Ryan thought. He was an ace marksman, but the Scout was never made for really long-range sniping. It was a long shot, and he reckoned he had misread the crossing wind.

He felt no disappointment. He hadn't truly expected to hit his target.

But then he didn't have to.

"Naughty, naughty," came Hammerhand's voice. It sounded more amused than angry, though the man could have just been a good actor. *Had* to be, considering his position and his rocket rise to it. *"I come to you with the open arms of friendship, and you try to chill me? Not cool, Lone Calf. Not cool. So it looks like death for all for you. Bloods, draw blood!"*

"That was cold, Cawdor," Helga shouted up at him. "Triple smart. But cold. I'll remember that."

"Not a problem," Ryan replied. "But keep in mind that to do anything about it, you've got to stay breathing."

With an angry snarl of engines, the half-dozen wags that had been waiting for the Blood boss's time limit to run out surged forward across the fifty yards that separated them from the settlement's first outbuildings.

"So as of now, it looks as if we're all on the same side for the duration."

"Damn your eye!" the proprietor roared. "All right, everybody. Defensive positions! Like it or not, we've got a fight on our hands!"

Ryan sighted in on the driver of the lead wag, a topless, battered Toyota Land Cruiser. He fired. The wag was hardly more than a hundred yards off and making almost straight for him—a gimme shot, after the one he'd just tried. He had aimed for the driver's shaved head, right between the lenses of her sunglasses. When he got the scope lined up again, he could see the vehicle slowing and a man standing up to lean over the back of the driver's set to grab the driver by the shoulders. The driver's head lolled back.

"Didn't miss that time," Ryan said.

Shots cracked from the attacking wags. Other shots, distinguishable by their lower tones because they didn't come from blasters pointed *at* Ryan, answered from the ville. Behind the first wags the whole mass of vehicles, horses and coldhearts began to advance, raising a shrill many-throated yipping that froze Ryan's blood.

But not his brain and actions. "Best get back down under cover, Jak," he called. "We're exposed up here."

Jak nodded and slid on his butt down the eastern slope of the roof, as if the slightest misjudgment wouldn't splat him on the street like a bug on a windshield. He caught himself, and swung as lithely as a monkey out of sight beyond the roof's edge.

Slinging his longblaster, Ryan followed at a much less breakneck speed.

Someone cut loose with a 5.56 mm blaster just below him. "Coming through!" he shouted between 3-round bursts.

"Holding fire, Ryan!" he heard Krysty yell.

A moment later she was helping him clamber in the window.

She hugged him briefly, then she looked him in the eye.

"Ryan, that was cold."

He shrugged. "It worked, though. There's not much chance the locals are going to power us down and turn us over to the bastard now, is there?"

She sighed and shook her head. "As much as I hate to admit it, you're right."

"It happens."

Jak was at the window, blasting into the street with his Python. Mariah, who had passed the night with Mildred to give Ryan and Krysty a little privacy—J.B. had bunked with Doc—had come into the bedroom the couple had shared. She just naturally gravitated toward Krysty. Ryan was ace with that; the redhead acted like a control rod for the temperamental girl.

Mariah sat on the bed, huge eyed with worry, twisting her hands in her lap. The others were interspersed among the other five rooms on the top floor.

The roar of wag engines from the street below was powerful and immediate. Ryan could smell the exhaust fumes. He moved quickly to the window next to Jak.

A stream of wags was rolling past the big compound structure. The Bloods seemed to be circling the big building. A brisk fire was being exchanged between the painted coldhearts in the open-topped trucks and the Spotted Elk defenders.

"The locals didn't manage to keep the bastards out long," he said.

Not that he'd expected them to. If they weren't total stupes, most of the ville's population would simply lie low and hope Hammerhand didn't follow through with his promise to raze the place and chill them all. Ryan reckoned he might not. He'd won a rep as a triple-hard man in his rocket rise to fame and increasing power over the past few weeks. But he also showed no sign of loving to deal out either death or pain when he didn't have to.

Rumor even said he'd had the delegation of elders from his former tribe who'd done something to piss him off chilled before he had them skinned and their hides sent home.

And he had also won a name for smashing absolutely

flat anyone who stood in his path, then stomping them into the ground. Ryan had few illusions as to which category the Bodacious Creek Trading Post defenders fell into, including him and his friends.

"You can leave off shooting," Ryan told Jak when the albino stopped to reload his huge revolver. "Save your ammo for when the bastards get inside and rush us."

Jak frowned, shrugged and put away the refilled blaster. Then he brightened.

"Got knives," he said.

"Yeah," Ryan said. "Go watch the stairs."

"Coldhearts not inside yet."

"They will be shortly," Ryan said.

Chapter Twenty-Five

The shotgun roared and kicked J.B. in the shoulder. A pair of Bloods riding in the back of an open Jeep Cherokee began thrashing and spurting blood.

"These are some persistent sons of bitches," he remarked to Doc as he pulled back to reload. The two of them were shooting from the window of the second room south toward the staircase from Ryan and Krysty's room, on the east side, directly overlooking the rutted dirt street.

"Indeed," Doc remarked and triggered another 3-round burst from his M4.

No fire was coming their way. Circling like vultures, the coldhearts were shooting exclusively at the ground floor of the main trading-post building, as were the Bloods who had scrambled onto the roofs, some flat, some peaked, some crazily slanted, of the buildings surrounding it. They were clearly exchanging brisk fire with Helga Spotted Elk and the other defenders. And had just as clearly been ordered to avoid doing any shooting that might risk hitting the goal of this whole mass attack: Mariah.

Nonetheless J.B. pulled back out of sight behind the windowsill to stuff buckshot shells into the long in-line magazine beneath the barrel of his M-4000 scattergun. He didn't want to take the chance of somebody taking an opportunity shot while he stood there in plain view, distracted, like a simp. Plus good habits were good habits for a reason, and to keep good habits you had to avoid varying from them. Just like checking the chamber of a blaster you had just taken hold of, even if somebody had just checked it before handing it to you.

The roar of blasterfire was stupefying. J.B.'s highly tuned ears could even pick out the snarl of automatic weapons. He wondered where the coldhearts were getting all that ammo. The air was thick with shouts and screams; the smell of powder, both smokeless and smoky; lubricant and fuel, all burned; as well as the reek of guts voided in fear, the relaxation of death, or plain torn open.

He poked the Smith & Wesson out the window again. As before, he found what could be called a "target-rich environment." The coldhearts had poured into town and were washing around the trading post and hotel like floodwaters.

He lined up the sights on another open wag. Like the rest of the attackers, its occupants, male and female, were dressed in a dizzy variety of random scavvied garments, modern manufacture and bits of decoration ranging from wild hair, and face and body paint to feathers, scraps of fur, cartridge belts, leather straps and less identifiable objects.

He blasted into the crowded pickup bed. At that distance, about thirty yards, the shot pattern spread out to somewhere upward of a foot. It was enough to poke .24-caliber holes in two or three people—if he was lucky, four. His object wasn't necessarily to chill any of the coldhearts. He was trying to wound as many as possible, to take them out of the fight, or at least reduce their efficiency, and to force other Bloods to do something to get them to healers for first aid. Or barring that, to mess with coldheart morale simply because they *weren't* getting help.

Trader had always been strict in his teaching: no chilling for chilling's sake. And in this case, chilling wasn't the most efficient way to cut the odds facing them.

Not that it seemed to matter. J.B. had no clue what Hammerhand had said or offered to this mob to get them so fired up to bring him one little girl—although having seen her in action, he could well understand why the Blood boss wanted her. At this rate, even though their stocks were plentiful, they'd run out of rounds long before Hammerhand ran out of willing blasters, even counting on the morale multiplier, which old Napoleon said was three-to-one, a figure J.B. always found on the light side.

He heard hammering on the frame of the open door behind him. Somebody wanted to attract his attention without flat barging in and risking collecting a belly full of buckshot.

He pulled back around with his back to the wall and his weapon held muzzle up. Doc was currently away from the window in the process of reloading his carbine.

The newcomer was Ricky, his cheeks colorless and his eyes big and wild. "They're storming in through the back!" he said breathlessly. "Already got inside the kitchen."

Ricky and Jak had been stationed in a room on the west side of the top floor, mostly to keep an eye out for just such eventualities. Although since Ricky had his replica DeLisle in his hands, he had likely been handing out hot-lead grief to the coldhearts on that side, just to keep their minds right.

"Such was inevitable," Doc said.

J.B. nodded. "We're not doing more than pissing in the ocean here anyway," he said. "Time to brace ourselves for the rush and the real fighting. Has Ryan heard yet?"

"Jak told him."

When J.B. and Doc stepped out, the others were gathered in the narrow corridor, even Mariah, ignoring the two grown women's efforts to shoo the pigtailed child back into the shelter of Ryan and Krysty's bedroom.

Ryan had slung his Steyr and held his SIG blaster in his left hand and his big, broad-bladed panga in his right.

"We need to get ready to pour fire down the stairs," he said. "Krysty, let me borrow your M16."

"Not a chance," the redhead said firmly. "Nor my Glock. I'd just as soon meet danger faceup than hunching back of the front line where I might get another ten seconds of life if the Bloods break through."

"It is kinda romantic how Ryan keeps trying to shield you from danger every now and then," Mildred said.

Krysty shot her a quelling look, but the stocky healer was hard to quell, which was one reason J.B. felt about her the way he did.

She turned her attention on Ryan. "Do we have an exit strategy here, *kemo sabe*? I know you're not counting on us running out of bad guys before we run out of bullets."

Ryan peered down from the top of the stairs. His brow was furrowed in concentration. From the look on his face, he wasn't liking the banging and screaming he was hearing from downstairs. Jak stood beside him, quivering with eagerness like a pup who smelled a catamount.

"I mean, get out on our own legs," Mildred persisted, "and not roped together by the necks or anything."

"Hold on until night," Ryan said, "then sneak out."

"It's worked for us before, Mildred," Krysty said.

"Yeah. But right now it seems kind of like that 'hang on until dark' thing is not looking too workable."

"I can help," Mariah said.

"I know," Ryan told the girl. He didn't look at her. "I don't want to get dependent on you, though. You've hauled our chestnuts out of the blast furnace a number of times now. But somehow we went all these years doing it on our own, up to the point we met you."

"Are you willing to lay down your life to prove a point, Ryan?" Doc asked.

"I didn't think you were all that attached to life yourself, Doc. Funny you should ask that."

The old man shrugged. His chin had sprouted white stubble, which made him look even older than he usually did.

"Please do not misinterpret my intent. It is a question asked purely out of curiosity. Inasmuch as that would be a substantial departure for you."

"Well, I won't say no to survival. But we've always stayed alive as a team, everybody doing their part. Not one of us relying on another all the time."

Jak brought his head up, whipping his long white hair way from the shoulders of his camo jacket.

"Coming now!" he said.

RYAN HUNG BACK a few steps up the warped-plank floor of the hallway. He was feeling none too pleased with the choice, but it was the practical one.

The stairwell opened up on the south end of the hall,

on the left-hand, or eastern, side. It was built to rely on the wall of the structure itself for support, probably to economize both on space and building materials. Like the kitchen and gaudy annexes and the rest, the upper stories had been added onto the Bodacious Creek Trading Post and Hostelry over the decades. That was plain to see.

The fact played both for them and against them tactically. A freestanding case that switched back along the north-south axis rather than one wall would have allowed room for all of them to stand around and blast downward, possibly clear down to ground floor. But it would also allow the invaders more scope to shoot up at *them*. And while Ryan was slide-lock certain the Bloods wouldn't try any of the tricks that would have been obvious had they just been looking to rub out the little group, like filling the floor below with blasters and just shooting upward through the wood floors until they could be sure they'd riddled everything larger than a particularly lucky mouse, he couldn't feel confident they wouldn't open up if they saw clear targets that clearly weren't a little girl.

There was just room for the four people with full-auto blasters to line up, either leaning over the rail or at the head of the stairs: J.B., Mildred, Doc and Krysty.

"Eyes skinned," Ryan said to Ricky and Jak, who waited with him in the corridor back from the stairs. "The only way the bastards can come is up those stairs, so—"

"No!" It was Jak, his ruby eyes blazing. "Climb outside!"

"Fireblast! What was I thinking!"

The answer is, you weren't, he told himself savagely.

But in a brief thought he realized that was another example of what he'd meant to Mariah, that they couldn't come to rely on just one person. Not even him.

"Right. We need to spread out and start cycling through the rooms and the far end of the hall, checking for somebody trying that." It wasn't likely, he calculated, but he didn't want to get back-shot because of relying on what he thought the enemy would do, rather than on what they could. And if they got frustrated at taking casualties trying to bull up the stairs...

"Mariah? Can you give us a hand on this?"

She nodded so hard her pigtails whipped up and down. She was painfully eager to do her part, even if it didn't entail any terrible reality-distorting mutie power.

"Then let's start rolling," he said, then turned to move to the window of the bedroom where Krysty and he had spent most of last night not sleeping.

Would it be their last night? He couldn't help but wonder.

Chapter Twenty-Six

Krysty saw a head topped with a blue and pink dyed Mohawk appear at the foot of the stairs on the landing below. It looked upward at her.

Dark eyes with yellow stripes painted beneath them went wide in a dark face—a heartbeat before Krysty shattered that face with three point-blank 5.56 mm slugs.

Through the ringing in her ears she heard startled curses, then worried shouts. She could also hear muffled shots and other noises that she guessed came from the bottom floor. Apparently some of the defenders continued to hold out down there. But just as obviously the coldhearts were focused on being the first to grab the prize, even with the mopping up in progress.

She shouted, "Back!" as a hand holding an MP5 with its stock folded poked its way into view and cut loose blindly, straight up the well.

The unseen shooter ripped off three bursts, somehow keeping control of the weapon despite using one hand, and that with the wrist turned in an uncomfortable, weak position. Or so Krysty guessed, because none of the bullets came up through the floor or even hit the railing.

Then during a break came a yellow flash, a single echoing shot and a thump.

"Hold your fire, you taints!" a man's voice yelled. "We want the girl alive and unharmed. That means no blasters!"

"But Loco," another male voice protested. "They's waitin' on us up there, with machine blasters and shit!"

"Who said you were gonna live forever, Wings? Now—*Bloods, draw blood!*"

Evidently the little inspirational speech, such as it was, worked better on the Bloods than it would have on Krysty. Or maybe the lust for glory and renown—and even a warrior's death—helped switch whatever common sense members of the Plains' fastest-growing crew of coldhearts possessed in the first place.

Because here they came in a rush, swarming into view from beneath her feet, trampling the body that had slumped on its back with half a face staring up with a single, perpetually astonished eye. The first few slipped on blood and brains spilling out of the shattered cranium.

She dropped the lead man with a burst to the head to the top landing and fired right into the face of the coldheart now in the lead from not much more than six feet away. He toppled backward onto the two right behind him. Krysty got a brief impression of the man's face looking as if its bearded features were being sucked into a black hole where the nose used to be. Then the two struggling with the floppy deadweight chill went down screaming and spraying from multiple hits from bursts fired by Doc and Mildred in hellish counterpoint.

For a moment the Bloods kept pushing on, clambering over the dead and thrashing wounded. A confused tangle of leather and sweaty skin writhed to halfway up the stairway, like a mating ball of giant rattlesnakes.

Krysty switched to single shot after a second burst. So did Mildred and Doc, who was a fast learner despite his appearance as a doddering old man. There was no point in wasting cartridges.

The rush faltered, then stopped. A couple of injured Bloods were dragged back moaning and howling. At least six stayed motionless on the steps. The bodies were too intertwined for Krysty to count.

"Time to reload," J.B. advised.

"You first, John," Mildred said. "Yours takes longer."

He grinned at her and pulled up his Mini UZI on its sling. "Fastest reload," he said. "New York carry."

"Not usually applied to longblasters," Mildred said, popping the partially spent magazine out of the M16 and pulling a new one out of a jacket pocket.

"Everything holding?" Ryan asked, slipping out of the room right behind Krysty.

"So far," she said. "Only tried once yet."

He nodded and crossed the hall to check the west side for ambitious wall climbers. Beyond him she caught a glimpse of Mariah crossing the other direction. She had a pink spot on her cheek and a big smile. She seemed to be having fun.

It was a game for her. For now.

Gaia, please help me keep it that way for her. But in her belly Krysty knew that was a prayer even the Earth Mother couldn't answer.

"This time, hang back," she said. "Wait for my word."

Doc and Mildred looked at her in momentary confusion. "I like the way you think, Krysty," J.B. said with a quick grin.

He had let go of his Mini UZI to reload the shotgun

after all. He finished, chambered a shell, then topped off the tubular magazine.

A rising pitch and volume of shouts from below clued Krysty to the next rush. She clicked the selector switch back to 3-round-burst mode and on they came.

This time she let the lead, a gaunt, incredibly tall black woman, scramble up the hump of chills that remained of the first attempt. Other coldhearts followed hard on her moccasined heels. When she was within a few steps of the top floor, Krysty shouted, "Now!"

J.B. pivoted onto the top-floor landing and fired his recharged M-4000 into her chest so close her vest was smoking when she toppled backward.

Krysty, Doc and Mildred ripped short bursts into her followers.

Already burned once, the Bloods recoiled almost at once, leaving one form writhing and three chills atop the heap. The stairway looked as if somebody had doused the walls with a couple gallons of red paint. The bodies were slimed with gore.

The well had already filled with that old, familiar smell, half slaughterhouse, half unlimed outhouse. Krysty, at least, had never gotten used to it, no matter how many times she came across it or how much time she spent in its unwelcome company. And it would only get worse until it got better.

Somebody was shouting authoritatively from out of sight on the floors below. The chill on the bottom started to slide out of view from overhead as a Blood snagged an ankle and hauled on it. J.B. threw a shot that way, but the coldheart ducked back too fast.

The chill vanished. The pile slid down. A leg flopped out of sight onto the second floor. Somebody had to have grabbed it, too, because that body vanished, as well.

The rest of the pile of casualties slid and tumbled to the base of the stairs. Despite a few shots and dark muttering from J.B., the rest were cleared away with hoes and a rake, presumably looted from a trading-post shed.

"How's it going?" Ryan called from behind.

Krysty looked back. He smiled and gave her a wink. She winked back.

"Still breathing," J.B. said.

"They're up to something down there," Mildred stated.

"I expected them to resume their headlong assault up the stairs," Doc opined, "once they had gotten them cleared of bodies."

"That's what I mean," Mildred said. "Somebody wised up."

"What else can they do?" Doc asked.

"If they look long enough, they'll find something," Ryan said. He waved at Jak, Ricky and Mariah, who had come out into the hall to see what was going on. "Back to window watch. Trying to outflank us is the most obvious thing to do."

Jak pointed right at Krysty. *"Gren!"* he screamed.

She spun. Sheer reflex or Gaia's subtle prodding caused her to bring up her left hand, fast, in a protective gesture. By luck she whapped something round and hard with the back of her hand, causing it to fall back down to the second floor.

"Flash-bang!" J.B. yelled. "Duck and cover!"

Letting her M16 drop—her sling kept it from hitting the floor—Krysty turned her face to the wall and pressed her hands against her ears.

The flash-bang went off with a splintering crack. The accompanying flash lit the grimy fly-specked wall in front of her. That species of gren was intended not to harm, but to stun its victims with a combination of a blast of intense high-frequency sound and a dazzling burst of light.

Even though she avoided the direct brunt of those effects, the sheer shocking power of the blast made her focus waver ever so slightly.

Not for long, though. She grabbed the longblaster again and started turning back to the well. Even though the flash-bang had gone off in the Bloods' own faces, she expected those who weren't stunned to charge up the steps immediately.

She heard Ricky shout, "More grens!"

Then motion blurred out of the stairwell before her eyes. Something exploded against the right side of her head.

It was as if a shaped charge had gone off in her head. She fell against the wall, dazed and half-conscious.

To his complete surprise, Ryan saw a big half-naked Blood vault the banister right in front of Krysty and, with his body almost horizontal, kick her in the side of the head with a massive black boot.

"Krysty!" he shouted. He turned back from the door of the bedroom he'd been going into, bringing up his SIG handblaster in his left hand.

The big coldheart landed directly in front of him, grabbed the SIG's muzzle with his right hand and, by twisting it toward the back of that hand, tweaked in straight from his grip.

"You are worthy opponents," the man said with a

huge white grin splitting his boot-leather colored face. He threw the blaster down and struck at Ryan with the steel-handled hatchet he held in his left hand.

Ryan fell into the bedroom and slid back into the bed. The gleaming blade cleaved air. The big Blood paused with his head and upper torso inside the door while several more flash-bangs went off with a ripple of thunder cracks that dwarfed the blasters that had been firing in the enclosed space.

The bedroom and the coldheart's own bulk shielded Ryan from the worst of the effects. The coldheart barely blinked.

Instead he drew a second one-piece steel hatchet from a brightly beaded holster at his right hip and charged at Ryan.

The one-eyed man brought his boots up and fired a double heel kick just below the Blood's beadwork belt. The shot hit true. It wasn't aimed at the big bastard's nuts, but rather against his pelvis.

Ryan did not feel bone break, which was a shame, because that would have meant the coldheart's legs would quit working altogether—they just, mechanically, wouldn't pick him up again. But he achieved the desired effect: he shot his assailant's center of gravity right out from under him. His legs shot out behind, and his big block chin and a bare right shoulder slammed the floorboards pretty much in unison.

As he jumped to his feet, Ryan heard blasters going off in the hallway and a tumult of confused shouting. He saw bodies thronging behind the fallen coldheart, and his heart dropped to the bottom of his stomach.

But the Blood bounced right straight up, still grinning, though his big white grin was rimmed and twined with blood. He rushed Ryan, aiming a long, looping overhand swing of the hatchet in his right hand at his opponent's head.

Without having to form conscious thought, Ryan realized the Blood warrior's intent was that Ryan block the skull-splitter stroke with his panga. Or get his skull split. Either one.

If Ryan did block with his heavy knife, the coldheart was going to chop off or break his right arm with his left-hand hatchet. And after that, he had pretty much clear sailing to however he wanted to chill his enemy.

Instead Ryan skip-stepped to his left, not crossing his feet in the process. He aimed a backhand cut at the coldheart's right shoulder.

The big bastard was fast. He twisted and went down to his left knee, catching the panga in his crossed hatchets. Steel sparked on steel.

The Blood snapped his hands apart, attempting to scissor the panga between them to pluck it from Ryan's grasp, much the way the man had his blaster. Ryan saw that coming. No sooner had the blades rung off each other than he turned clockwise, pulling the panga blade straight back out of jeopardy.

He made use of his turning momentum to launch a thrust kick with his left boot. The Blood tucked his right forearm against his chest, taking the blow there. Propelled by Ryan cocking his own pelvis back as he kicked and turning on his plant foot, it wasn't so much hard as forceful. It knocked the coldheart sprawling on his side.

He rolled away from Ryan's attempted heel stomp and scrambled to his feet facing him. Ryan swung the panga backhand for his enemy's face. The man brought up his right-hand hatchet vertically to block. Then he lashed out with the weapon in his left hand.

Ryan danced back. He found himself teetering briefly as the edge of the bed caught him at the backs of his calves.

Seeing his opponent's momentary loss of balance, the coldheart bull-rushed him.

Ryan snatched up the scratchy wool blanket and threw it over the coldheart's head and shoulders, then he dodged to his right.

The Blood, blinded, blundered into the bed, tripped on it and fell on his face on the straw-filled mattress. Resilient and agile as always, he immediately pushed up on his brawny arms.

Ryan reversed his hold on the panga. Holding the hilt in both hands, he plunged the broad blade down between the coldheart's left shoulder blade and spine with all his strength and weight.

Though it did come to a point, of sorts, the massive African knife was not really meant for stabbing. But it punched through skin, muscle and bone, to gash open the left lung and cut the heart almost in two. The man's body heaved once, then he uttered a gargling roar that ended in a bubbling whistle. He slumped down lifeless, half on the bed, half off.

Putting a foot on the middle of the chill's back, Ryan wrenched the panga free. He turned back to the door.

The room exploded in blue-white light and a sound so loud it was painful.

Chapter Twenty-Seven

Eye dazzled, ears deafened by a ringing like gigantic temple bells, Ryan swayed. He barely felt whatever hard thing it was—rifle butt, table leg, or bat—that clubbed him down to the floor and pounded him mercilessly on the ribs. The panga was yanked out of his hand as more blows landed on his skull.

He was dazed, nauseated and tasting blood when he was dragged by a male and female pair of Bloods out into the hall. He saw several of his companions lying pinned beneath several coldhearts apiece, including J.B. and Krysty. Doc lay slumped against a wall with the visible side of his face a bruise. A Blood woman danced around swearing and flapping her gashed and bloody palm as a burly man hammered a laughing Jak to the floorboards with the butt of a Mossberg 500 pump shotgun.

All this Ryan made out through balloon-like purple patches floating in his vision. Gradually his eye cleared. The intolerable ringing dwindled to a sort of roar.

From the last bedroom on the west side, a large male Blood with black leather straps crossed over his hairy chest like fetish suspenders came out dragging Mariah by both pigtails clutched in a paw. He stopped and called something. Ryan heard blobs of sound but no words.

Mariah grabbed the Blood's wrist with both hands.

He ignored her, laughing. Somehow she twisted her head around and sank her teeth into the hand that held her hair.

Ryan heard the coldheart's roar of surprised pain, although dimly, as though he had a blanket on his head. He yanked his hand away, then used it to backhand Mariah to the floor.

"Bad call," Ryan heard himself say inside his own skull.

The girl instantly sat up. Blackness streamed from her eyes. It spun itself around the big Blood, who was so startled he froze.

In an eyeblink a cocoon of swirling blackness enveloped him. Bits of pale skin and swatches of blood whipped around the cloud.

Ryan's hearing returned almost fully in time for him to hear the coldheart's shriek of unendurable agony.

Two scraps of black leather, still joined by a steel buckle, bounced off one wall with a musical sound.

"Stay down!" Mariah shouted.

Ricky, who was being held up by a pair of Bloods while a third punched him in the stomach, sagged abruptly to his knees. The cloud jumped up, gouged through the ceiling into the attic and swept forward with its base at a height of five feet.

This time it cut all three coldhearts apart and dropped their lower halves intact to the floor. Ryan wondered if she meant to do that, or if it was even something in her control.

Both hands that had been holding Ricky's wrists fell to the planking. The youth threw himself down on his face and covered his head with both hands.

The coldheart who sat astride Jak, pinning his arms

to his sides with her leather-clad thighs and methodically punching his face, had turned her spike-haired head at the sound of her comrade's dying scream. Now she saw the cloud plunging toward her face and opened her mouth for a scream of her own.

The cloud took her head first. Somehow it sucked her right up off the supine Jak, shredding her as it did.

"Mariah—" Ryan croaked.

She didn't hear him, or if she did, she gave no sign. The girl was on her feet now, her right arm stretched out in front of her, controlling the devil vortex's dance with a hand like a white spider. She had a feral light in her eyes and a slight, twisted smile set on her lips.

He rotated his head the other way. The coldhearts were beginning to galvanize to life. It was already too late. Ryan saw one man with long hair and an eagle feather at his nape jump off one of Krysty's arms and bolt into the nearest bedroom. Ryan faintly heard glass shatter as he evidently flung himself right through the window.

The cloud expanded until it was as wide as the hall and swept down it to the stairs at waist height. A few legs and hands and weapons hit the warped planks. A chunk was gouged out of the west-side wall as Mariah stalked by Ryan. Then the cloud had shrunk down to scarcely larger than the girl herself. It passed over the rail, hovered briefly, then dropped out of sight as she began to walk down the stairs.

"Ryan!" he heard Krysty say. That restored energy to his limbs, if not stability to his gut, nor his brain inside his head. He staggered up and lumbered down the hall toward her like a grizzly bear loaded to the eyelids on speedballs.

She sprang up, too, and stumbled toward him. Their foreheads came together with a crack.

His head spun freshly and his stomach did a slow roll. Involuntary tears streamed from his eye as he hit his knees hard.

She was on her knees face-to-face with him. They leaned their foreheads together, more gently this time, and both began to laugh.

"Are you two good to go, or are you having a romantic moment?" he heard Mildred ask.

"I'd say neither," Ryan said. "But I reckon we've got to go anyway."

He was aware there had been screaming downstairs. Now that had stopped. Instead he heard wild shrieks pealing from the street to the east, a crash. A *whoomp* of igniting fuel.

"Fireblast!" he exclaimed. Krysty was already back on her feet. Well, she was younger than he was. She stretched down a hand and reminded him how strong she was by hauling him right up onto his pins as if he weighed no more than Mariah did.

"Here's your blaster," Ricky said shyly from behind. Ryan turned and the youth pressed the grips of the SIG into his palm. He closed his fingers around it. "Jak's got your panga."

"Thanks," he said. "Now everybody grab what weapons you can, because we need to get downstairs in a hurry."

"DARK NIGHT!" J.B. said.

They were in what had served for the lobby of the hostelry and the main trading-post floor.

It was now well on its way to being open air. The

whole east wall was simply gone, along with some of the ceiling. The rest of the ceiling sagged alarmingly.

"I sure hope this whole place isn't about to come down on our heads," Mildred stated.

The ruined room was full of chills. Sadly Krysty recognized some of the Spotted Elk clan among the dead, although most were clearly coldhearts. Helga herself lay facedown across the counter, pinned there with a bayonet through her broad back.

The presence of several dismembered bodies suggested that the cloud had done its work before bursting through the wall.

"Clear," Jak called, crouched just inside what remained of the wall to the street. Then, "Out here!"

Despite the possible danger, Krysty sprinted out. The sky had clotted with clouds, dark and convoluted and menacing. But they didn't approach the darkness or the menace of the black funnel cloud, now as tall as the trading post itself, that was walking down the dirt street. It was sucking in the chills and debris as it went. In its wake the bottom half of a Blood wag burned with orange and blue fire. Its top had been sheered clean off, along with the top halves of several Bloods.

The girl followed her nightmare creation. She had her arms out to her sides and was skipping and dancing.

"Fireblast!" Ryan exclaimed. "She's enjoying this!"

He shouldered his Steyr Scout. Krysty grabbed the short barrel and shoved it up. "Ryan, don't!"

"Don't tell me you're still protecting her."

"No." She looked him in the eye. "You."

He nodded, then lowered the longblaster.

The cloud clipped through the southern end of the

gaudy, then cut through the storage area and yard behind the compound building.

"Our wags!" Ricky exclaimed. "They're back there!"

"We can get new ones," J.B. said. "Not so easy getting a new *us*."

The girl vanished, dancing through the ruins. Krysty trotted after her. After a brief hesitation, she sensed her lover following her.

"Eyes peeled, everybody," Ryan cautioned. "That cloud may be the worst threat in the ville, but it's not the only one."

Nevertheless they moved rapidly in the open to the end of the street and around the corner. They steered well clear of the half-eaten annex.

Not even Jak seemed eager to lope ahead as he usually did. He stayed just behind Ryan, alongside his friend Ricky.

The devil's vortex stalked straight west through the ville, leaving a path cleared almost to the ground and on either side slumping ruin. Mariah skipped behind it, waving her hands gaily in the air.

"Where are the coldhearts?" Doc asked, blinking myopically in the morning sunlight, cloud filtered though it now was.

"Living ones?" Ryan asked. "It looks like they're bugging out."

Krysty could see wags driving west across the prairie in apparent panicked flight. What she could see of the mass of fighters, horses and machines beyond them had already started moving in the same direction.

Four people burst out of a collapsing house—a man, a woman with a baby in her arms and a little girl. Krysty could see their fear clearly.

Unfortunately they bolted directly into the path of the black whirlwind.

"Ahh, no!" Mildred cried out. "Those're civilians."

The cloud subsumed the fleeing family without slowing.

"What is she doing?" Ricky moaned, as childish but insane-sounding laughter pealed to the sky.

"I know what she's doing," Krysty said in a broken voice. "She's hitting back. Making the whole world pay for every blow she's taken, every groping at midnight or out behind the shed. Every contemptuous word. The being kept like a slave but treated with less love and respect. She's trying to make everyone feel her pain.

"I know that feeling. Even if I'd never give in to it."

Ryan came up and placed a gentle hand on her shoulder.

"Krysty…"

She turned and rested her head against his shoulder. "I know. And you're right. But for Gaia's sake, don't try to chill her yourself. Promise me you won't—and J.B. either."

"Do I look triple stupe to you? J.B., mebbe."

"Count me out. Got precious little hankering to see that cloud from the inside."

"Oh, boy," Mildred said gustily, shaking her head. "You guys. Joking at a time like this—"

"You know a better time, Mildred?" Ryan asked.

"I guess not."

"Come on," Ryan said. "We need to follow her. At a safe distance."

"Can there truly be such a distance?" Doc asked.

"I don't know. Let's stay back fifty yards and hope for the best."

He started forward. The others followed.

"Ryan," Krysty asked, "what are we going to do?"

"Wait until she gets enough of it out of her system to settle down on her own, I guess. Unless you got a better idea?"

Krysty shook her head. Her sentient hair had uncurled itself from the tight cap of curls it usually formed around her head in times of immediate danger. But its tips lashed nervously across her shoulders, like agitated snakes.

"What if she doesn't settle down," Mildred asked, "and decides to make that 'making the whole world pay' thing all too literal by—I don't know—having her cloud eat the whole damn planet?"

"Good question," Ryan said.

He worked the action, opening the bolt far enough to catch a glimpse of dull yellow cartridge brass inside.

"At that point, I guess we do what we can. Because it won't be like we got a lot left to lose."

Chapter Twenty-Eight

Hammerhand looked from the line of wags streaming away from the ville, and the fat four-story black tornado that seemed to be devouring it behind them, to the youth dying on a tarp on the hill near the settlement where his command wag sat parked.

Mindy Farseer crouched beside him. She looked up at Hammerhand and shook her head.

"Says Joe didn't make it," she said.

"The cloud?"

She shook her head.

"One-eyed man…chilled him," Little Wolf moaned. He had his head on a rolled-up wolf pelt. His chin, neck and the front of his skinny bare chest were coated in blood. "Fought him…faceup."

"Sounds like Joe," Mindy said.

"Yeah. This one-eyed man must be a stud to beat Joe at his own game." Hammerhand shook his head. "I'll mourn later."

He saw a wag powering toward him between a couple of sorry-ass lean-tos. Bloods appeared from somewhere and flung themselves at it, desperately trying to grab a handhold as the black death-cloud bore down on them. Although the open cab and bed of the truck were so overstuffed with fugitives, it looked like a big troop of monkeys gathered on a small rock, the occupants reached out to them.

The whirlwind of Void caught the vehicle from behind. It seemed to stop. Bloods turned and threw up their hands in futile fear as the swirling shadow swallowed them.

The fuel tank blew. Red and blue flames briefly whirled about the black cloud, then they, too, were gone.

"Fuck," Mindy Farseer said.

Hammerhand braced in case the monstrous thing came on. Instead it turned and spiraled back through the little ville. Buildings that it struck disappeared. Those it merely brushed against collapsed.

"Send up red flares," he said.

"How many?" Mindy asked.

"All of them." He looked around at the small headquarters staff he had on the low hilltop with him. "Everybody else, start saddling up to ride out of here."

"Do we need that?" Mindy asked. Red flares were the retreat signal. "Looks as if everybody's bugging out already."

"I don't want any more of my people than necessary eaten by that thing," he said. "It's time to cut stick and go." He was glad he'd only sent a small fraction of his total force into the place.

"You can't!" exclaimed Dr. Trager, who had been hovering nearby like a pesky, lumpy bird. "You can't just run away!"

"Watch me."

"But the girl—she's within your grasp!"

"If you want to run up and try grasping that black whirlwind, knock yourself out. I'd love to see it, actually."

He turned his face abruptly from the annoying little whitecoat. "What about the kid?"

"He's boned," Mindy said. "Not just that both femurs are smashed. But it seems like at least one of them got rammed clean up through his hipbone into his belly. He's pulped and bleeding out inside."

She shook her head. "Must have landed triple bad. I didn't think a couple-story drop would even do that to a person."

"Give me…blaster…please," Little Wolf croaked. Every word bubbled out through fresh gut blood. It was painful to see and hear. "Die…with weapon…in hand."

"Right. Lend him yours, Farseer."

"Why me?"

"You're handy."

Shaking her head and muttering, she drew her Beretta 92, checked the chamber, put it back on safety and passed the 9 mm blaster to Little Wolf.

He had trouble grasping it. With another peevish look at Hammerhand over her shoulder, Mindy folded his fingers about it until he took hold. He nodded his thanks.

"Hammerhand, you've got to listen to me—" Trager pleaded. He actually reached out as if to grab the chieftain's arm, but his grubby fingers stopped short and trembled.

"Tell…my aunt… I died a…warrior."

Hammerhand heard the slight but unmistakable click of a safety lever being switched off. From the corner of his eye he saw Little Wolf raising Mindy's handblaster to aim at himself. Or trying to. His arm wavered wildly. Smoothly Hammerhand drew his Smith & Wesson M29. The revolver belched orange flame and noise. A .44

Magnum bullet hit the kid at the inner corner of his right eye and blew the back of his skull and most of what it had been holding in all over the wolf pelt.

Mindy jumped to her feet. "What the fuck?"

"You can take your blaster back now," Hammerhand told her.

"Did you know he was going to do that?"

"Of course. Have him wrapped up and loaded on a wag. The kid's earned a warrior's send-off."

She knelt and recovered the Beretta. "He wasn't a bad kid," she said, shaking her head and wiping away the blood his gory hands had gotten all over it with a torn-up hank of grass so it wouldn't ruin the bluing. "But busting your own ass all to nuke jumping out a window to escape doesn't strike me as a double-heroic end."

"I'd say it was triple smart," Hammerhand said. "You of all people know a real warrior picks his battles. Or hers."

"But—"

"The fall didn't kill him. He died at the hands of a chief. Right?"

Mindy uttered a short, sharp sigh. "Yeah." She stood. "Leo, Red Sky, you heard the man. Wrap the kid up and get him in a wag. Might as well use that wolf skin, because it's not good for much else now."

"You have to get her!" Trager shouted. Hammerhand felt spittle on the side of his face and had to fight down the urge to choke the life from the vile little creature.

"Enough," he said sternly. "I had four members of my birth tribe's Council killed, skinned, salted and sent back to the rest as a hint to my family to get back out of my face. One of them was my own uncle. So if I'd do that to my own blood, what do you think I'll do to a random whitecoat who stumbled out of the wilderness for not being able to take a nuking hint?"

Dr. Trager's face went satisfactorily pale behind its perpetual coat of grime and hoary stubble. But he did have something resembling balls, Hammerhand had to admit. He pointed back at Lone Calf, where the black monster wind seemed to be trashing the pathetic buildings on the far side of the main Bodacious Creek Trading Post.

Hammerhand was pleased to see the wags he'd sent to patrol the far side of the settlement were powering back across the prairie swells, too.

"That power!" the whitecoat cried. "It's like nothing on Earth. It's like nothing *ever*! You can't let that slip through your fingers!"

"Believe me, little man, I know. And I don't intend to. But doing it your way will only get us all eaten by that black, swirling devil."

"What other way is there?"

"I'll come up with something. All right, Bloods, let's ride!"

THEY FOUND HER sitting on the road just past the outskirts of what had been a thriving if crudely cobbled-together ville, on her knees. She was drawing pictures in the dust and humming to herself.

The black devil's vortex had gone—wherever it went.

The humming had a tune, Ryan realized. But he didn't recognize it. He signaled for the companions to spread out left and right. Just in case.

Gotta leave some of us alive if it all goes sideways here, Ryan thought.

Survival, no matter what, was just that deeply ingrained in him.

"I know," she said without turning her head or even looking up as they cautiously approached. "I have to go away now."

Ryan looked at Krysty. A tear ran from her green left eye down her pale-pink and perfect cheek. But her head was high, her jaw resolutely set.

"Yes, Mariah," she said. "You do."

The girl nodded. She stood up, turned and marched up to Krysty. She threw her arms around her and hugged her fiercely. Krysty hugged her back. But as strong and as loving as the red-haired woman was, she couldn't muster more than a stilted, awkward effort. The girl let her go, turned right about and walked directly away from them.

"That's it?" Mildred asked. "She's not even waiting for us to consult each other?"

"She knows if she's lost Krysty, she's lost us all," Ryan said.

J.B. looked at him meaningfully. He shook his head.

When he reckoned she'd gone far enough not to hear, with the wind blowing brisk, hard spatters of rain hitting their faces as they watched her go, he said gently to his friend, "She did save us all back there. I won't have her back-shot."

"I didn't think you were so sentimental," Mildred said. Then her eyes widened. "I'm sorry, Ryan, Krysty. That came out meaner than I meant it."

"Nothing shaken, Mildred," he said. "Not sentiment. Standards. I'm not a coldheart. This is all the slack I mean to cut her. But I hope our paths don't cross again."

Krysty went to Ryan, buried her face in his chest and wept fiercely. He hugged her back fiercely.

When her sobbing subsided, she stepped back, shook her hair and smoothed the tears from her face. Then she leaned up and kissed Ryan on the lips.

"What now?" Mildred asked.

"I have to admit, I'm a bit worried," Ricky said. "I mean, I don't have any idea why it worked out this way. But it seems like four or five times recently, we've gotten into trouble that we'd never have gotten out of without Mariah's help. What do we do now that she's gone?"

J.B. pondered that a moment. He took off his round glasses and began to polish them with a handkerchief. "I reckon that we'd never gotten clear without her wading in. The first time, with those Buffalo Mob coldhearts, yeah. Mebbe. But these other times, I reckon we'd have found a way to pull through on our own."

"Even this time?"

"We always have, so far," the Armorer said. He held his glasses up to the clouded sky, inspected them through a squint, then settled them carefully back on his nose. "We're good at it. Mebbe you noticed."

"Also," Mildred said, "we wouldn't have been *in* this latest fix, except for her."

"Then why did she intervene with such frequency?" Doc asked. "I understood that it pained her to make use of her power."

"It hurt her less each time," Krysty said. "At least after she joined up with us. She told me that."

"She was protecting Krysty," Mildred said. "She felt mighty protective of her."

"Me, too," Ryan said.

"And—" Krysty frowned and licked her lips "—she

started liking it. The feeling it gave her, to use all that power."

Ryan shrugged. "That's the problem with power," he said. "Starts out, mebbe you don't want to use it, but then you keep coming up with more reasons why you've got to. For the greater good and all. Then, well, it just gets to feeling so rad-blasted good, you can just hardly help yourself. And then you're using it all the time."

The girl was already out of sight. Jak came trotting in from an angle. Ryan hadn't even noticed him slipping away.

"Heading away," he said quietly. Ryan knew who he meant.

He turned his back to the rain, toward the sorry ruin that was all that was left of Lone Calf.

"Best get back, see if we can get our gear out of Bodacious Creek Trading Post without the whole thing caving in on us," he said. "Then shake the dust of this place off our boots in a hurry."

"What about the injured?" Mildred asked. "Or helping victims dig out?"

Ryan shook his head. "They're going to have to look after themselves. Yeah, that's harsh. But at this point, we need to look out for ourselves—they're more likely to lynch us than welcome our help."

Mildred set her jaw. "You're right," she said. "Again."

Chapter Twenty-Nine

"Where are you going, little sister?"

The girl just stood there in front of them in the middle of an immense expanse of prairie, open except for scrub dotting the green grass, staring at Hammerhand and his Jeep Cherokee with eyes like two holes pissed in a snowbank.

"Look at her," Mindy Farseer murmured from behind the wheel. "She's nothing but skin and bones. I don't think she's been eating."

She shook her head.

"Dark dust, I don't think she's even been drinking. Look how she's shaking."

He'd had scouts watching the whole time. They'd seen her walk away from the wreckage of Lone Calf after parting with the one-eyed man and his crew. At his orders, they'd shadowed her since, under strict instructions not to let themselves be seen.

He suspected they hadn't had much trouble with that part. They were way more scared of her than they were of him. He didn't blame them.

And in that whole time they hadn't once seen her eat or drink. Even when she happened to wander in clear sight of a running stream. She just walked on alone, out into the wasteland.

"Right," he said. "Mebbe she'll be receptive and not just disintegrate me."

He stuck his head out the window. "Hi. You're Mariah, right? I'm Hammerhand. I just want to talk to you."

She blinked, then frowned. "I know who you are," she said in a raven's croak. "You tried to kidnap me."

"Yeah. Well. That was a misunderstanding, okay? I promise, I'm not about to do anything without your permission. So, can I get out?"

She nodded.

"Okay. Moving slowly, here."

"Mebbe—I hate myself for saying this—but mebbe if she's trying to chill herself by wandering around out here without looking for food and water…is that such a bad thing?"

Aside from the fact Trager would pitch a fit? Although Hammerhand had to admit that wouldn't be a bad thing at all.

"Do we want to trust that'll happen, just like that, though? What if somebody else happens across her before she dies? There's worse people than us out here, you know."

"Like Trager's whitecoat pals."

"Affirmative."

Slowly he opened the door. He maintained eye contact with the girl the whole time. Her clothes were rumpled and dusty, and even her pigtails seem to hang in defeat.

"You sure this is a good idea?"

"Nuke, no. But I never expected to die in bed anyway."

Deliberately he stepped out into the grass. He took a step forward, leaned against the side of the wag's snout and crossed his arms over his chest. He wore a sleeveless cotton shirt this day. It was warm, though mostly overcast.

"I'd like to take you along with us, if you're willing," he said.

"Why would you want something like that?" she asked listlessly.

"I want to help you," he said.

"What do you want from me? Nobody wants to help me without wanting something from me."

"I'll be honest with you, Mariah. I'm not different. But I'm not pretending either.

"You're an outcast. I'm an outcast. You have special skills. I do, too, if not exactly in the same league. I reckon we can help each other, mebbe."

She just stared at him.

He unfolded his arms, raised a hand and made a two-fingered come-ahead gesture at Mindy. She got out of the car slowly, her brown eyes wide.

She gave him a quick *you have* got *to be shitting me* look.

He grinned at her.

"This is my friend Mindy Farseer. She'll help take care of you. There's another nice woman named Corn Blossom in the back. She'll help you, too. We'll give you food, water. Get you out of the sun."

"I don't want food and water."

"How about someone to be nice to you? I tell you what. They'll be kind. They'll take care of you, and you can come back with us to my tribe for a few days. Then, if you don't feel like staying, you can leave. No strings. How does that sound?"

He was gambling that she missed human company

and was a sucker for a pleasant voice. And what he told her was true—mostly.

She hesitated.

"You're lonely, right? Bet you've been lonely a long time. We'll treat you kindly."

For the first time, her face, which remained pale despite being unshielded from the sun's burning rays, showed sign of emotion: she frowned.

"The people I was with," she said, "they were nice, too. Until they made me leave."

So that's the way you turned it around in your mind, he thought. The scouts had told Hammerhand it looked to them like a mutual parting of ways. Or as much as you could tell through good field glasses at two hundred yards.

"Did they, ah, did they tell you what they wanted from you?"

"No."

"Well, I will. I want your help. But you can be my guest as long as you like. *I'm* not a poor wanderer scuffling for my next meal. And you know that's true."

"Yes."

"So how about it? Let Mindy put you in the wag, and then Corn Blossom will give you a nice drink. Much as you want. And honey."

She moistened her lips. "I like honey," she said.

"You're a smooth devil, boss," Mindy said softly from right beside him. "Slick-talking a poor, crazy, half-dead little girl."

"Shut it."

But he could see Mariah hadn't decided. There was no give in her. He found himself admiring that. It was clear she had a power of determination by the course she'd set herself. Starving and drying yourself to death deliberately took a degree of willpower he wasn't sure *he* had.

"You can help me," he said. "We're going to bring peace to the Plains, at last."

She stiffened.

What the nuke was wrong with that? he wondered.

"The whitecoats said that, too. I didn't believe them. They were bad. I could tell."

He exchanged sidelong glances with Mindy.

"Where did you happen across these whitecoats?"

"Driving. From one ville to another. This big round shiny thing like a mirror just appeared in front of us, and a bunch of men in black with these blaster things got out. Then two whitecoats got out. They wanted me to go with them."

"And you didn't."

She shook her head. "I made them leave me alone."

"I'll just bet you did, honey," Mindy muttered.

"I tell you what, Mariah," Hammerhand said. "See Mindy, here? That blaster she wears by her side? She's triple good with that. And if I do anything—anything—that makes you uncomfortable, she'll pull it right out and chill me dead."

He turned to Mindy. "You heard me. I so command."

"Don't think I won't, boss. I'm tempted to anyway, on general principle. For getting me into this."

"You can thank me when you're marshal of the Northern Plains."

Mindy made a sour noise, but then she stepped toward Mariah and held out her hand.

"I'm Mindy, like the man said. I'd like you to come with me, please."

For a moment he thought she might actually bolt. And I'll shoot her right straight in the back of her head, he thought. I am not letting her wander loose all over the world, with a belly full of mad and a power like that.

And come to think about it, her trying to flee would be the second-best outcome. If she decided he was a threat after all, or that she just plain didn't like him...

The girl nodded, then she swayed. Mindy was instantly at her side, supporting her with a hand around her shoulders.

"It's all right, Mariah," the woman said. "Come on with me. Can you walk? I'll help you walk. That's right. And you'll like Corn Blossom. She'll take good care of you."

She escorted the child to the rear of the wag, steering a course wide of Hammerhand. As they passed, she shot him a death glare.

"Women," he said under his breath, as Corn Blossom, a sturdy middle-aged Arapaho woman, got out to coo over the girl.

Then he grinned. No stopping you now, boy, he told himself. Unless of course she ups and chills you.

"So, DO YOU really think this is a good idea?" Mildred asked her friend.

"Which one, Mildred?" Krysty asked cheerfully.

They were rolling through a beautiful morning with Ryan at the wheel, down into the green Missouri River Valley in search of the ferry to take them across. Actually, it was just a raft on a rope strung bank to bank. But it would carry their wag, or so the trader-talk said, and they needed to cross the run-off swollen torrent on another courier gig.

"Hanging on around here," Mildred said. "Instead of clearing out as fast as we can."

Between them the bed was stacked with their packs and supplies, secured by crisscrossings of coarse hemp rope. One of their wags had not survived Mariah's Lone Calf outburst. Or at least the engine compartment and the front part of the cab hadn't. They could all squeeze into the front and back seats together, being as they were already pretty friendly and all. But that wasn't comfortable. And anyway Mildred had thought it might be time for a good woman-to-woman talk with her flame-haired friend.

"I'm not sure what's a good idea," she said, "and not just about this. Sometimes I'm starting to feel as if it just doesn't make any difference what we do…if we're just doomed to wander the Deathlands forever."

"You're not afraid of running into the girl again?"

Krysty hesitated. "I hope to see her again, to tell you the truth. I miss her."

"You're not scared of her?"

"I don't think she'd hurt me. We were close, which is why I feel so bad about sending her away."

"Then why'd you suggest it in the first place?"

Mentally, Mildred kicked herself. That came out way harsher than I wanted, she thought. Ah, well. I always did have a lousy bedside manner.

"I was scared for the rest of you. That's true. But more, I was afraid what it would do to us. Being with her the next time she lost control and killed a bunch of innocent people and ruined the lives of others. And the time after that. At what point do we become complicit?"

Some might argue we already were, Mildred thought. But she held her tongue. She could see how torn up

Krysty was about the end of her increasingly tight relationship with Mariah. And the way it had ended.

"But about staying in these parts, mostly in what was South Dakota, back in the day," she said instead. "If we don't bug out, shouldn't we try to, well—*do* something about her? Instead of letting her run loose with all that power that seems to control her more than she does it?"

"How?"

Mildred shook her head and sighed. "Got me there."

"Ryan's right," Krysty said. "This is an easy life for us. Even if it's not exactly settled. I guess this is the best thing to do for now. Until we can't. Or until—"

"What?" Mildred prodded after a pause that seemed likely to stretch to infinity.

"I was going to say, 'something better comes along,'" Krysty said. "But we *know* that's not going to—"

The sound of somebody slapping the outside of a wag door made them look around. Ricky poked his head out the driver's-side rear window.

"Ryan says to tell you two to wake up back there," he called. "Ferry's in sight!"

Looking around, Mildred saw it, too.

Her heart sank. It was to a "ferry" what some crazy mountain man's lean-to was to the White House. Calling it a "raft" seemed stretching the point.

"It's not just a job, they tell me," she said with sigh. "It's an adventure."

"ALL RIGHT, GIRLS," Hammerhand said, sticking his head into the cool interior of his personal tepee. "Put some clothes on. You got company."

"But you like us this way," whined one, a skinny, freckled redhead.

"Yeah," the shorter, curvier dark one said.

"Yeah, Shelley, I do. Now I want you two to put some nuking clothes on. I got a little girl for you to take care of, and I want you to treat her right. So make yourselves decent, for Spirit's sake."

"A little girl? We're not babysitters," Shelley said.

"You are now."

"Wait, a little girl?" the brunette asked. "That's disgusting."

"It's not *like* that, Prairie Fire. I don't want her for her body. That's what I have you two for."

He backed out and turned to find Dr. Trager standing right behind him.

"You got her," the little man stated. "Outstanding. You can give her to me now. I'll see that she gets to my associates."

"That's a negative."

For a moment the shabby, greasy little whitecoat looked as if he actually did not understand what those words meant.

"What?"

"She's not going anywhere. Except with me."

"But that's ridiculous! You promised you'd get her for us."

"I promised I'd get her. That's a little bit different."

"But you gave me to understand you'd hand her over once you obtained her."

"Well, mebbe. Now I'm not doing that."

Trager started to become visibly angry. "After all we've given you," he began, "all we've done for you—"

"You need me bad. That's clear. And you did before you had any idea Mariah and her little power even existed."

"What are you going to do with her?"

Hammerhand gave him a big grin. "What you and your friends have been setting me up to do all along—take over the Plains. And when I'm done, mebbe I'll feel nice and grateful, and turn her over. Now get out of my sight."

"But—"

"Now."

The whitecoat turned and scurried off. Hammerhand watched him go. He's going to be trouble, he thought. Well, what else is new?

He turned and signaled to Mindy who sitting behind the wheel of the Cherokee with Mariah and Corn Blossom in the backseat. He had had her park the wag twenty-five yards from his tepee to give everybody a little room while he announced to his current main squeezes their new duties.

The wag was surrounded by a grim phalanx of a dozen of his most loyal followers—mostly originals from his small, scrubby-assed renegade band, or early recruits. A crowd of Bloods had gathered at a somewhat nervous distance to peer at the new passenger in curiosity and fear.

And sometimes hate. They'd lost dozens of Bloods in Lone Calf, and most of them had been chilled by the innocuous little girl sitting huddled against Corn Blossom's soft, capacious flanks.

The wag rolled slowly toward the big tepee, which was painted with imposing symbols of power, like bears, tigers and dragons. Hammerhand had always liked dragons.

As it came to a stop, an ugly rumble came from the crowd, which had grown to north of a hundred.

"There's the witch who chilled so many of our people!" a voice rang out from somewhere prudently back in the press.

Hammerhand's sec team looked to him. They were eager and seemed ready to go and root out the loudmouth.

He shook his head. Instead he climbed up on the wag's hood and held his hands up.

"New Blood Nation, listen to me," he called in his best buffalo-bull voice. "I understand your pain. We've all lost someone.

"But let's all try looking at this square, shall we? We tried to kidnap her. We did. I should know. I ordered it. She fought back, the best way she could. And yeah, it was effective. But honor to both sides."

"Is that really how you see it, boss?" somebody called.

"It really is."

That won a chorus of assent, if not as full-bodied as he'd like. He decided to press on.

"This is not the first time we have welcomed into our clan those who have fought against us, who have fought well and chilled some of us, even. You, Iron Bear—you chilled three of our people when we fought your Ka'igwu raiding band of the Missouri River. And I myself saw you, Xunyi, kill four at Coyote Springs, including a warrior in hand-to-hand battle. You fought bravely until overpowered.

"And did we seek vengeance? No. We welcomed you with open arms."

He spread his arms wide, open palms toward the sky.

"Because you joined us, of your free will, you have become our blood. True Bloods. It is only those who betray us, or those who defy us, who feel the Hammer."

He raised his right hand and clenched it into a fist.

"So it is that, when this girl asked to join us—" he had to hide the truth "—I agreed to take her in and let her earn her place among us. And you all know what power she has to offer our Nation.

"And it's how it's going to be. Make no mistakes, my brothers and sisters, this girl is under my protection. And if you lift a hand against her, I will remind you that I am not called 'Hammerhand' for shits and giggles!"

This time the cheering was widespread and lusty enough that, as Hammerhand turned left and right, luxuriating in it, he gave Mindy a nod and a wink through the windshield. She opened the door and called to the chief of his sec detail, a sandy-haired young man called Travis Sweetwater. He quietly formed his crew into a perimeter between the crowd on one side and the wag and lodge on the other just in case.

Corn Blossom opened the rear door and got out holding Mariah's hand. That still brought some hissing and catcalls, but Corn Blossom was widely respected as a healer, which helped. Mindy squired them both quickly inside the tepee.

He gave the brethren and sisters a bit more of a rousing rah-rah speech—cracking jokes about where they had all come from, what outcast outlaws they were and, of course, their victories, of which there were many. He had fun with it, and they ate it up. That was nothing new, and he felt fully comfortable with it.

He'd always been persuasive, and once he found he liked talking to crowds, he quickly made himself good at it. That more than anything had caused him to get the boot from the Kainawa band: not just that he was considered subversive to their holy tradition, but that he was so rad-blasted good at swaying others from it.

He left them laughing and calling for more, just the way he liked to. They chanted his name as he ducked into the tepee.

"I want to see how you're—" He stopped speaking abruptly.

His two female companions had Mariah ensconced amid a pile of furs they used as a bed. Prairie Fire had put on a doeskin dress. Shelley had more or less draped herself with a buffalo robe instead of actually getting dressed. But it was a gesture, and despite the flashes of pale freckled skin that kept coming out when she moved, Hammerhand was willing to accept it as a start.

The pair already had Mariah's night-black hair unwound from its tight, skinny pigtails and were combing it out and cooing over her. The girl looked a little nervous, but she was staying put and seemed to be relaxing and enjoying the attention.

She ignored him, which suited him fine.

"Why didn't you tell us she was so adorable?" Prairie Fire asked.

He shrugged. The black-haired woman gave him a how-like-a-man sniff.

You didn't see her siccing her pet devil tornado on our people like a rabid dog, he thought, and rubbing out most of the ville she was in in the bargain. He did not say any such thing.

Mindy scowled and was clearly about to enlighten the pair. Hammerhand caught her eye and shook his head.

She shot him a spear-tipped look, then she wheeled and stalked out.

Fine ass, he thought as he watched her go. Shame

she's so tight with it. But it was the right of every Blood to sleep with whom they chose. Rape was a chilling offense and not reluctantly enforced. No skin off his ass. His problem wasn't women telling him no. It was having to tell so many no. Or he'd never get any conquering done.

The mission came first. Always.

And his current mission seemed well accomplished. Even if it took longer and cost more than he'd ever dreamed.

He nodded pleasantly. "Well, I'll leave you ladies to it. Treat our new member well. Welcome home, Mariah."

She looked at him but gave no other sign.

"Wait," Shelley called out as he turned to go. "Have somebody come up with some decent clothes for her. This dress she's got on smells like the hide of a two-days-dead goat."

Chapter Thirty

"If you won't let us avenge our murdered brothers and sisters—if you won't let me avenge my sister—against that monster, then you aren't worthy to lead your own nation, Hammerhand."

The sun shone hot. The wind whispered in the tall grass. Hammerhand stood alone toward one side of the open patch, gazing calmly into the furious black eyes of the warrior who faced him within a circle formed by a growing, nervously excited throng of Blood onlookers.

His challenger was another Blackfoot—a Sikiska, or what some called a "true" Blackfoot. Like many of the North Plains First Nations he was tall—a mere two inches shorter than Hammerhand—and spare, with wide muscle-roped shoulders. He wore only buckskin pants, his weapons belt and an eagle feather in his black ponytail. His craggy features were painted red from the eyes up, dead white below. He had at least three confirmed kills to his belt, every one hand-to-hand.

All told, he was a serious chiller. People were tense.

"Is that your last answer, Three Suns?" Hammerhand asked. Like his opponent, he wore only a belted knife and a pair of pants.

He knew many in the Nation still harbored hatred in their hearts for Mariah and festering resentment against Hammerhand for insisting she become one of them. So when the inevitable challenge had come, he had welcomed it.

"It is," Three Suns said. "Now and forever."

"Forever's a long time, my friend. So be it. Do what you must do, Blood."

Three Suns whipped out his hunting knife and raised it over his head.

Hammerhand was already in motion the moment steel cleared sheath. He crossed the intervening space in three lightning steps. He caught the still-rising knife arm beneath the triceps with his left hand. His right hand he brought slamming down onto Three Suns' forehead in a furious hammer fist.

Bone crunched. Three Suns' eyes rolled up in the red half of his face. The knife fell from his hand, and his legs folded beneath him.

The onlookers gasped. The front of his forehead was dented in by the brutal force of the blow.

Hammerhand shot his hands above his head in triumph, which gave him a pretext to wag his stinging fingers. Nuke! I need to practice that shit more often, he thought.

The crowd erupted into chanting his name, and he marinated himself thoroughly in their adulation.

"SHE SAYS YOU can come in," Mindy Farseer said, poking her head out the flap of Hammerhand's tepee in the early-morning light. "She wants to see you."

It was the early morning of the second day since Hammerhand had brought the strange and dangerous girl to his tepee. The day before, he had quieted down the lynch-mob talk with his brief but impressive performance in his duel with Three Suns.

He had spent the past couple nights in a borrowed yurt with Miao and Gracie, another pair of women from his volunteer harem. And remembering their smooth-bodied beauty and almost-matching green eyes, he couldn't think he'd gotten the worst of the bargain. This morning he reckoned it was time to check in on Mariah.

"You don't seem triple pleased about this," he said to his lieutenant.

She emerged and stood up. "I'm confused," she said. "Is that ace with you? I don't really know what to think about all this. Or feel."

"Whatever you say, Mindy. I know you're there for me, whatever happens."

She looked around. Nobody was near enough to overhear.

"What is this going to do to us, Hammerhand?"

"Either make us an empire or destroy us. I don't see much middle ground there. If that's what you mean."

She shook her head. "It wasn't, but whatever."

Mindy started to walk on.

"We're after the good here," he called after her. "The power to do good. And if what we do is righteous, the way we do it is righteous, too!"

Without looking back she waved and kept on walking.

Shaking his head and grumbling under his breath, Hammerhand turned, stooped and entered the lodge.

It was dark inside and still warm against the previous night's cool temperature with trapped body heat. It had a comforting feel and smell of home.

Mariah was dressed in fine doeskin. Her hair hung free, black and lustrous. A couple of giggling girls of about her own age were showing her how to play rock-paper-scissors. Of course there were children in the Nation; it was truly shaping up as that. Mariah wasn't exactly taking part, but she was watching with interest, with something that might hint at a smile on her thin lips.

A spill of orange hair from beneath a heap of buffalo robes indicated Shelley was still sacked out. Prairie Fire nodded a greeting to Hammerhand and went back to stirring a pot of rabbit stew brought fresh from the fire outside.

The two girls looked at him wide-eyed as he approached. "Give me a few minutes with her, will you, ladies?" he asked. They nodded quickly, hopped up and scampered out.

Mariah gazed at him as he sat down across from her, none too close. He didn't want her to feel crowded. For any number of reasons.

"Your old friends betrayed you," he said. "You know that, don't you?"

For a moment she frowned so ferociously he feared he had overplayed his hand. I fear no man nor power on this Earth, he thought. But I don't see there's shame in fearing her power. Whatever it is, it isn't of this world.

Then she nodded. Tears ran from her eyes.

He nodded. "So you're with me? Please?"

She nodded, then she raised her head and her eyes were clear, if red. "Yes. I am with you."

He nodded and stood. "Right. Then I say to you, Mariah, I will be big brother to you, and the Blood Nation will be your family, for so long as the sun keeps crossing the sky!"

THE COMPANIONS STOOD in the grass of a knoll and watched the old trader and his heavily laden mules make their way across a rolling landscape yellowed by the early-evening light. A herd of pronghorns watched the procession pass from a rise to the east.

"So Hammerhand's got himself a 'young witch who can summon the power of the storm to blast his foes,'" Ryan said, shaking his head.

"You think that's Mariah?" Ricky asked.

"Of course it is," Ryan said. "Who else could it be?" He scratched his ear. "Hammerhand got her after all. I should've expected that, I suppose."

"He's forcing her to work for him against her will," Krysty said. "He has to be!"

J.B. snorted. "How you reckon that's possible?"

"But she fought against him, when he tried to kidnap her."

"Mebbe he asked nice this time," Ryan said. "He seems like a smart man."

"Why would she ever join him, though?"

"She probably got to feeling we'd abandoned her, after a day or two by her lonesome," Mildred said. "You know how loneliness works on a body. Especially when you've finally started to get used to friendly faces around you for the first time in your life. He could've won her over just by being willing to take her in."

"But she was the one who said she had to go away."

"And we didn't exactly try to talk her out of it. Not even you." Mildred shook her head. "We weren't willing to accept what her power was…making her become. I bet he's eager to embrace it."

"So, what now, Ryan?" J.B. asked.

"How do you mean?"

"Do we keep doing what we're doing or try to do something about this new situation?"

"Do something? Like what?"

"Seems like the girl's kind of our problem. An ambitious dude like Hammerhand could do a lot of damage with power like she packs. Mebbe we should do something about one or the other."

"A daunting task," Doc said, "either way."

"Doc's right," Ryan agreed. "I'm not ready to throw my life away just yet, or even this line of work, truth to tell. I like this break from jumping all over the place to nuke knows where. We've got it easier than we have had in a long time, just being errand runners. Hammerhand hasn't come after us so far. Until and unless he does, I think we keep on doing what we're doing."

"But won't Mariah make him too powerful?" Krysty asked.

"Mebbe. But remember *why* we had to go our separate ways. She got so she couldn't control her own power anymore. So now I'd say she's like a stick of dynamite that's commenced to sweat nitroglycerin. She's a bigger threat to Hammerhand than anybody else mebbe."

"Mebbe," J.B. echoed.

Ryan shrugged. "When do we ever get a better answer than 'mebbe'?"

No one could find anything to say to that.

"You with me on this?" he asked them. They all nodded, agreeing to continue working as they had been.

"Right," Ryan said. He took a deep breath. "Now let's forget about *mebbe*s and *might-have-been*s and start looking for a good place to camp for the night."

Chapter Thirty-One

"You've broken our deal!" Dr. Trager said accusingly.

"I don't see it that way," Hammerhand said calmly. He stood with legs braced and arms crossed over his chest.

They stood in a clearing on the side of a small forested mountain in the Black Hills. The New Blood Nation was currently camped in the next valley.

After a lull, its numbers had begun to increase again, once Hammerhand had demonstrated Mariah's terrible power against a notorious baron who had defied him. There had been few survivors from the ville, a necessity that Hammerhand regretted. But the point had been made.

Apparently, it hadn't been lost on Trager's pals either. Not that Hammerhand expected them to give up.

"You agreed to work with us in exchange for our help," Trager explained carefully, as if Hammerhand hadn't been there. "We have given you a great deal of help."

"And?"

"We tasked you to get the girl for us. You contrived to secure her, for which, believe me, I and my associates admire you. But you refuse to hand her over."

"And?"

"This is clearly unacceptable! And I'm afraid I must demand that you honor your agreement with us."

"You do, do you? Look, I know your friends are triple powerful. Not just from the stuff they've given us or done for us, and yeah, all that's been a huge help. But the way they faked that vision I had on my little quest, that prophesied your coming. Come to that, I reckon they must've bribed that Lakota shaman to steer me up Rocky Top in the first place. Word is, neither she nor her daughter have been seen since not long after I consulted her. Funny coincidence, huh?"

"I fail to see what any of this has to do—"

"For all your power," Hammerhand said, "you need me. That's why you went through all that happy horse-shit to rope me in. You want me to conquer? I'm doing that now. And that creepy little girl is definitely making it easier.

"And speaking of which, she told me some white-coats tried to grab her and carry her into some kind of weird magic-mirror thing. That didn't turn out so well, I hear. So if you're thinking of puffing out your chest and trying to bluster me into giving her over, save us both the time. She's with me, and I've got use for her. So she stays."

Hammerhand grinned. "Mebbe you can take measurements from a distance, or something."

"You misunderstand, mighty Hammerhand," Trager said, pouring on the oil to his most obsequious manner. "I'm here to, you might say, sweeten the pot."

"Oh?"

Trager dug into the messenger pouch he carried. Hammerhand wasn't concerned he'd come up with a weapon.

Until he did: a handblaster. But not like any blaster Hammerhand had ever seen. It looked as if it were made of plastic, with a dull not-quite-white finish. It looked streamlined, rather than blocky the way a blaster usually did.

He did not let his sudden spike of concern show in his face or his posture. If you think you're going to jack me at blasterpoint, little man, he thought, you're in for an unpleasant surprise. An even more unpleasant one.

And if he chilled Hammerhand—well, not everybody would be sorry to see that happen, even in the New Blood Nation. But even the least sorry to see the head man go would be among the most eager to punish the man who murdered him, undoubtedly in creative ways.

"What's that?" he asked. "A toy ray gun?"

Trager smirked. He could tell he had made an impression.

"You're almost right, mighty Hammerhand."

He half turned, raised the handblaster, aimed it and squeezed a stud on the front of the grip. A bright red line appeared between its muzzle and a humped gray boulder the size of a yearling buffalo calf.

Sizzling and popping sounds broke from the stone, then it split. It looked as if a gouge many times larger than the beam had eaten through it. It seemed to have turned a volume of the hard rock to dust.

"Okay, now that's seriously cool," Hammerhand said, impressed despite himself. "What is it?"

"A laser pistol," Trager said proudly. "Just the down payment on what we're willing to give you in exchange for the girl. Think of what you could do with a hundred of these things."

Hammerhand nodded thoughtfully. "Can I see?" he asked, holding out his hand.

"Of course, of course."

The whitecoat handed over the weapon. Hammerhand turned it in his hands. It was surprisingly lightweight for the punch it packed. But it still had enough heft to feel like a weapon, not a toy.

He aimed it at a ponderosa pine and pressed the trigger stud. The beam lanced into the reddish bark.

The tree trunk exploded. The upper part tipped over and fell down the slope with a rustling crash, leaving a smoking stump.

"The beam flash-heats the sap," Trager said, "causing a steam explosion."

Hammerhand nodded.

"I do appreciate the offer," he said. "But it still looks to me as if I've got all the power I need to do all the conquering I can handle with the help of Mariah. So you can keep your fancy blasters. Because I'm keeping her."

"But with this pistol you can blast through a boulder!"

"So? With her, I can blast through mountains."

Trager began to sputter furiously. Hammerhand held up a palm.

"Save it," he said. "Now that I've got her, I don't reckon as to how I need you at all anymore. Or your scaly whitecoat 'associates.'"

"You mean you're just casting me aside?" the little man shrieked, spraying spittle from his stubble-surrounded mouth.

"Looks like it, old hoss."

"This isn't over!" Trager shouted, shaking his fist at the Blood leader.

Hammerhand was turning the laser pistol over admiringly in his hands. He looked up.

"As a matter of fact," he said, "it is."

He shot the whitecoat through the beady left eye. The balding head behind split along the seams that held the cranial cap to the rest of the skull as flash-boiled steam blew holes in the scalp. Trager fell, flopping.

Hammerhand looked down at the blaster. "Cool."

He tucked the weapon into his belt and took off down the hill at a swinging lope. This day was shaping up to be a good one, he decided.

"WHAT THE NUKE happened here?"

The wind moaned as though mourning for the torn and devastated land.

"Don't you know, Ryan?" Krysty asked him. She felt a numbness in her soul that seemed to radiate throughout her body. "*She* happened."

He grunted. "Yeah."

The plains in this area showed more relief than in a lot of other places here, the hills a touch steeper, the valleys lower. They were strewed with chills and gangs of crows and ravens squabbling with the battalion of vultures that swooped down to avail themselves of the all-you-can-eat buffet of carnage.

That wasn't what frightened her, indeed shook her to her core. That was just the aftermath of battle. And if it had clearly been a big one, by Deathlands standards, it still was nothing she hadn't seen before. She'd seen worse. They all had.

What scared her were the gouges dug in the flesh of Mother Earth, too deep, regular sided and raw with relative newness to be the work of any manner of natural erosion. And some of them were a good fifty yards wide.

"Who were these people?" Mildred asked.

"Somebody who pissed off Hammerhand way past nuke red, I'd say," J.B. stated. They had stopped the wag near a creek at the southern fringes of the carrion field and stood beside it in the slanting afternoon light.

"Wow," Ricky said. "Look at that ridge. It's like it just stops all of a sudden. Mariah must have eaten the whole end at a bite with that cloud of hers."

"Does she really have that kind of power?" Mildred asked. "That's got to be thousands of tons of earth. Just gone like that."

"You saw what she did to Lone Calf," Ryan replied. "What do you think?"

"I should have seen this coming," Krysty said, "from the way she gouged and devastated the Earth when we cleared the muties out of that field." The realization sickened her to her soul.

"She was giving us a hand," Ryan said. "I didn't think anything about it beyond that at the time. I wouldn't go blaming yourself for not doing so, Krysty."

She just shook her head. How could I be so blind? she thought.

She knew the answer, though: Just like Ryan said—she helped us in our need. That was all that mattered to me, too.

"Survivor," Jak called.

They all looked around. Jak had his handblaster out and was crouched a hundred feet or so east of the others. He seemed intent on a low mound topped with yard-high grass.

"Check it," Ryan said. "Everybody else, blasters up, eyes skinned."

Jak circled to the south, then cautiously approached the rise.

"No danger," he called after a moment. He tucked the Python away beneath his jacket. "Come see."

A man lay on his back on top of the mound. The grass had hidden him from view. He was a tall man, brown skinned, with black hair tied behind his head, and he wore a deerskin vest and canvas pants. From his hips down he was horribly mangled, as if something had crushed him. Flies buzzed in a thick cloud of decaying-blood stench. The gore that had stained the grass and ground around him had turned almost black.

"Water," he croaked.

Mildred approached and gave him her canteen. As he drank greedily, Adam's apple bobbing, the physician turned to her companions and shook her head slightly. There was nothing she could do for him.

"That's not Mariah's work," J.B. said.

"Wag rolled," the man said, letting the hands clutching the water bottle drop to his breastbone. "Got me. Never…stood a chance…anyway."

"Who were you?" Ryan asked.

"Káínawa."

"Blood band of the Blackfoot Confederacy," J.B. said. "Original Bloods, I guess, as opposed to Hammerhand's bunch."

At the mention of the name the mortally wounded warrior turned his head and spit bloody saliva into the crushed-down grass. "Renegade," he croaked. "Monster. Of-offended Council. Came to…reclaim…our name."

"What happened?" Ryan said.

"The witch…girl. Black…tornado. Ate the Earth. Ate…us. Will eat…the whole…world…"

His eyes closed and his head lolled to one side. For

a moment Krysty thought he had died. Then she saw that his chest was still heaving.

"We know," Ryan said quietly.

The eyelids fluttered, then opened wide. Dark eyes looked beseechingly from one of them to another.

"Please," he whispered. "Warrior's…dea—"

The crack of Ryan's handblaster cut him off. The strong-featured face sagged to the side again. The eye that hadn't been imploded by a 9 mm bullet seemed to show a look of peace, not pain or fear.

"Right," Ryan said.

He holstered the weapon and cast his eye over the slaughter grounds.

"I was wrong," he said.

"About running?" Mildred asked. "Because something tells me we should be running right about now."

"You heard the man, Mildred," Krysty said. "The black whirlwind will eat the Earth someday if Mariah isn't stopped."

"That's what I was wrong about," Ryan said. "I let myself hope it wouldn't come to this. Reckoned she'd fight Hammerhand until she got chilled."

"How could anybody chill her?" Mildred asked. "That black dust devil eats bullets as easily as it eats everything else."

"She doesn't have a black cloud to protect her," J.B. said. "She'll die just like anyone."

"What do you intend to do, Ryan?" Doc asked.

"Settle this ourselves," he said.

"But that means going up against the whole, what, fake–Blood Nation even to get to her!" Ricky exclaimed. "What chance do we have of pulling that off?"

Ryan fixed him with his lone blue eye. It looked as bleak as Krysty had ever seen it in all their years together.

"Slim chance is better than none," he said. "Let's ride."

Chapter Thirty-Two

Krysty lay on her belly on the east side of the low ridge's crest, then crawled forward the last couple feet to the top.

"There he is," Ryan said. He handed her the binos. The afternoon sun beat hot on her back.

"What's he doing?" she asked.

"Haranguing."

The others crept up, keeping low in cover and mostly silent. Jak was nowhere to be seen, but that was to be expected.

Below them the Blood forces and their tents filled up a broad bowl of a valley. "It's like there's ten thousand of them!" Ricky said.

"Their numbers are certainly intimidating," Doc said. "How might he summon a force so immense out of the sparsely populated Deathlands, even after all he's done and won? Far less feed for them."

"I wonder that, too," Ricky said.

"A mess of them are gathered to hear whatever he has to say," Mildred remarked. Krysty handed her the glasses.

Recruits continued to flow to the charismatic leader in his current camp in a broad valley among the painted mesas and wind-swept gorges of the Badlands. Especially now that he had hold of a power that made him unbeatable, or seemingly so. The companions had infiltrated most of the way here by masquerading as followers.

The more distinctive of them—Ryan, Jak and Krysty—had disguised themselves with hats and dark glasses, plus clothing with a distinctly different look from what they usually wore. Feeling left out, Doc, Mildred and Ricky had dolled themselves up like landlocked pirates with colorful bandannas tied around their heads.

Even J.B. got into the spirit of things by swapping his trademark battered fedora for a somewhat less battered felt cowboy hat. Temporarily.

Ryan had judged their wag was not unusual enough to merit trying to disguise it or swap it for a different ride. And so it had proved. They had rolled within a few miles of the mustering point where Hammerhand rallied his growing clan to face his even-more-rapidly growing enemies with scarcely a look cast their way.

And the enemies definitely gathered, and big-time, if the rumors that flew among the prospective Blood recruits were even half-true. The Oglala out of Pine Ridge had raised much of the large and powerful Lakota Nation to strike down the upstart Hammerhand. Equally alarmed, the Cheyenne and Arapaho were said to be mustering against the renegade Bloods from the northwest. And some even claimed the coldheart bands of the farther eastern Plains, many fleeing the worsening conditions in the heartland, were forming an unlikely and undoubtedly unstable alliance to deal with the new threat growing east of the Black Hills.

Of course, with Mariah on his side, Hammerhand had little to fear, even from a number of potential foes that dwarfed anything likely seen in the Deathlands in recent times. That was why she and her friends had embarked on this desperate last-ditch mission.

It was Krysty who told the others that if Mariah's power kept growing, as it obviously was, it could potentially cause as much destruction—or more—than skydark. Her heart had dropped at just how much traffic was heading the same way they were—people in wags, on horseback, even on foot. Ryan had said nothing about the numbers of coldhearts, adventurers and refugees with no place better to go who were flocking to Hammerhand's side. But he did seem to hold his jaw more set than usual driving among them.

When they got closer, though, they slipped away into the wooded hills under cover of night. They ditched their disguises and cached the wag under dead brush that had collected in a narrow draw. Ryan intended to slip in on foot, to reconnoiter the camp and see the lay of the land.

He intended for them not just to do the necessary job, but to get out alive. Krysty prayed to Gaia that might be possible, but she had her doubts. It seemed to her that they were embarked on a suicide mission.

But there were no doubts that the job they meant to do needed doing.

Now they were no more than two hundred and fifty yards from the heart of the encampment. Krysty couldn't hear Hammerhand's oration, but every time he scored a point, the enthusiastic crowd's response beat at them like surf.

"How could we get so close without getting spotted by patrols or sentries?" Ricky asked. "I mean, they know this terrain. It's their home turf."

"Not necessarily," J.B. said. He took off his wire-rim spectacles, held them up to the bright blue sky and squinted critically at them before polishing the lenses with a handkerchief and sticking the glasses back on his nose. "Most of them are not from around here, most like."

"Hammerhand, it is said, was born into the Blood branch of the Blackfoot Confederacy, in what once was Canada," Doc said.

"A camp this size usually gets sloppier about security than a smaller one anyway," Ryan said. "Numbers kind of go to their heads."

"There she is!" Mildred exclaimed, peering through the big binocs.

Krysty looked down at the distant platform, which seemed to be made up of planks laid over a foundation of big rocks, where Hammerhand held forth, and her heart sank.

"You sure that's her?" Ricky asked, squinting.

"It is," Krysty said. "I don't need the glasses to tell."

Even at two to three hundred yards, there was something unmistakable about the short, slight form. Maybe it was the way it held itself, at once fragile and defiant. The way the girl who had appeared to be dwarfed by Hammerhand's massive frame was dressed could hardly have been more different from the way they'd always seen her. She wore a white dress with some kind of colored figuring on it, and her raven-wing hair hung unbound across her shoulders. It contrasted all the more sharply with the pallor of her face.

"She's got a lot more hair than I ever would have thought," Mildred said. "But yeah. That's Mariah."

Ryan peered through the telescopic sight of his Steyr Scout. "This is going to be easier than I thought."

He snugged the forestock of the longblaster down in a clump of grass for stability and began adjusting his position as if getting ready to take a long shot.

"What are you doing?" Krysty asked in alarm.

"Getting ready to end this."

"Hammerhand or Mariah?" J.B. asked.

"Mariah," Ryan said. "Got no particular problem with Hammerhand."

"He may have one after this," J.B. said.

"We'll burn that bridge when we come to it. Now, everybody get ready to power out of here."

Tears filled Krysty's eyes. She blinked them clear. She would not look away. Is there a better way than to kill a little girl? she thought. Someone I was close to? Someone who trusted me?

If there is, why can't I see it?

But she knew that Ryan, as hard as he could be, would never do such a thing himself unless it was a matter of life and death. She saw him inhale deeply, then release half the breath and hold it. Her own breath caught. She knew what came next.

"Up there!" Ricky cried as Ryan's finger tightened deliberately on the blaster's trigger.

Krysty looked up to see a red dot, bright even in the daylight, arc across the sky right over their heads.

RYAN KNEW IT had all gone to hell even before the bullet left his weapon.

The shot was easier than the one he'd taken at Hammerhand at Lone Calf to bring an end to the chances the inhabitants would hand over Mariah to him. He didn't bother wondering how much misery and trouble everyone would have been saved had they actually just gone ahead and done so; that was passed. He had lined up the reticule, adjusted for range and wind on the girl's chest and fired.

Even as the longblaster kicked up with recoil he saw the black cloud form instantaneously around both her and Hammerhand. She'd been practicing.

As he brought the longblaster back down with a fresh cartridge chambered he broke focus enough to look for what had excited Ricky—and alerted Mariah to the presence of danger.

"Fireblast!" He saw the red flare burning down the sky toward the near outskirts of the Blood encampment.

"Behind!" Jak called from down the slope from them.

"Cover!" Ryan ordered by reflex. He already had a good guess as to what had happened.

He spun. A mesa with steeper sides rose behind the ridge they had found for a vantage point. He knew at once that a Blood patrol had spotted them from there and fired the signal.

Lying on his back, he raised the longblaster as confused shouting broke out from the Blood camp. He swung the scope to bear on the mesa. It was slightly lower than their ridge and, by luck, had fewer rocks for cover.

A party of four warriors was hunched down. Ryan saw a lever-action longblaster in one man's hands, a man with long unbound hair, a blue shirt and bare legs. Ryan quickly targeted him and fired.

The man jerked as dark spray flew out the back of his chest.

"Mildred, Ricky," Ryan called, naming the two best distance shooters, "get fire on those bastards. Everybody else, form a perimeter, find the best cover you can and dig in."

He followed his own orders. Thirty feet to his left a cluster of reddish rocks lay just shy of the ridge's crest line. He dived into it, and laying down his blaster, began gouging at the ground with his panga.

As he did, he heard fire outgoing from the ridge, and the many-throated roar of warriors charging toward them from the massive Blood encampment.

Chapter Thirty-Three

Ricky knelt behind an outcrop slightly larger than he was about forty feet down from the ridgeline. He had the long-range sight flipped up on his reconstructed DeLisle longblaster. It was mostly for lateral aiming; its elevation was still calibrated for the relatively high-powered .303 cartridge the original weapon was chambered for, not the slow, fat .45 ACP pistol round it shot now. His tío Benito had always talked about making a new flip-up sight. But the coldhearts had chilled him first, along with Ricky's family and most of his home village of Nuestra Señora, and carried his adored older sister, Yamile, off to slavery.

Luckily, Ricky had a fair amount of practice shooting the longblaster at distance—so long as the "distance" was no greater than 200 yards, or preferably one hundred and 150. After that he might as well have been chucking rocks. And even at those ranges the 230-grain bullets had a very similar trajectory. Luckily, the small mesa they had been spotted from was little more than sixty yards from his lie-up.

A dark figure was sprawled in the yellow dirt. Another person knelt nearby and started firing a Mini-14 toward the ridge and Ricky's scrambling companions even as he watched.

That made him Ricky's target. He set the elevation

slider for the distance appropriate to his weapon's ballistics, lined up the iron sight on the riflewoman and fired.

She jerked. From her reaction he gathered the slug had taken her high in the right chest, right below where her arm was angled as she blazed away. She let go of the wrist of her 5.56 mm longblaster's stock to clutch at herself, experimentally almost, as if she wasn't sure what had happened to her.

From his right Ricky heard the blasts of another weapon discharging, shatteringly loud. Mildred had hefted an M16 and fired controlled 3-round bursts at the coldhearts below.

A third crouching scout, who aimed what looked like a cowboy-style single-action handblaster, went down writhing and moaning. By that time Ricky had a fresh round chambered and was switching his aim to the fourth, a man with short red hair and a beard.

One thing his DeLisle wasn't suited for was suppressive fire. It was functionally silent at this range or anything close to it, but the combination of seeing a comrade hit plus Mildred's loud longblaster made more than enough impression on the survivors. The woman Ricky had shot turned to flee. Her comrade grabbed her by the back of her patched army jacket to help.

Ricky still might have brought one down, though moving targets were obviously trickier than stationary ones, but he wasn't naturally bloodthirsty. They were, as his idol and mentor, J. B. Dix, would have put it, "heading in the right direction." And Ricky already had a sinking sensation of certainty that he was likely to find himself faced with more bad guys than he had bullets before the day was out.

He started to rise as he heard Ryan's longblaster bark toward the hordes onrushing from the Blood camp.

"STAY WHERE YOU ARE, kid!" J.B. called. Ricky froze, then obediently tucked himself prone behind the cover of his rocks.

The Blood camp lay due west. They'd been spotted from a height to the east. Krysty lay behind the crest five yards to Ryan's right. The Armorer had stationed himself ten yards or so to Ryan's left and down seven or eight from the ridge crest, set to cover the south flank. Ricky lay twenty feet or so downslope. North of Ricky, Jak crouched behind a scrubby juniper. Upslope and north of him lay Mildred with her M16. Doc had taken position with his M4 carbine covering the south flank, about midway between Mildred and the top of the ridge.

It was far from an ideal situation. With seasoned skill, all seven had found hard cover—rocks or the ridge itself—to shield them from the direction they were covering. They had also placed their packs near them, both for additional shielding and easy access to ammo and other supplies. It was a reasonably tight, efficient perimeter and secured the high ground. The craftsman in J.B. approved.

What made it less than ideal was the fact that they faced somewhere between five hundred and one thousand enemy fighters, by J.B.'s calculation. Those were worse odds than they'd been up against in Lone Calf, at least after Ryan's cynical ploy forced the inhabitants onto their side. And that was leaving aside the nightmare scenario: that Hammerhand had possession of a weapon that quite conceivably could end up dwarfing the whole nuclear arsenal that had scorched the world and brought on skydark, to judge by the damage Mariah's power had done against the original Blood band.

J.B. put that out of his mind. There was a lot of fighting to do between now and then, whenever *then* happened to be. He focused his whole being on that and keeping himself and his friends alive.

As long as he could anyway. But that was the deal everybody woke up to every day.

THE BLOODS ROLLED up and over the lower mesa that stood between the companions and the camp like a wave of angry human flesh.

They're like an army of soldier ants, Krysty thought. And they're not even the biggest threat we face.

She heard Ryan's blaster roar from her left. She sighted in on the front ranks and began to rip at them with 3-round bursts.

Bloods fell, rolled, died. Survivors thrashed their arms and legs in pain. Others came, flowing around the wounded rather than simply trampling over them.

Krysty was a seasoned warrior—as seasoned as any of them, except for Ryan and J.B. She knew from experience that meant the Bloods weren't fully committed to this attack. They were eager but not full of the single-minded fanatical zeal that would have led them to stamp their own brothers and sisters into red paste in the fury of their assault.

It was their numbers, she reckoned. They knew as well as their enemies did that they could eventually prevail. Why throw your life away when the odds were stacked so heavily on your side?

She heard the snarl of a full-auto 9 mm weapon as J.B. shifted up to the ridgeline to add the fire of his

Mini UZI to her M16 and Ryan's Scout longblaster. With so many targets, they inflicted brutal losses with just three weapons.

And sure enough, that wave of flesh faltered. It stopped and receded over the rise, leaving a good twenty dead and wounded behind.

But some of them continued down to take cover in the brush and the rocks between the high spots. J.B. yelled a warning, calling her attention to others slipping around the south end of the mesa.

"Flanking!" he shouted before slipping back down to his original lie-up.

"Everybody else, brace yourselves," Ryan called. "They're going to surround us before they try again!"

THE FIRST VISIBLE attacker crept down a nearly dry streambed that ran around the back side of the ridge. He was a young man with long black hair, bound only by an Apache-style headband. He was bare-chested and crouched low over a remade Remington 870 pump shotgun.

His head exploded and he dropped to the ground. Chunks of brain like curiously formed dough slopped into the streambed as red stained the whisper of water.

Blasterfire answered furiously from a stand of willow saplings ten feet behind the scout. Jak was already in motion, soundless and unseen, making for a fresh hidey-spot he'd picked out in advance.

He was grinning. They might lose this fight, but he planned to enjoy it as long as he could.

"HAVE AT YOU, caitiff rogues!" Doc roared as he stood to his full height from beside a big rock and blazed

3-round bursts into the coldhearts advancing up from the eastern end of the ridge.

Three of them went down. He could see eight or ten others promptly turn around and dive for the cover of rocks and brush.

One of the fallen Bloods raised a handblaster and aimed at him. Doc shot her once through the head. He did so without a heartbeat's hesitation and only a twinge of regret as he ducked into cover to reload.

At most times chivalry was dead in this poor, tormented world. He had learned that with brutal clarity within hours of being dumped into it by the vile predark whitecoats.

"That was foolish, Theo," he said to himself as he rammed home a fresh magazine and, by habit, tucked the partially depleted one in his pack. "Exposing yourself like that."

Still, he felt mostly exhilaration and only partly because of the still largely unaccustomed thrill of firing a fully automatic weapon. The likes of which had barely come into existence when he was snatched from the bosom of his family.

Oddly, the sky was clear blue and free of the usual colorful chem clouds. The sun was warm. His nostrils were full of the scents of moist growing grass and blooming wildflowers.

What was it the Indians had said, back when he was young? "Today is a good day to die."

He felt that now. He was at peace with it.

What hope he had was that his friends might somehow pull through against all probability, as they had done before often enough.

And, even less likely, accomplish their terrible but oh-so-necessary task.

The coldhearts began to shoot blindly in his general direction. He started to peek around the flank of his rock to look for targets to shoot back at.

And his blood was turned to ice streams in his veins by the sound of an electro-amplified voice booming out from beyond the ridge's bulk, *"Bottle them up, Bloods, and hold your ground. No point wasting your lives. The Black Wind Walking will take care of them for you!"*

"FIREBLAST!" RYAN EXCLAIMED.

The voice was coming loud and clear from beyond the mesa, well out of his line of fire. Hammerhand had learned his lesson at Lone Calf, it appeared.

"This is a bad bunch, Bloods," the voice said, half-banteringly. *"Lethal as a ball of rattlers on a hot day. We've rumbled with them before. We know you, Ryan Cawdor. Oh, yes, we do!"*

"You don't know what you're messing with, Hammerhand!" he shouted back. He stayed low, well aware a group of Blood blasters was dug in at the foot of the ridge.

"Oh, but I do. The power to change the world. Make it a better place. Don't you want that?"

"Make it better," Ryan called, "or destroy it."

Hammerhand laughed.

"Whichever. Doesn't it take the power to do one to pull off the other? But I'm not here to jaw about ethics. There's somebody here with a bone to pick with you and your crew. A chilling bone. Mariah, honey? Time to do that voodoo that you do."

Deliberately, almost as slowly as the setting sun, the black cloud rose into view beyond the mesa top.

Ryan found himself terrified at the sight, but not frozen nor panicked enough to bolt or flail wildly instead of actually fighting. He'd learned years ago to ride out the adrenaline jolt of awful and immediate danger and the fight-flight-freeze reflex it tried to trigger in the brain. He could almost view the fear like a detached third party.

Except he still felt it.

The black whirlwind began to move across the mesa toward them, slowly and inexorably, almost at a walking pace, it seemed to Ryan.

"Mariah," Krysty called out. "Are you sure you want to do this? We were friends. We took you in."

"You were *friends,"* the unseen Hammerhand taunted. *"Until you threw her out to die alone in the wasteland. That kind of ended the whole 'friendship' thing.*

"But tell us, Mariah. How do you feel about the people who betrayed you?"

"I hate them."

The chilling words pealed out in a high, girlish voice.

What made them a hundred times more chilling was that they clearly came from within the cloud. Mariah was walking in the eye of her black cyclone of total devastation.

She clearly meant to do the job of vengeance up close and personal.

"Why not come out and face me yourself, Hammerhand?" Ryan yelled.

"Are you triple stupe, Cawdor? I know what a longblaster is. I'm not some ignorant stone-age savage. I

know you're a crack shot, and I know that I can't slap a 7.62 mm round out of the air with my dick."

"I'm calling you out, then. Just you and me. Mano a mano."

"Oh, nuke no. That's what I have an army for, friend. And even better, that's what I've got the greatest hammer in the history of the whole entire world for. Which my little sister is fixing to drop square on top of you."

The whirling cloud crossed the hill, then inexorably descended. Bloods jumped up from cover and fled to either side of its path.

"Ryan?" Krysty asked.

"They're not the threat now. Save your ammo."

He was glad she didn't ask what she should save it for. But then again, always before, there had been a *what.*

"Stay clear of that thing, people," Hammerhand said to his warriors. "Just keep them bottled in up there. Hold your fire unless they try to escape. Let the girl have her revenge for her broken heart."

The black whirlwind advanced across the little valley. It began to climb the ridge toward Ryan and his companions.

He felt no fear now, only sickness and rage at his complete and utter helplessness.

"Mariah," Krysty called, "please don't do this to us. We're sorry we hurt you."

"You did hurt me!" the cloud screamed at them, wild with rage. The whirlwind grew taller and broader. And faster. "I trusted you! I thought I'd found a family at last. And—and you rejected me! I'm going to kill you all for it!"

Krysty stood.

"No," she said. "I won't let you hurt my friends."

"Krysty!" Ryan shouted desperately. "What the fuck are you doing?"

To his horror he saw her march purposefully downslope.

Directly toward the cloud of complete oblivion.

Chapter Thirty-Four

Terror greater than any she had ever known filled Krysty to the point it felt as if she were about to explode.

She held out her arms to the sides. "Gaia! Earth Mother! Hear my prayer!" she cried. "I beg of you—lend me your strength!" Krysty urgently repeated her plea, and then the power of the Earth Mother flooded her being.

The unstoppable force of Gaia pushed out the fear. It was soothing in a way, yet Krysty also sensed rage smoldering within, as if Gaia knew this was one of the greatest threats the Earth Mother had ever faced.

"Krysty!" Mariah screamed. For the first time she sounded like herself instead of a teenaged Fury. "Get back! I—I'll chill you last!"

"You won't chill any of us," Krysty declared. Her voice boomed with an unfamiliar menace.

But then, it wasn't really her own voice anymore.

"I won't stop! I'm warning you!"

The blackness was swirling mere feet ahead of Krysty now. She could feel it. Not hot, not cold. Not even the wind of its violent spinning. But a sense of nothingness. Of *negation*. Not merely nothingness, but...antisomething.

Uncreation.

Without the least hesitation she walked into the black cloud.

It hurt. It felt the way she imagined being burned alive had to hurt. The pain seared her skin, her eyes. It permeated her flesh, her bones. Her being.

And yet—she remained. She was not destroyed. She felt Gaia's strength, Gaia's will, opposing the force of uncreation.

She was aware that she slowed. It was like wading through molasses over her head—molasses that still burned like furnace flame. It took all of her strength joined to that of the whole world to continue.

But she did. One foot after another.

She felt her strength began to fail. Her body wasn't being torn apart—not yet. Nor did the strength of the Earth Mother fade. But she was a frail vessel still—and channeling Gaia drained her energy in a way nothing else did. She felt her physical strength failing.

Another few heartbeats and I will fall. And die. And then my friends will die.

And then the world will die.

I—will—not fall.

And then she broke through. A few feet of air surrounded a startled-looking little girl in a white dress.

"Krysty?" Mariah asked in disbelief.

She stepped up to the girl. Feeble though her own shell was, the righteous strength of Gaia still clung on. It had the strength to crush her. To destroy her. To end the evil she had brought into the world and could continue to bring.

Instead she took Mariah in her arms and hugged the frail form hard against her breasts. She felt the skinny little body begin to tremble uncontrollably.

"Mariah," she whispered, "I love you."

And then her strength was gone, and the blackness rushed in to claim her.

RYAN STOOD IN plain view of most of the New Blood Nation. He didn't care if anyone shot him down.

Not when he had just watched the woman he had loved for years, his life mate, walk right into her inevitable and terrible death.

The black whirlwind vanished.

Mariah stood in the middle of where it had been, just twenty feet downslope.

Impossibly, Krysty was there, too. She was on her knees, slumped against the girl with her arms hanging loose. And Mariah was clinging to her with tears streaming down her face.

"Krysty," she was sobbing. "I'm so sorry I tried to hurt you."

Mariah couldn't support the woman's deadweight. Krysty's body slid from her grasp to slump on the soil of the Earth whose strength had somehow carried her through the cloud of annihilation.

Grimly, Ryan raised his longblaster.

"Dark night!" exclaimed J.B., who had joined his old friend to face death with him. "She's still breathing, Ryan!"

So she was. He had only one eye, but it was eagle keen.

"What's going on?" he demanded of Mariah. "Why didn't you chill her?"

"I tried!" the girl wailed. She knelt to cradle Krysty's head in her arms. "But I couldn't. Because—in spite of everything—she loves me!"

"What in the name of glowing night shit is going on?" Hammerhand roared.

He wasn't talking through a loudspeaker now. He'd come up onto the top of the little mesa between his enormous camp and the ridge where his enemies were dug in to watch the fun. A mob of his most loyal warriors surrounded him in a dense human shield. Ryan had no shot at him.

His voice boomed naturally out of that prodigious chest of his to be clearly audible from where he stood. "Why aren't you chilling them, girl?"

She turned her face to him. "I won't! You used me to do—to do terrible things! And I'm through doing that!"

"Blast them down!" Hammerhand ordered his warriors. "All of them! Starting with the traitor witch!"

Ryan's racing heart suddenly seemed to be beating in slow motion. Once. Twice.

And then the whole basin valley seemed to fill with fire flowers. Muzzles flamed from the bottom of the ridge and the mesa.

But the black cloud was suddenly there again, as wide as the ridge. The bullets all vanished without a trace.

The cloud narrowed again. It began to move once more, back down the slope. Mariah walked close behind.

"Shoot it!" Hammerhand shouted. "See if you can blast through it to the girl!"

The New Blood Nation obeyed. Those who didn't simply turned and ran for their lives.

Hammerhand drew a blaster from his belt and aimed it at the black whirlwind. A line of pink light suddenly appeared between its muzzle and the swirling void.

"Laser blaster," J.B. said in awe. "Read about them

in a couple of predark novels. Didn't know they were for real!" He sounded impressed in spite of himself.

"Cool," Ricky called from the ridgetop.

Ryan had run to Krysty's side. He barely beat Mildred. As he gathered his lover in his arms, she was checking her pulse and feeling her cheek.

"She's alive," Mildred announced. "Not…fine, maybe. But this seems just like the other times she's passed out after calling on Gaia. She's come out of it okay all the other times. So she should be okay now."

Her eyes almost pleaded with Ryan. "I hope?"

"She will," Ryan said. "She's too tough to chill."

He looked back. The cloud was walking its hideous way straight up the mesa now. It spun its funnel of devastation barely a hundred feet from Hammerhand.

"Why?" the Blood chieftain cried. "Why are you doing this, Mariah? I took you in when they pitched you out!"

"They tried to stop me from turning into a monster," the girl said. She didn't seem to be shouting, but Ryan heard her plainly just the same. "You took me in *because* I was a monster. And you made me worse.

"So now you die, Hammerhand!"

In disgust he threw down the laser blaster. He did not run. Instead he tore off his fine buckskin shirt and cast it aside. Then he spread his brawny arms wide, threw back his head and began to sing in a language Ryan didn't understand.

The cloud swept over him. Ryan thought he could see a few shreds of flesh and blood spin by. Then the last of Hammerhand was gone from the world, as completely as if he had never been.

"Singing his death song," J.B. said. He took off his

spectacles and polished them. "Say what you will about him, that's a *man* who just died right there."

"I'm just glad he's dead," Ryan rasped and lowered Krysty to the ground.

As one the New Blood Nation turned and fled. Ryan couldn't blame them.

The cloud winked out again. Mariah turned and raced back toward them. Her pale bare legs seemed to twinkle beneath the hem of her doeskin dress.

"Shall I blast her?" J.B. asked.

"No," Ryan said. "We got nothing to fear from her now."

"Are you sure?" Doc asked.

The others were all gathered on the ridgetop now, Ryan saw. Even Jak.

"Yes."

Ryan almost jumped out of his skin. "Krysty!" he said. "Don't even talk."

"I saw it, you know," she told them, struggling to lean up on one arm. "I was floating above the world. But through the kindness of Gaia I came back. I'm so tired."

Mariah ran up to them and tried to throw her arms around both her and Ryan.

"I'm sorry," she sobbed. "You were right, and I'm sorry."

"It's okay, Mariah," Krysty said. "I won't leave you now."

And then Ryan heard Ricky yell, "*¡Nuestra Señora!* It's *them* again!"

LIKE EVERYBODY ELSE, Ryan looked where the boy pointed.

A giant mirror, easily a dozen feet top to bottom by ten wide, had appeared in thin air beside the ridgetop.

It cleared to what seemed to be a window to another world: a dark unnatural womb lit by screens and blinking, multicolored lights.

"It is time to end this farce," the bald male whitecoat said. He stretched out a clawlike hand. "Come with us now, Mariah."

She turned to face them, holding her fists clenched by her sides.

"I won't," she screamed. "I never will."

"You have no choice, child," the female whitecoat said.

"If you refuse," the gaunt man said, "we promise we will hunt your friends down and destroy them. Whatever it takes, and then we'll collect you."

"You have to sleep sometime," the woman stated. "So come with us now, Mariah."

She smiled. At least, Ryan reckoned, she thought that was what she was doing. It looked more like the expression you'd see on the face of a chill who had not died easily.

"We don't care what you do to us," Krysty said. She battled to her feet. "We're not letting her go with you! She stays with us."

"Yeah," Ryan added. To his surprise, he meant it.

"No."

He started down at the girl.

"Mariah, what are you saying?" Krysty asked.

The girl looked at the portal that hung in the air. "I'll go with you if you promise to leave my friends alone."

The whitecoats glanced at each other. "Oh, we do," the gaunt man told her. "We have run the projections. They are of little or no consequence in this timeline."

"Come with us, Mariah," the woman said.

Mariah stepped forward. "I'm ready."

"Wonderful!" the whitecoat said. "Shaughnessy, lower the Aperture to the ground so that our new subject—I mean, our new guest—can cross over."

"Yes, Dr. Sandler."

"Ryan," Krysty said. She swayed. He caught her around the shoulders and held her as if he'd never let her go. "We have to do something!"

He shook his head. "Her choice."

The strange portal touched the ground a few feet downslope from them.

The woman held open her arms in a ghastly parody of maternal welcome. "Mariah, come to us!"

Mariah walked forward through the gateway.

She stepped into the other world, then she turned to face her friends.

"Goodbye," she said. "I love you."

"Goodbye is right," Dr. Sandler told them. "Major Applewhite, destroy these genetic culls."

"No," Mariah said. "You won't."

Suddenly it was around her: the black cloud, swirling. The tall black-armored man who had stepped up at the whitecoat's command screamed horribly as he was sucked in.

"No!" the female whitecoat shrieked. "You can't do this! Baronial America will be delayed or canceled completely on this timeline! All the work we've—"

Her words ended in a crescendo of wordless agony.

The cloud began to expand. Techs screamed as it devoured them. Electricity sparked from violated panels.

"You little fool!" Sandler howled. "This is a sealed environment! You don't know...what are you—!" Sandler shrieked in horror.

Mariah turned. "Goodbye," she said again. "I love you. Think happy thoughts of me."

There was an explosion of white light. The portal winked out.

"Well," J.B. said, "that's something you don't see every day."

Krysty slumped to the ground. Ryan only just caught her in time to stop her shoulders and head from hitting the ground.

Somehow she rallied to lift her head.

"Farewell," she called to the sky where the strange gateway had been. "And thank you for all you've done for us. And wherever you are, keep believing, and mebbe we'll be together again someday!"

The redhead looked back at her lover.

"Ryan," she breathed, "for the first time, I have—*hope*."

Krysty slumped. She was well and truly out cold now.

"Bloods're running," Ricky reported.

Ryan glanced up and saw that it was true. The basin had all but emptied of visible humanity.

"Ace on the line," he said. He squatted and gathered Krysty's limp form in his arms. Then he stood.

"Let's get out of this place," he growled.

And so they did.

* * * * *

UPCOMING TITLES FROM

THE EXECUTIONER
DON PENDLETON'S

KILL SQUAD

Available March 2016

Nine million dollars goes missing from a Vegas casino, and an accountant threatens to spill to the Feds. But with the mob on his back, the moneyman skips town. Bolan must race across the country to secure the fugitive before the guy's bosses shut him up—forever.

DEATH GAME

Available June 2016

Two American scientists are kidnapped just as North Korea makes a play for Cold War–era ballistic missiles. Determined to save the scientists and prevent a world war, Bolan learns he's not the only one with his sights set on retrieving the missiles...

TERRORIST DISPATCH

Available September 2016

Atrocities continue in the Ukraine and the adjoining Crimean Peninsula, annexed by Russia in March 2014. With no end in sight, a plan is hatched to force American involvement by sending Ukrainian militants to strike Washington, DC, killing civilians and seizing the Lincoln Memorial as protest against their homeland's threat from Russia. Can Bolan bring the war home to the plotters' doorstep?

COMBAT MACHINES

Available December 2016

What began in a Romanian orphanage twenty years earlier, when a man walked away with ten children and disappeared, leads Mack Bolan and a team of Interpol agents to fend off a group of "invisible" assassins carving their way across Europe...toward the USA.